HLAND
ON

LESTE
RCLAY

OLIVER
HEBER
BOOKS

THE CLAN SINCLAIR LEGACY

Highland Lion
Highland Bear (Coming May 17, 2022-Preorder Now)
Highland Jewel (Coming Aug 2, 2022- Preorder Now)

SINCLAIR FAMILY TREE

Liam Sinclair m. Kyla Sutherland

    b. ***Callum Sinclair*** *m. Siùsan Mackenzie* (SH-IY-oo-san)

    b. Thormud Seamus Magnus Sinclair (TOR-mood SHAY-mus)

    b. Rose Kyla Sinclair

    b. Shona Mary Sinclair

    b. ***Alexander Sinclair*** *m. Brighde Kerr* (BREE-ju KAIR)

    b. Saoirse Sinead Sinclair (SEER-sha shi-NAYD)

    b. Nessa Elise Sinclair

    b. Mirren Louise Sinclair

    b. ***Tavish Sinclair*** *m. Ceit Eithne Comyn* (KAIT-ch En-ya CUM-in)

    b. Ailish Elizabeth Sinclair (A-lish)

    b. Tate Henry Sinclair

    b. William "Wiley" Matthew Sinclair

    b. ***Magnus Sinclair*** *m. Deirdre Fraser* (DEER-dreh FRA-zer)

    b. Maisie Blair Sinclair

    b. Blake Magnus Sinclair

    b. Torquil Lachlan Sinclair

    b. ***Mairghread Sinclair*** (Mah-GAID) *m. Tristan Mackay* b. "Wee" Liam Brodie Mackay

    b. Alec Daniel Sinclair

    b. Hamish Kincaid Sinclair

    b. Ainsley Maude Sinclair

PREFACE

Welcome to *The Clan Sinclair Legacy*, a spinoff from my *The Clan Sinclair* series. As you join the second generation of this remarkable family, you may recognize heroes and heroines from the first series. For some of you, it may be a chance to become reacquainted with old friends. For those who haven't read *The Clan Sinclair*, take heart: all of my books can be read as standalones, so you don't have to read the earlier series to enjoy this one. Many readers of the original books wondered what would become of the couples from my *The Highland Ladies* series. Fear not. The children of several of those couples will have their chance to find love with the younger Sinclairs and their Sutherland relatives over the course of my next twenty books.

The Clan Sinclair Legacy takes place roughly twenty years after *The Clan Sinclair* and about ten years after the final installment of *The Highland Ladies*. In my first series, I never explicitly stated who ruled Scotland at the time; however, King Robert the Bruce and Queen Elizabeth de Burgh appear throughout *The Highland Ladies*. By the time this new series would take place, the Bruce is dead, and his son, David II, is on the throne.

You will discover more about King David's complicated reign in later books in this new series.

Highland Lion begins this new adventure with the oldest grandchild of Laird Liam Sinclair. "Wee" Liam Mackay is the son of Laird Tristan Mackay and Lady Mairghread Sinclair, the only daughter among four brothers (*His Highland Lass*). I've found the Clan Sinclair history fascinating and complicated since I began research for my very first series. As with my other books, these stories are fiction. The characters and plots are products of my imagination, but they're based on accurate history that I spend countless hours studying. In some cases, I condense events for the sake of the storyline. That is the case in this book.

Orkney is an archipelago in the Northern Isles of the North Sea and are near Scotland's northeastern coast. It lies only ten miles from the Caithness coast, and modern-day ferries make the crossing frequently. In this story, I include *birlinns*, West Highland and Hebridean boats that followed the Norse longboat style but were smaller. For lack of a better option, I have my Highlanders use these vessels, even though they hail from the eastern Highlands.

During the peak of the Viking Age, the eighth and ninth century AD, Norwegian settlers made their homes on Orkney and its neighbor, Shetland. The Norwegian king annexed the islands and officially made them part of Norway in 875 AD. From about 1100 onward, the Norse *jarls*, who governed locally through their holdings as Earls of Caithness (Earls of Orkney in some sources), pledged their allegiance to both the Norwegian and the Scottish crowns. In 1231, the Earldom of Caithness, the region in which Castle Dunbeath was built and includes both Orkney and Shetland, was granted to the son of the Earl of Angus by the Norwegian king, Haakon Haakonsson. The earldom passed to the Sinclairs in 1379, who were barons of Roslin, near Edinburgh. Since this story takes place in roughly 1336, I took creative license with the transfer of governance to the Sinclairs.

The islands didn't come under Scottish rule until 1468, roughly one hundred and twelve years after this novel takes place during the reign of King David II. This is another historical event with which I used creative license for the dates. At the time of the transfer of ownership, Christian I of Denmark and Norway used the islands as a collateral of sorts against the dowry he owed James III of Scotland when the latter was to marry Christian's daughter, Princess Margaret. The dowry was never paid, and King Christian forfeited his claim to the islands.

I use these events as the catalyst for the story. Our hero, Liam Mackay, travels to Orkney during the transfer of governance. He represents his grandfather, Laird Liam Sinclair, the Earl of Sinclair, as I also make him the Earl of Orkney. I have Laird Liam Sinclair adopt the title of the Earl of Caithness to follow earlier tradition. While traveling to the island of Rousay, our hero encounters a Norse trader. After the decline of the Viking Age and the adoption of Christianity, thralldom —Viking slavery—became far less prevalent. For the sake of this plot and our villain, I rely on the fact the practice was rare, but still possible.

Discovering the Norse history in Orkney presented some interesting challenges. Several sites on different islands bear the same name. For example, the village of Skaill on Rousay, which I reference, is a site where archeological remains have been found and studied. However, that village name appears on other Orcadian islands. It also doesn't correlate to where the Bay of Skaill is located. Thank heavens for maps, because it was confusing. All of the locations I include in this story are real, with documented connections to the Norse settlers. The Orcadian names were drawn from census data from the 15th, 16th, and 17th centuries. I chose the surname Isbister because I liked the sound. I later discovered that there is a village of Isbister on the island called Mainland. That worked well for my plot, since surnames were frequently derived from the homesteads upon which families built their lives.

I think one of the best parts of authorhood is the adventure I take whenever I set out to research new events and places. I fall down rabbit holes and travel back in time. I hope you enjoy the artifacts of these journeys, and I hope this preface gives you historical perspective to better enjoy this tale.

Happy reading,
Celeste

CHAPTER 1

$\mathscr{L}$iam Mackay gazed at the bustling Orcadian village of Skaill, on the isle of Rousay. He thought of how it reminded him of his clan's village, outside the walls of Castle Varrich in the Scottish Highlands. As he crossed the dock, he noticed the massive longboats that Norse traders sailed to conduct trade on the island. With his father's jet-black hair and emerald eyes, few would believe Liam had Nordic heritage, but it had connected his family to Orkney for ten generations. He swept his eyes over the crofts nearest the marina of sorts. He watched as a tall blonde woman stormed out of a house and slammed the door shut. The fury on the woman's face made him think of his mother when she was angry with Liam and his younger brothers and sister. But the woman before him, statuesque and voluptuous, couldn't resemble his petite brunette mother any less. Her tall stature belied her curves until she leaned forward to fill a bucket at the well.

"Elene, come back here. We are not through speaking," an older woman called from the doorway to the croft Elene Isbister left. The younger woman continued to fill the bucket as though no one spoke to

1

her, but Liam watched her face grow red, and it wasn't from exertion. His path carried him toward the well, but he could have continued past to reach his destination. Instead, intrigued by the stunning blonde and the scene playing out before him, he stopped at the well as the woman finished raising the bucket. She poured the contents in her own pail before letting it drop back into the cavernous pit. Unaware of Liam, she jumped when he stepped forward and grasped the crank.

Liam's emerald eyes met deep sapphire, the shade of the Highland sky in autumn. Liam observed the surprise, then wariness, in her gaze as she stepped away. He drew the full bucket to the ledge and dipped the community ladle into the cool water. As he sipped, Elene took two steps back before turning away, disconcerted by the handsome stranger. However, her feet grew roots as the older woman stormed toward her. Liam kept his head down as he lowered the bucket, chiding himself for his nosiness but unwilling to move away. The older woman glanced at him dismissively before settling her attention on Elene.

In Norn, the language of Orkney, the woman continued her chastisement. "I didn't tell you that you could leave. We were in the middle of talking."

"No, Mother. You were in the middle of talking, and I was in the middle of not wanting to hear any more. I cannot believe you're considering marrying him."

"Not considering. I've already decided. When Gunter returns in a sennight, we will wed. Then we will all move home with him."

"Home?" Elene scoffed. "Norway hasn't been our people's home in ten generations. And you are a fool if you believe he will allow me to remain."

"You're old enough to marry."

"Getting married is a far sight different from being

sold!" Elene made to step around her mother, but the older woman was just as quick.

"You exaggerate."

"And you believe a slave trader over your own daughter."

"Gunter is not a slave trader. You would smear his name because you aren't getting what you want, you selfish child."

Clearly not a child, Elene stood to her full height as she gazed at her mother, who was at least two inches shorter than her daughter. "Selfish," she repeated her mother. "I hadn't realized Katryne and Johan raised themselves."

"I am their mother."

"But I raised my brother and sister. I lost my chance to marry while you lost yourself in barrels of mead." Elene swung her glare at Liam, who'd remained near the arguing women while he spoke to his two ship captains. Despite speaking Gaelic, Liam sensed Elene knew he understood her conversation with her mother. It explained her accusatory glare.

"That was my grief."

Elene released a dismissive puff of air. "That was your habit. You haven't missed Father in years. You welcomed Petyre into our home almost every night, and Father hadn't been dead two moons."

"We need a man to provide for us," the older woman sniffed defensively.

Elene gawked at her mother before she laughed. "We do not need a man to provide for us. You might need one because you can't stand to be alone for more than a day. But I work our fields and hunt out supper. Petyre, and now Gunter, come into our home and eat the food I provide. I should have accepted Duncan's offer before he grew fed up with waiting."

"You didn't love him."

3

"You mean like you love Gunter?"

"I do love him," Elene's mother insisted.

"More fool are you," Elene muttered.

"Come inside. You're causing a scene."

"I'm not the one yelling. And I can't. I must bring Bess this water, feed the chickens, muck out the stalls, then milk Bess. I haven't time to argue when I know you refuse to believe me."

"He is not going to sell you!"

"He will. Or he'll force me to bed him. He will not feed and clothe another adult without getting something in return. He told me."

"Liar," the older woman hissed. Elene stared at her mother, not recognizing the woman she'd become in the six years since Elene's father died. She nodded before turning toward the village barn. Liam watched her walk away before he continued to the mead hall in search of the village's chieftain.

"What was that all aboot?" Dermot asked as he came to walk beside Liam. He was the son of Clan Mackay's senior-most warrior and the clan's tánaiste before Liam rose to the position. Dermot was the best sailor in the clan and captain of the Mackays' largest ship. He was also Liam's friend since they were both in the cradle.

"The mother is remarrying a Norse trader, and the daughter doesnae like it." Liam shrugged, unwilling to admit how witnessing the exchange unnerved him. He wasn't sure if it was the conversation itself or the alluring blonde woman, but he was certain he wouldn't forget it. "It's none of ma business. We're here to represent ma grandfather."

Dermot glanced over his shoulder before returning his gaze to Liam. He said nothing, but he doubted his friend would merely forget the young woman. He'd watched Liam and the Orcadian woman stare at one another, and he'd known Liam only half paid attention

4

while he spoke to Dermot and Alfred, the other ship captain. They entered the mead hall, the warm air easing the chill they'd faced during their days at sea. It was summer, but a strong Atlantic breeze always buffeted the Northern Isles, and the waters had been choppy during their passage.

"Liam Mackay!" A bass voice boomed across the hall as a mountainous man with red hair and a fur cloak approached. If ever anyone doubted Orkney's connection to the Norse raiders of yore, this man put that doubt to rest. Androw Eunson resembled his Viking forebearers. He greeted Liam with a loose embrace as the men clapped one another on the back.

"Androw, how are you?" Liam asked in Norn, any hint of his Gaelic or Scots accent unnoticeable.

"Keeping well." The chieftain rubbed his barrel belly with a hearty chuckle. "It's been years since you visited Skaill. You're usually in Kirkwall with your family." Androw looked beyond Liam's shoulder, expecting to see Laird Liam Sinclair, the younger man's grandfather and namesake.

"Grandfather sent me as his representative."

"Ah. Wee Liam is not so wee anymore."

"Aye, well, I believe I shall bear that moniker for years to come. My grandfather is still as strong as a bear and looks more like my uncles than my grandfather."

"True, true. Come. Sit. Join us for the midday meal. You've arrived just in time." Androw elbowed Liam's belly in jest. "Someone has fed you well. You've filled out since the last time I saw you."

"That was nearly five years ago." Liam waggled his eyebrows and grinned. "I was a lad then. Now I'm a man."

"Is that so?" Androw returned Liam's grin. The man was closer in age to Liam's father, Laird Tristan

5

Mackay, than Liam's grandfather, the Earl of Sinclair and Orkney. Androw had teased Liam throughout his childhood visits to the archipelago that he resembled a herring while his male relatives were sharks. "Been swinging that sword, have you?"

Liam playfully scowled, but his grin was irrepressible. "Something like that." Liam accepted a mug of ale from a curvaceous woman who offered him a welcoming smile. He nodded and handed her a coin but kept his attention on Androw as Dermot joined the rest of the Mackay men at a table below the dais. While the woman was attractive, he hadn't traveled to Orkney to tup barmaids. Despite that resolve, an image of the angry blonde he'd watched only minutes earlier flashed to mind.

As Liam accepted the seat to which Androw gestured, he unclasped his own cloak and let it drape over his chair. The air was brisk but not unbearable. His *breacan feile*, or great plaid, was more than enough now that he no longer faced the bracing sea air. He accepted a trencher with his favorite Orcadian patties, a mixture of mincemeat, tatties, onions, and spices rolled together and fried. Its distinct flavor and texture, from the combination of the beef and potatoes, was something no one in his area of the Highlands ever replicated, despite how his mother and aunts tried. The Orcadians swore it was their cattle. Liam accepted a bere bannock made from beremeal, an ancient form of barley, and happily began his meal.

He'd taken three bites when the mead hall door opened, and the blonde woman from the well entered. Elene scanned the crowd before turning her attention to the dais. Liam registered her surprise when she saw him seated beside Androw, a trencher already before him. He knew all traders were the chieftain's guests, so Liam hoped her surprise was more personal. It cer-

6

tainly was for him. The woman approached the dais and dipped her head to her chieftain.

"Elene," Androw greeted. "Have you met our guest, Liam Mackay?"

"Hello." Elene's tone was softer than it had been when she argued with her mother, and it had a near-melodic tone as she turned her sapphire gaze toward Liam. In poor Gaelic, she offered, "Welcome."

"Thank you." Elene's eyebrows shot to her hairline when Liam responded in Norn. Her cheeks flushed red as she realized that, as she'd feared, he had understood the entire conversation he'd overheard. Her gaze hardened, the accusation clear. Liam's cheeks heated, and he offered her a guilty smile.

"Have you met?" Androw asked, looking between the pair.

"I overheard a conversation I wasn't meant to understand," Liam confessed in Norn.

"You mean Elene's argument with her mother?" Androw rolled his eyes. "The entire village heard."

Elene's jaw set, and Liam wondered if her teeth might crack from how tightly he saw them clenched. "Forgive me for interrupting. I will seek you later, Androw."

Liam wondered for a moment what Elene meant. Something passed between the older man and younger woman, and Liam felt a stab of emotion that he realized was jealousy. He shifted his attention to his patties, preferring to eat than watch what he assumed were lovers exchanging glances. He looked out from under his eyelashes as Elene turned away. There was something about the way Elene carried herself—with confidence and grace—that appealed to Liam. Even when she'd argued in public, she hadn't raised her voice. She'd remained collected; it was her mother who sounded like a harpy.

"So you already met my mother's cousin's grand-daughter," Androw surmised in Norn.

"We didn't really meet. We—encountered one another."

"You witnessed the argument, you mean."

"I don't think she appreciated that I understood it."

"I doubt it. We're used to it, especially her family, but I doubt she liked a handsome outsider watching and listening."

"It seemed—contentious." Liam chose his words carefully as he spoke to the Skaill chieftain. He trusted Androw, had known him most of his life, but he was there to conduct business, not gossip.

"Elene is a good woman, and she's dedicated to her family. Her younger brother and sister adore her, and rightfully so. But her mother is a self-centered woman and has been since we were children. When her husband died, she turned to the drink. Now she intends to remarry a Norse trader and move her family back to Norway. Since Elene is unwed, she has no choice but to join her mother and soon-to-be stepfather. There is little I can do, and she knows it, but I'm certain she was here to seek my help again."

"Has she not reached her majority?"

"She has. But she couldn't manage the farm alone, and once her mother marries, it becomes the Norse-man's property. She would have nowhere to live and no means to support herself. I wouldn't let her work here, and she would never agree to do so."

Liam watched Elene take a seat with a nearly ado-lescent girl and boy, who he guessed were the siblings he'd heard mentioned. He watched as she passed food to both before she served herself. She laughed with the surrounding people, but her eyes darted to the dais sev-eral times. But she never looked at Liam; she only watched Andrew. It still made him wonder about their relationship.

"You can stop trying to guess. Yes, she's beautiful, but so is my wife. Elene is family, not a woman I would bed." Liam swallowed, nearly choking, not appreciating that his thoughts were so obvious. "You needn't fear. If I hadn't known your father since we were lads, I wouldn't read your expressions so easily. You have your mother's keen mind, but you think just like your father did when he courted your mother. I made a brief visit for just a couple of days while your Sinclair family was still at Castle Varrich before your parents' marriage. I was there two days, but it was obvious how attracted your parents were to one another. Your face resembles your father's, especially since you watch Elene the same way your father watches your mother. I doubt you'd want to hear this, but Elene and Mairghread are very similar."

Liam scowled. Andrew was right. Liam didn't want to think of his mother when he thought of a woman who made his rod thicken. He'd made the fleeting comparison when he first saw Elene, and he knew Andrew was right after how he watched Elene converse with her mother. She'd been succinct and forceful while remaining calm, though her flushed cheeks spoke of her anger.

"Then she is a woman to be admired." Liam raised his mug to his lips, then paused. "From afar."

"That's likely for the best. Gunter Haakonsson isn't a man known to forgive anyone he believes is encroaching upon his trade. If he learns of your interest, or worse, Elene's interest, he will seek her and punish her."

"Was she right when she told her mother that Gunter intends to sell her?" Liam fought to keep his voice level as he grew anxious. When Andrew didn't respond immediately, Liam's piercing gaze bore into the chieftain. His anxiety rapidly morphed into anger, both at the faceless Norseman and his family's friend.

"I suspect he might. The slave trade is uncommon these days, but Gunter acts like a slighted lover where Elene is concerned. I think he was interested in her, but she rejected him. Now he is after her mother for spite. Selling her as a bed slave to some other Norseman is the type of revenge he would seek."

"And there is naught you can do?" Liam sounded incredulous.

"Ever since Gunter showed an interest in her, then made clear his intent to marry Inburgh, no man has dared come near her. No family will take her as a servant."

"Can't you protect your people from him if they did?"

Androw turned a warning glare on the younger man, not appreciating the insinuation that he couldn't control what happened in his village, that he was at the whim of a Norseman.

"Until your grandfather officially becomes the Earl of Orkney, I am still beholden to the Norse and pay fealty to them. Gunter is the king's younger brother."

Liam sat back in his chair, suddenly understanding the gravity of Elene's situation and the precarious position in which it placed Androw. He could understand a prince's interest in Elene. She was beautiful, clearly intelligent, well spoken, and appeared strong enough to survive childbirth. The only reason for the Norseman to take an interest in a middle-aged woman with three children was to gain something far more valuable. Liam wondered if it was truly to sell Elene or force her into his bed as she'd predicted to her mother. Androw had little recourse to deny Gunter Haakonsson anything for as long as the Norse controlled Orkney.

Liam withdrew a scroll from his sporran and unrolled it, smoothing the creases before he slid it toward a watching Androw. "This is the deed. King David signed it a fortnight ago, agreeing to accept Orkney and Shetland in appeasement for King Haakon Haakonsson's debts. My grandfather is the Earl of Orkney, and King David is now your sovereign."

"This won't endear you to anyone."

"I didn't think it would. But the people know my grandfather and my Uncle Callum. They know they're two of the most trustworthy men alive."

"That's not what causes the chilly reception. The Norse traders won't return. That means lean times for people who rely on the Norse to buy their crops."

"We provide just as much trade for Orcadians as the Norse do, and my grandfather accounted for that. The Earl of Angus has agreed to increase trade and keep their close ties to the islands. You know the Mackays are connected to this land, just as they are to Castle Varrich."

"I know that, and you know that. Even people on the isles know that. But that doesn't mean the Norse will make anyone's life easy."

"Then the Norse should have considered that before they failed to pay a dowry." Liam swept his gaze over the gathered villagers. He noticed that most stared, or at least glanced, at him frequently. The only person studiously ignoring him was Elene, who faced him but never looked at him. When she looked toward the dais, she offered Androw a challenging glare.

"That may be, but Haakon Haakonsson is in Norway, and you are the one here. Tread lightly, my friend. I do not want to explain any bumps or bruises to your mother. Lady Mackay terrifies me." The enormous redhead chuckled, a booming sound that bounced off the walls. Liam cocked an eyebrow, knowing Androw only half-jested. The man would be wise to recall Mairghread Mackay was the best knife thrower in all the Highlands, defeating her oldest brother Callum year after year at the Highland Gatherings. While Callum reigned as the men's champion for nearly two decades, it was undisputed that Mairghread was likely the best in all of Scotland.

Androw's laughter and clap on Liam's back was a genuinely friendly gesture, but Liam understood it signaled to all in the gathering hall that Liam was a welcome guest. He was certain they would need the reminder in the days to come.

CHAPTER 2

*E*lene pretended to focus her ire on Androw throughout the midday meal, but she couldn't ignore the brooding Highlander who sat beside her chieftain and distant relative. She noticed each of his expressions, reading them with ease despite not hearing the men's conversation. When Androw looked at her and spoke, she observed Liam's concern, then anger. She assumed Androw explained the situation with Gunter and her mother, Inburgh. His mien turned shrewd as he handed a scroll to Androw to read. She knew not what the scroll decreed, but she suspected it was about Orkney's impending transition from Norse to Scottish rule.

Intertwined for centuries, Orkney had belonged to the Norse since their early conquests, but men of mixed Norse and Scottish ancestry governed them and Shetland. The Earl of Sinclair—now also the Earl of Orkney—and the Earl of Angus both held Norse lineage a few generations back. With the new position, the Earl of Sinclair and Orkney would be known as the Earl of Caithness.

It surprised her to hear the young man introduced as a Mackay, since she'd assumed he was a Sinclair.

She'd met some when she was a young girl when they passed through Skaill before venturing to other parts of the archipelago.

"Elene, did you hear me?" Katryne tugged on Elene's arm. "Can we go down to the water's edge to gather whelks and cockles?"

"You must wait for the tide to go out. I don't want you to slice your fingers off if you can't see what you're doing." Elene looked down at her younger sister, a near-mirror image of her own face and their dead father's. The earnest, deep-blue eyes pleaded with her, and there was little hope she could refuse Katryne or Johan. She'd loved wading into the chilled Atlantic waters, digging her toes into the sand as she searched for the shellfish. She still accompanied them often to search for spoots. She didn't feel either her brother or her sister was old enough at ten and twelve to handle the long knife needed to pry the razorfish from the sand at low tide.

At ten years Katryne's senior and twelve years Johan's senior, Elene had felt more like a mother than an older sister for half her life. Inburgh miscarried several pregnancies between Elene and Katryne, and the village midwife told her to stop trying after she nearly died birthing Johan. It was only a few years later that the siblings' father, Thome Isbister, died. Within weeks, Inburgh abandoned the children in favor of alcohol, and only two months after her husband died, she took a lover. She ignored nearly all her duties to cater to a man who eventually got himself killed by falling from the gristmill and cracking his head open while drunk.

While girls her age were still playing games and chasing one another, Elene was at home, cooking every meal and learning how to manage a farm on her own. After being kicked more than once, she learned how to milk their cow. Neighboring men took pity on her for the first few years and brought their own plows and horses to help her till their land. Eventually, she grew strong enough to manage their horse and plow alone. She'd cared for her mother when she was too inebriated to make it to her bed. Elene struggled when her siblings were still very young to hide their mother's alcoholism from them, but she'd given up after Inburgh flew into a rage at her in front of Johan and Katryne while glugging mead from a wineskin.

Elene glanced toward the door, picturing the Highlanders' ships docked in the bay. She longed for a means to escape, and the birlinns appealed to her. They would take her away from her life of verbal abuse and drudgery. A life where she took care of everyone, but no one took care of her. She finally let her full gaze rest on the Highlander as he and Androw rose. Their eyes locked, and something sparked between them. They stared at one another for a protracted moment, and Elene had an overwhelming sense that she could trust the stranger. Then she chided herself for thinking she could trust anyone.

She couldn't trust her mother. She couldn't trust Gunter. She couldn't trust that Androw could, or would, help her. None of her neighbors would. Her brother and sister were too young for her to entrust her wellbeing to them, especially since they depended on her for theirs. With an even heavier heart than before the meal, Elene rose and followed Katryne and Johan from the mead hall. They raced together toward the shore while she turned toward their croft.

Elene avoided entering her home, knowing her mother would still be inside. Instead, she made her way to the back of the building, to the lean-to where Bess stood in the shade alongside their gelding, *Belget*, who she'd named greedy for how he had nursed constantly as a newborn foal. She drew him from the shade and harnessed him to their two-wheeled cart. With the reins in one hand and the wheelbarrow's handle in the other, she urged the cantankerous old horse out to the fields. She walked along the rows of potatoes, looking for the yellow-fleshed ones that were ready to harvest. She toiled for two hours, gathering a barrowful of the root vegetable, before steering Belget back to the croft.

I would be glad to never see a plow again in my life. I don't even like tatties, yet here I am, harvesting more of the damn things. They taste like the dirt they come from. Would that I could walk into the sea and float away.

After unharnessing the gelding and transferring the potatoes into baskets, Elene wiped sweat from her brow. She was sticky, and her gown clung to her back and breasts. She wished for nothing more than a dip in the freshwater loch only a half mile from the village. She would have to content herself with a drink from the village well for now, but she planned to slip away to bathe before nightfall.

"What's happening?" Elene asked a neighbor as she entered the village center. A crowd gathered, blocking her way to the well. In the center, she spied Androw and the Highlander. Androw held a sheet of parchment, presumably the one Elene watched Liam hand to him during the midday meal. Before the neighbor answered, Androw spoke.

"It can come as no surprise that our time as Norsemen and -women has ended. We are now Scottish, and subjects of King David II," Androw proclaimed. Elene watched as Liam attempted not to wince. It was hardly the introduction she would have offered, even to a man who eavesdropped on her argument, however public, with her mother. "Liam Mackay, Laird Tristan Mackay's son and heir, and Laird Liam Sinclair's grandson, is here officially to accept governance of Orkney on the Earl of Caithness's behalf. He and his family have long ties to the Northern Isles, so it is easy for the Sinclairs and the Mackays to understand our Norse heritage and traditions. We shall celebrate this eve!"

Liam noticed Elene the moment she stepped into the crowd. But his attention whipped back to Androw in horror as the chieftain bluntly announced yet another power that felt foreign to them would rule the Orcadians. He understood the Norse culture felt more familiar to the islanders than anything Scottish, despite how the two cultures had blended as the people from both regions settled Orkney and its neighbor, Shetland. He prayed he would report a smooth transition when he returned to the Sinclairs at Castle Dunbeath. This was the first mission where he commanded entirely on his own. He'd led patrols on both Mackay and Sinclair land, and he'd accompanied his family to court frequently. But he'd begged his father for a chance to prove himself, and it was his grandfather who offered the opportunity.

It shouldn't have surprised Liam that he didn't make the announcement, but he'd planned what he would say from the moment he stepped aboard the Mackay ship bound for Rousay, then Mainland, the largest of the Orkney Islands. He'd intended to begin by reminding the Orcadians that the Sinclairs had Norse family ties, just as they did, and that the Sinclairs were a long-established presence on the islands. He'd hoped to remind them that he'd been visiting the islands since he was a child, that he'd taken his first steps in Kirkwall just before his first saint's day.

Instead, he faced an angry crowd who resented his presence. He understood it stemmed from fear of the unknown. He supposed it wasn't too late to make the speech he'd planned.

"Hello." Liam sought Elene, the only familiar face among the crowd. He locked eyes with her, and he sensed she didn't realize she offered an encouraging nod. But it gave him the confidence he suddenly lacked. "It has been five years since I last visited this part of Orkney, but as you can tell, it isn't the first time I've spoken Norn. I have spent much of my life traveling here. I even took my first steps outside St. Magnus Cathedral in Kirkwall. I feasted alongside your kinsmen in Snusgar, as a guest in the chieftain's home, the last time I was near here."

Liam paused, surveying the crowd, hoping his speech was well received. When no one came after him with a shovel or a sword, he plowed on with his gaze once more locked with Elene's.

"My grandfather, Laird Sinclair, chose me for this journey to share the news that after decades of travel and trade, he is now the Scottish king's designated leader on Orkney. Many of you know my grandfather since he was King Robert the Bruce's frequent delegate here to represent Scotland in negotiations with the Norse. You know him to be fair and wise, a man renowned not only as a warrior but as a leader. I am honored he chose me to stand here in his stead."

Liam shifted his gaze from Elene and swept it over the gathering once more. While no one appeared openly hostile, most were dismissive. He assumed they were unimpressed by him or the announcement. If their daily lives changed little, they wouldn't care that Orkney now belonged to Scotland. However, he noticed several people dash nervous glances at the Norse longboats that left the bay with the tide. Liam had met none of the Norse traders, but he'd seen them moving around the dock when he arrived. Their suspicion and dislike had been nearly palpable.

When he looked back, much of the crowd had dispersed, clearly unmoved by his speech. Androw stood talking to Elene, leaving Liam wondering what he should do. He supposed he would return to his ship and ensure his men unloaded all the goods. He was certain they had, but he could think of nothing else to fill his time before the evening meal in a few hours. He couldn't very well stand in the village square alone.

"Liam," Androw called and gestured to him to come stand with Androw and Elene. When Liam neared, he dipped his chin to Elene. He wondered if the heat his cheeks exuded made them match the shade of pink Elene's cheeks grew as he approached. He doubted it looked as fetching on him as it did her. "Since you have met but only briefly introduced, I suppose I shall perform the courtesy. Liam Mackay, this is Elene Isbister."

Before either Elene or Liam could say anything, Androw spun on his heel and called out to men near the gristmill. He left the pair staring at one another. Again. Elene wished to melt into the ground. She hardly felt presentable, with her filthy gown still clinging to her. She knew her hair was a mess, and dirt filled the space beneath her nails. She glanced away, embarrassed but unable to escape without saying something. It was Liam who blurted out the first thing that came to mind.

"I apologize for earlier. I know I shouldn't have listened to your argument, and since I did, I should have —" Liam shrugged. "I suppose I should have let you know I understood. I didn't mean to be rude or deceptive, but I suspect that's how it appears."

"It did." Elene raised her chin, but she struggled to feel imperious when she caught a whiff of herself. "I feared you might, but I told myself there was no way you could. I didn't know who you were—are."

"Feared?" Liam shifted, feeling uncomfortable at the notion Elene might fear anything about him.

Elene looked at her feet, miserable that Androw trapped her in a conversation that hardly fit the one she imagined as she worked in the field. This was hardly charming, or even amusing. It wasn't seductive and alluring. It was humiliating.

"It's embarrassing that a stranger listened to what we said. It's even worse that you understood. I should go." Elene couldn't bring herself to meet Liam's gaze.

"I was fearful too," Liam confessed. "I still am. I didn't like what I heard. And I admit Androw explained some of it to me."

Elene was certain that flames danced around and singed her ears. She could only imagine just what her talkative distant cousin shared. It took a moment for her to register that he admitted he was scared on her behalf. She forced herself to look up, and a shiver raced along her spine when their eyes met. The overwhelming sense that she could trust Liam once more flooded her, even though her conscience screamed that she was a fool.

"Is there really no way for you to stay?" Liam's words broke into Elene's thoughts.

"Short of marrying someone in the next fortnight, no."

Elene's words hung in the air. Neither knew what to say. Liam didn't want to imagine Elene in another man's arms, in his bed. But neither could he make an offer. Elene furthered her embarrassment when she feared he thought she expected him to ask. Liam opened his mouth to say he wished he could help, but he feared how Elene might interpret it. "I'm sorry if my arrival complicates things, since the Norse who arrive next won't be pleased that I'm here."

"You're staying for a fortnight?" Elene doubted that was the part that was supposed to catch her attention the most.

"Yes. I have other parts of Rousay to visit, but I shall leave my birlinns docked here. I have smaller curraghs to take me between the closest islands, too. I'm not just representing my grandfather, I'm delivering grain my father sold in the spring."

Elene nodded, debating what to say. "I wish you well." The words sounded flat to her ear. She smothered her grimace, feeling tongue-tied and obtuse in front of the most desirable man she'd ever met.

"Thank you. I wish you the same." Liam and Elene watched one another until they accepted there was nothing more to say. Elene forced her feet to carry her home, even though she still loathed returning to the croft. Liam trudged to the dock. He looked back just as Elene turned toward him when she reached her door. Liam fought the unexpected urge to cross the village and kiss Elene. They went their separate ways, even tried to ignore one another at the evening meal, but thoughts of one another plagued them the entire evening.

Elene eased the door closed behind her before lifting her skirts and hurrying away from her croft. She'd laid out her soap, drying linen, fresh chemise, and shawl while she made supper for her mother. Inburgh hadn't attended the evening meal, opting for a jug of wine instead. Feeling guilty that their argument likely spurred Inburgh's latest intoxication, Elene prepared a meal she doubted her mother would touch, then went to the gathering hall for her own food. But she felt compelled to tend to her mother, despite how she loathed doing so. Guilt and duty drove her most days, exhausting her more than the physical labor of running their farm.

While she longed to escape her life, she settled for escaping her home and running to the freshwater loch just beyond the village. As she approached the water, she looked toward Snusgar, recalling Liam saying he'd feasted there the last time he'd been to her part of the island. She wondered if they'd ever met as children. She scoffed, reminding herself that she wouldn't easily forget the striking combination of jet-black hair and emerald-green eyes. Even if Liam hadn't been so attractive five years ago, which she doubted—she doubted he'd ever been unattractive—she would have still remembered a Scottish boy who had such unusual features.

As she approached the loch's shore, she slipped behind a boulder that she always used to shield her as she undressed. Water lapped at its base on one side, making it possible for her to slip into the loch without being noticeable. She folded her soiled clothes, intending to launder them once she finished bathing. She couldn't bring herself to put on clean clothes while her body was still filthy, not wanting two sets to wash since it would leave her nothing to change into. With her only clothes folded and out of the water's reach, she snatched her lump of soap and waded into the brisk water. Even in summer, the loch's water never warmed because of its depth. She swam out to where she could no longer stand and allowed herself to drop beneath the surface as she worked her fingers through her braid. Kicking her legs, Elene surfaced and tilted her head back, her hair floating out around her.

"If I hadn't met you today, I would think you were a selkie."

Elene splashed and dipped below the surface, unprepared for the male voice. Her head popped back out as she twisted to find its source. She breathed a sigh that she hadn't been floating on her back with her breasts in the air like she often did—like she would have done if Liam didn't startle her.

"What're you doing here?" Elene recognized the question as an accusation, but she resented anyone being in her nightly sanctuary, even if it was Liam. She told herself that her nipples tightened further from the cold, not from knowing Liam tread water, naked, only a few yards from her.

"The same as you. The water isn't warm, but it's clean and nowhere near as freezing as the Atlantic." Liam grinned but grew serious when Elene didn't return the amusement. He looked around, wondering if she'd come alone. "I'll leave if you are expecting —privacy."

Elene's mouth dropped open, understanding Liam's implication. "I'm not married. The only privacy I expected was to be alone."

Liam drifted closer, unaware of what he was doing, until he stopped himself with just enough distance that the moonlight didn't illuminate their naked bodies to one another. "You come here alone? In the dark?"

"You're here alone."

"And I've been wielding a sword since I was five."

Elene cocked an eyebrow, finally amused.

"You and Androw both," Liam grumbled. "That wasn't what I meant. My sword may be on the shore, but I have three dirks on me right now. Are you carrying any knives?"

Elene glanced down without thinking. She couldn't see beneath the water's surface to where Liam tread. She caught herself and looked up, his grin back in place. Feeling testy once more, she snapped, "No."

"Then only one of us is prepared if someone attacked. And only one of us is a likely target."

"Yes. You. Only one of us is unwelcome here." Elene blinked several times, shocked at the snideness in her tone.

Liam's arms stopped moving, but he remained above the surface. "Be that as it may, you said yourself that a Norseman wishes to sell you. A beautiful, naked woman is an easy target for any man, especially one who already wishes you harm. He might kill me for taking his trade, but he'd do a far sight worse to you. You'd wish you were dead."

"I already do most days," Elene whispered. Liam swam closer, hearing her confession.

"Elene." It was Liam's turn to keep his voice low. "I already finished bathing. I'll swim back to my clothes and leave you alone. But I'm not leaving here. Take as long as you want. I'll stand guard, then walk you back."

"Why?"

"Because it's the best I can do."

Tears filled Elene's eyes, unprepared for the rush of emotion. No one had offered to protect her since her father was alive. She swallowed the lump in her throat and nodded. Liam turned away, dipping below the surface, and swimming underwater. When he surfaced, he was much farther than Elene expected. She watched him wade out of the water, his muscular form moving with ease. The water shimmered on him beneath the moonlight, but he was too far for her to make out any sculpted details—or to see the part that made her most curious. As she ran the soap over her body, she wondered what it would feel like to have Liam's hands roaming over her. When she washed between her legs, she lingered, circling her finger over the tiny bundle of nerves she'd discovered by accident at thirteen.

The first time she'd brought herself to release had

been the product of an accident and curiosity. Now it was purposeful as she looked in Liam's direction. He'd ducked behind a boulder of his own. She wondered if he had a drying cloth with him, something that she could have been running over his chiseled body. She'd watched in awe as his shoulder muscles bunched and relaxed while he was in front of her. She bit her lip and moaned as pleasure surged through her. Wishing she could linger and pleasure herself a few more times, she knew she needed to be considerate of Liam's time. She hurried to scrub her hair, then dashed back to her clothes. She rushed to launder her filthy ones then donned her clean ones.

Liam pressed his back against the boulder, hiding himself from Elene's view. He turned his head and glanced around the edge of the enormous rock. He could see she faced him, but he was certain she could no longer see him. Knowing she was naked in the water had immediately brought his cock to life. It had twitched with annoyance when he swam closer but stopped before they could touch. He'd spied her watching him leave the water, and the ache in his bollocks grew unbearable. Now he peeked at her as he wrapped his hand around his rod and stroked.

He heeded his father's warning about having too colorful a past before marrying. Tristan's past had hurt Mairghread several times over the years, even endangering her while they were still courting. Tristan warned Liam and his brothers, Alec and Hamish, that there were few things more dangerous in life than a scorned woman. Taking his warning to heart, all three men had gained enough experience to know what they would do when they took wives, but none were the rakes their uncles Callum and Tavish had been. The two Sinclair brothers had echoed Tristan's warnings to their own sons, having caused their own share of pain to their wives.

As Liam eased his overwhelming desire for a woman he'd met only hours ago, he wondered if he should find a barmaid in the mead hall to further assuage his need. It was a rarity for him to indulge in women or alcohol. But he suddenly felt like he needed one or the other to fill the unexpected longing he had for the unusual blonde for whom he now lusted. He groaned as Elene tilted her head back to wash the soap from her hair. He suspected she didn't realize how much of her breasts he could see. He wondered if she even suspected he watched her. Then he asked himself whether she was doing it on purpose to tempt him. Before he was able to formulate an answer, another groan tore from his throat as his seed spilled forth. With a sigh, he rested his head against the rock.

When he noticed Elene leaving the water, he hurried to dress. Only barely sated and annoyed at himself that he hadn't been guarding her like he promised, he gathered his sword and made his way toward Elene's private spot.

Someone could have attacked us both while I had ma hand wrapped around ma bluidy cock. I wasna supposed to be fisting maself. I was supposed to be protecting her. And from whom? The vera sort of mon I am. Och, I wouldnae force her. But I was certainly lusting after her. I still am. Bluidy hell.

Liam approached Elene's boulder as she stepped around it. She finger-combed her hair while she eased her foot into her slippers. Without forethought, Liam reached out and peeled away a lock of hair plastered to her neck. His knuckles brushed her throat and collarbone. They both froze.

"I'm sorry. I had no right to do that." Liam pulled his hand away.

"Thank you." Elene didn't want Liam to regret touching her. She wanted him to do it again. "I appreciate you guarding me." She didn't understand why Liam blushed. She assumed her thanks embarrassed him. Liam knew he blushed because he hadn't guarded her at all. He'd forgotten entirely.

"Earlier, you made it sound like you come out here often." Liam looked around. Since the island had very few trees, it exposed the loch on all sides. Anyone could watch Elene, but she would likely see them as easily as they did her. But the village was still half a mile away, and most men would easily outrun her and catch her if she tried to get away. They began walking back.

"No man is coming near me, Liam. The men in the village know Gunter has claimed me. He hasn't made it a secret that I'm his, one way or another. The other Norse traders won't come near me for the same reason. Who is going to stop the Norse king's spoiled brother? Gunter won't touch me because he can't sell me if I'm not a maiden. And he doesn't trust me not to kill him and escape while we're still here. He'll wait until I'm truly his prisoner."

"You're placing your safety on the assumption that no man believes he could force you beneath him, then force you to keep the secret. There are too many men in the world who believe they can do just that. Mayhap not the men you grew up with. I don't know. But traders from other islands and Norway come here all the time." Liam stopped them as they walked toward the village. He turned toward Elene. "I can't stop you. I won't stop you. If you wish to come back while I'm here, I will escort you. I think this place is your haven, your only respite. I don't want to take that from you. But I also can't ignore how fearful it makes me after what I learned today, after what you just said. I will always give you your privacy. I will bathe at another time."

"Why?"

Liam frowned. "I have a younger sister, Ainsley, and I have nearly ten female cousins on my mother's side. I'm also close with my mother's cousins' children. There are half-a-dozen more girls among them. I would never consider letting a single one of them come here alone, dressed or undressed. If they found themselves alone, I would hope someone honorable would help them."

"You assume I can't protect myself."

"No. I get the feeling you can protect yourself quite well—dressed and with a weapon, or at least not slippery. Your smaller size and being naked will put you at a disadvantage few people—man or woman—could easily overcome. I wouldn't let any of my boy cousins who don't yet train come somewhere like this alone, either."

"So you're not overbearing. You're just overprotective." The corner of Elene's mouth twitched.

"I think I'm just the right amount protective. I'm serious though. I won't stand in your way or invade your privacy. That was an accident tonight. But I will stand guard."

They stopped as they came to the edge of the village, just beyond the wooden wall. Nothing stirred, but both knew that didn't mean they couldn't be spied upon if they continued together. Elene stood on her toes and pressed a kiss to Liam's stubble. She surprised herself with her boldness as much as she did Liam. He turned his head in shock, and their lips grazed together. They froze, their noses a hair's-breadth apart. Elene's lips parted as her sapphire eyes locked with Liam's emerald ones. His hand brushed hers before it traveled up her forearm, then rested at her waist.

"I have never wanted to kiss a woman as much as I do you," Liam murmured, his warm breath caressing Elene's lips. She lifted her chin, bringing her mouth to his.

"Please," she breathed.

Their mouths fused together as Liam's hand slid to the small of her back and pressed her against him. Elene's hands grasped his powerful biceps, which flexed under her hold. She glided them up to his shoulders, then along his neck, until she cupped his jaw. Liam's free hand mirrored her movements as his other arm tightened around her.

The kiss was gentle, despite the simmering passion threatening to boil over. It was clear to both that it wasn't a first kiss for either of them. But it was their first kiss together. Neither wanted to hurry. Neither wanted to think that it might be their only kiss together. Their tongues tangled as they canted their heads as they pressed their bodies against one another. It was the soft cooing noise from a dunter, an Eider duck, which waddled from a patch of heather that finally broke them apart. They leaned away, but neither let go.

Elene glimpsed a longing in Liam's gaze that she suspected her eyes mirrored. When silence engulfed them once more, the need for another kiss subsumed them. The passion threatened to pour forth, but they both moved slowly, fearful any hurried movements might spoil the moment. Liam's tongue slid past Elene's teeth and caressed the inside of her cheek before it swept along hers. Just before he could retreat, she sucked lightly.

"Do that again, and it will be me who carries you off to my ship," Liam whispered with a groan. Elene repeated the arousing kiss, adding more force. His hand dropped from her jaw, his palm resting on her nape. The broad palm held her in place, and it was his turn to devour her. He kissed along her jaw until he came to her ear, where he nipped her lobe. "We should stop. We should go our separate ways. But all I want is you."

"Don't let go. Don't leave. I'll only embarrass myself and follow you like a lost kitten." Elene nuzzled his throat before licking and grazing her teeth over the heated skin. Their kiss erupted with the suppressed passion of only moments ago. She fisted the front of his leine, making certain he understood she didn't want him to go, as though neither her kiss nor her words proved it.

The sound of someone moving within the village broke them apart, both taking two steps back and looking in the sound's direction. It was a night sentry on the other side of the wooden wall. Without a word, they hurried through the gate. Elene glanced back as she moved away from Liam's side. She found him watching her when she reached her croft. She stood at her door until he turned toward the chieftain's home, knowing he was a guest there. Neither slept well that night.

CHAPTER 3

$\mathcal{L}$iam stepped onto his ship's deck after sorting sacks of grain seeds and barrels of whisky. He and his men spent the early morning separating the items into stacks and groups for each village at which they would stop. As he looked toward the shore, a tall woman with blonde hair caught his eye. He was too far to see her face, but her graceful walk and proud bearing told him it was Elene. He watched as she stooped to dig in the sand beside Katryne. The younger sister pulled something from the ground and held it up. Liam watched Elene nod before Katryne dropped her catch in a basket.

Liam stepped onto the dock and made his way to where the sisters continued to work. "Good morning," he greeted.

Elene looked up and shaded her eyes. "Good morning."

"We're hunting for scoot again," Katryne announced. "Elene brought her big knife, but I found all these myself." Katryne's cheeky grin showed her pride that she'd accomplished more than her much-older sister.

Liam peered into the basket and nodded. "You've done very well for such an early start."

"Take these back to the croft and clean them. Tell Johan that he must milk Bess for me." Elene stood and handed the basket to Katryne, who ran back toward the village. "Is everything all right aboard your *longa*?"

"Yes. We were just sorting through the goods and making sure we know what goes to which village."

"When will you visit the other homesteads?"

"In two or three days. We could go today, but the men earned some rest before they haul sacks and barrels. They deserve a couple nights' sleep on cots before sleeping on the ground after several days sleeping on the decks."

"That's generous of you."

Liam shrugged. "They're good men who work hard. I don't take that for granted."

"A nobleman who respects his warriors."

"A man who respects those who he leads and those who are older than him." Liam glanced toward the birlinns. "Dermot's my age, but the rest have known me since I was in swaddling clothes. At least one of them has wiped my runny nose after I've sneezed on him. I owe them a good deal."

"Sneezed on them?" Elene grinned.

"Mayhap not sneezed or a runny nose. But they've known me all my life, and they each helped me become a warrior. They trained me in the lists, and now train alongside me. There's time, so why not let them rest?" Liam shrugged again.

Elene nodded, unsure what to say next. Liam watched her, appearing equally uncertain. He tucked his thumbs into his belt to keep from fidgeting. He'd never been so nervous around a lass, but neither had he ever shared such an earthshaking kiss with one as he did with Elene the previous night.

"Than—" Elene started.

"I mea—" Liam spoke at the same time. He gestured for her to go first.

"Thank you for walking me back last night." Elene's cheeks heated. She didn't know if she should thank him for the kiss, too, or pretend like it never happened. The awkwardness between them wouldn't let either of them forget.

"You're welcome. And I meant what I said. I'll respect your privacy, but I still wish to accompany you if you go out alone."

"I appreciate that." Elene's gaze met Liam's, emeralds and sapphires sparkling in the sunlight. "I would like that."

"I thought to go fishing today. I want to offer Janet something since I will share their meals. Would you show me where the best spot is?"

Elene nodded, a smile playing at the corner of her mouth. "Do you have a pole?"

"Yes. On the birlinn. Do you?"

"Of course. Are you inviting me to stay and fish with you?" Elene cocked an eyebrow.

"I was going to, but you saved me from worrying that you might say no."

"But I didn't say yes. I just wanted to know if you were inviting me." When Liam's smile faltered, Elene giggled. The youthful sound surprised her, making her cease as her cheeks flushed brighter. Why was she blushing so often these days? She was certain she looked like a permanent hazel berry. "I'd like to come."

"Meet you here in five minutes?"

"Yes." Elene hurried to her croft, and Liam watched her cross the village before he recalled he needed to gather his own pole and tackle. They were soon walking along the beach, both enjoying the feel of sand between their toes while they carried their poles in one hand and their shoes in the other. "Just around those rocks is an inlet that's quite deep. The fish like to gather there."

Liam spied the spot and noticed there was a place between two rocks that would be wide enough for them to sit together, with their feet hanging over the ledge. They were quiet while they both set up their poles and dropped their lines into the water below.

"Has your family been on Orkney for many generations?" Liam asked. It was all he could think of to say.

"Yes. About ten generations on my father's side. Has your family always been at Varrich?"

"Yes. About as long as your family has been here. My however-many-ago grandfathers married a Norsewoman, actually. That man's cousin left as a young woman and moved to the Trondelag after the Norse raided her home. She married the jarl."

Elene's head turned as her brow furrowed. Something about Liam's story reminded her of the tales her father told. "Do you know this woman's name? The jarl's?"

"Lorna Mackay. It's quite the legend among my clan. She married Rangvald Thorson."

"Who had Erik Rangvaldson and married Freya Ivarsdóttir," Elene supplied.

"How did you know? Freya's brother, Leif, and his wife, Sigrid, had a daughter. She married the laird's son. Alex Mackay was Lorna's cousin."

"I didn't know that part." Elene's mouth turned down for a moment. "But I know they had friends. Bjorn Jansson, Tyra Vigosdóttir, and Strian Eindrideson."

"The Mackays helped them fight an enemy, Hakin Hakinsson. The legend says they fought in the Trondelag, but Hakin escaped to the Highlands, then Wales. The Norse followed them and enlisted the Mackays to help since Lorna bound them. Their victory was quite the Viking glory of their day."

"Yes. I remember something about Strian being separated from his wife, Gressa Jorgensdóttir, during an earlier battle." Elene grew excited to tell parts of her family legend, and she could tell Liam was eager to listen. They both marveled that their families were bound so many generations ago. "They found one another, but she wanted to return to Wales, where her captors sold her as a slave. Why would she want to go back there if she could return home with her husband?"

Liam continued with a part he remembered. He hadn't heard the story from his father since he was a young boy, but it flooded back to him as he shared it with Elene. "The legend says that each couple was a love match known across the North Sea. Freya and Leif's parents, Ivar Sorenson and Lena Tormudsdóttir, were as powerful and as in love as Erik's parents, Rangvald and Lorna."

Elene's gaze locked with Liam's, both feeling something indescribable and too overwhelming to discern. "The legend in my family is that Tyra and Bjorn married and had sons. Strian's wife, Gressa, was part Sami, and they had several sons but one daughter. That daughter married one of Tyra and Bjorn's sons. They settled here."

The pair stared at one another until a tug on Elene's line broke their concentration. She pulled the fish from the water and tied it to an extra piece of line. Liam watched as he thought about the story they'd told together, that their lives already overlapped.

"Do you believe in fate?" Liam blurted.

"I don't know," Elene answered as she dropped her line into the water again. She turned her head to look at Liam. "Do you?"

"Fate or God, I don't know. But someone or something guides our lives, takes us where we are supposed to be. It's our choice whether we accept that."

Elene opened her mouth to respond, wanting to tell Liam that she believed the same, but Johan called out to her. He dashed to them, explaining that their mother demanded Elene return to prepare their morning porridge. Elene nodded, too embarrassed to look at Liam. But she smiled when he offered his hand and helped her to her feet. Johan skipped ahead of them while Liam and Elene walked briskly.

"I like that our pasts overlap," Elene said as they walked across the village.

"Mayhap it is fate." Liam stopped outside Elene's door. "Should I meet you outside the wall after the evening meal?"

"Yes, please." Elene scanned their surroundings before she reached out and squeezed Liam's hand. She ducked into her croft before either of them could say more.

Liam looked behind him as he slipped through the wooden gate and looked in the loch's direction. It was only a moment later the gate opened again. He swung around, poised to grab his sword. Elene held her hands up in surrender, grinning at Liam.

"Do you need to protect yourself from me?" Elene whispered.

Liam's shoulders relaxed as he reached out to carry Elene's bundle. They set off for the loch in silence. When their hands brushed together twice, they linked their fingers, neither saying anything but both enjoying the touch. When they reached the loch, they faced one another, their hands still clasped.

"I'll stand behind that boulder until you're in the

water. Then I will move to where I can see more of the loch and the other side."

"Are you missing your chance to bathe for this?" Elene bit her bottom lip, feeling guilty.

"No. I will come back after you're done."

"Mayhap…" Elene trailed off when Liam shook his head.

"I may have dirks on me when I bathe but wading in with you leaves us both vulnerable. The reason I offered to protect you is because you're already vulnerable. It defeats the point if I am too."

"But it's an inconvenience."

"If I thought that, then I wouldn't have offered." Liam's lips twisted. "Well, I would have, but I wouldn't be enjoying being here with you."

Elene offered her thanks and ducked behind the boulder. She undressed, then peered around it until she was certain Liam wasn't watching. Despite having found each other naked the night before, she felt embarrassed that he might see her bare. She hurried into the water and dove beneath the surface. When her head emerged, she spied Liam looking around them and across the loch. She would have liked to soak, taken her time, but she didn't want to force Liam to stay awake too long. She knew they should both be abed—albeit in separate ones. Her lips pursed as she silently grumbled at that admission.

Five minutes later, Elene called to Liam. "I'm getting out now."

Liam turned toward her, having studiously avoided looking at her. His cock pulsed behind his sporran just thinking about being so close to Elene while she was naked. He didn't need to make it worse by seeing her so. "That was quick. I thought you'd like to linger."

"Not this evening." Elene swam closer to shore but waited for Liam to turn away. He put his back to her as she dashed behind the boulder and rubbed herself dry, toweling her sopping hair. She hurried to dress, once more not wanting to delay Liam and shivering in the brisk night air. When she was presentable, she carried her bundle as she approached Liam. He pointed toward a grassy knoll near the water's edge a few feet in the opposite direction from the village.

Liam led the way, unpinning the extra length of his plaid. When they came to the spot, he spread the woolen yards on the ground and offered Elene a place to sit. He gazed up at the heavens. "My mother taught my brothers, sister, and me ancient stories about the stars. She told us what the Greeks and Romans believed. She even told us about the Norse. I still love looking at them and remembering those nights all of us, including my father, would lie in the meadow outside our walls. We would tell the stories as we pointed out the clusters. We would make up ones for the stars we didn't know."

"That's a wonderful memory," Elene whispered. Liam reached out his hand and grasped hers.

"I'm sorry if that was insensitive. I know not all families are like mine."

Elene rolled onto her side, still holding Liam's hand. "Don't feel guilty about having a loving family and fond memories. I was old enough when my father died to remember many things from before it happened. He used to take me fishing at night. He taught me to navigate by the stars, and he told me those Norse legends, too. I used to take him mead and ale when he worked in the fields. He would let me walk in front of him, my hands on the plow just like his. It's how I knew what to do, or at least I thought I did. It was harder than it looked, so I was lucky neighbors helped me after he died. He would put me on his shoulders when we went to watch the Beltane bonfires. Back then, my mother didn't drink as much. She wasn't a happy woman, but she loved our family. She was kind when she taught me how to manage our home, and she was patient too. She would have too much mead or ale sometimes, but my father hid it from us. I didn't realize I'd seen her drunk until after he died. I recognized things she did, but she grew far worse once he died. But before that, we had an untroubled home."

"I'm glad you have that to look back on. We live in places where life is hard. The weather is fierce, and we often face too little food, too little heat, and too little time. Having something to think about that cheers you up is important. Or at least, I think so." Liam rolled to look at Elene. He pulled her wet hair over her shoulder, noticing that it was dampening the back of her gown. He wrapped a tendril around his finger before they leaned in for a kiss. They pulled apart to look at one another. Liam released her hair and cupped her jaw as her hand slid over his heart. They inched closer until their forearms pressed together. Their languid kiss remained as tender as the first.

When they parted to catch their breath, Elene asked, "What are your brothers and sister like? You've met mine."

Liam's grin revealed white teeth that gleamed in the moonlight. "Alec, Hamish, and I all look just like our father. We have his hair, his eyes, and his build. Alec is a year younger than me. Hamish is two years younger than Alec. Ainsley is the youngest, and she looks just like our mother. The older she gets, the more people confuse her for Mama. She's the smartest of all of us because she's patient and cunning, like our mother. Mama and my uncles have a dirk they pass back and forth. They use it when they bet against one another on something happening or not. Mama has had it the most times and always for the longest. She watches people, understands them, and plans before she acts or speaks. Ainsley is the same. Alec, Hamish, and I gave her a dirk for her saint's day."

Liam grinned as he remembered that day three years ago.

"It was Ainsley who said it would be what the four of us would use to bet. She looked so innocent. Before any of us knew it, she'd maneuvered Hamish into daring she couldn't hit a target if she stood sideways. We all know Mama trained her, and Mama is the best knife thrower in all the Highlands—not that Uncle Callum likes to admit it, since he's the best man. But Ainsley got us to agree. Not only did she keep the dirk, my brothers and I ended up mucking out her horse's stall and picking weeds for a sennight. Da laughed—hard, and Mama chided us for being so gullible. She told us of the time she played hide-and-seek with my uncles while she traveled with my grandparents. They feared they'd lost her or that she'd floated away in the river. She had my grandfather and uncles in a near panic. It was my grandmother who told her she had to come out and stop tormenting my uncles. She was the most patient and waited them all out. She was five." Liam chuckled.

"Sounds like the men in your family are very lucky to have your mother and sister."

"That we are, and we know it." Liam grew serious. "Naught is more important to me than my family. *Prima familia.* Family first. It's our motto among the Sinclair and Mackay families. It includes the Sutherlands too. My grandmother was a Sutherland, so my parents named my brother Hamish for my mother's uncle, Laird Hamish Sutherland. My mother and uncles are very close to their Sutherland cousins, and in turn, their children—my cousins and I—are very close to our Sutherland family."

"How many of you are there?" Elene wondered.

"Good question." Liam released Elene's hand to hold up his. "Mama and Da have four. All together my aunts and uncles have—" Liam ticked them off on his fingers "—twelve. Three each. Then, on the Sutherland side, there's another nine. So four and twelve and nine, that's five and twenty cousins. If you add in Mama, Da, my four uncles and their wives, my grandfather, his brother-by-marriage—that's Laird Hamish—and his three children, their mates, and his wife...that's four and forty. I don't know if everyone is done having bairns yet, so mayhap there'll be more before it's my generation's turn."

"Is that the entire Highlands?"

"Just about. Through our Sutherland relatives, we're connected to the Rosses, the Camerons, and the Mac-Leods of Lewis. Through my aunts, we're connected to the Frasers of Lovat, the Comyns, the Mackenzies, and the MacLeods of Assynt. I have a Lowlander aunt, and one Sutherland married a Lowlander. So we add the Kerrs and the Johnstones."

"Good Lord!"

"If you extend our Ross connection, you reach the Campbells too. So yes, pretty much the entire Highlands and a good portion of the Hebrides."

"And we're connected through Lorna Mackay and her family."

"Yes. I just remembered that Bjorn Jansson was Leif and Freya's cousin. They were related on their mother's side. His father was Lena's brother."

"That means his second cousin, Leif and Sigrid's daughter, married your great-however-many-back grandfather, Alex Mackay's son and Lorna Mackay's distant cousin." Elene lowered her voice to add, "Mayhap there is fate."

"I think so." They shared another kiss before they

heard voices. They scrambled to their feet, and Liam drew his sword. They moved to hide behind the boulder Liam used the previous night. Liam wrapped the plaid around Elene and tucked her head against his chest, shielding her from any prying eyes. The men passed, and Liam realized they were villagers doing night hunting. It wasn't long before the night air fell silent again. Liam whispered, "We need to head back."

Elene nodded, lifting her head from Liam's chest, regretting an end to the comforting position, but she knew he was right. They moved back to the path and made their way to the village. Liam watched as she passed through the wood portal and waited before he followed her. He watched the door to her croft close before he slipped into Androw and Janet's home to gather his belongings, then he returned to the loch for his own bath.

CHAPTER 4

The next two days were blissful for both Liam and Elene. Watching his men rest and socialize with the locals confirmed Liam made the right decision. Elene's mother took an unexpected reprieve from drinking, so there were no serious arguments between the two women. Elene toiled in her gardens, surprised when Liam silently picked up a basket and kneeled beside her to weed. They worked in companionable silence the day after he escorted her to the loch. Liam learned Androw told villagers he sent Liam to help Elene. He urged his villagers to think it was Liam's endeavor to show the people of Skaill that the Sinclairs valued the Orcadians. They sat together at the meals they shared, Katryne and Johan always present as chaperones of a sort.

The second day, Liam spent the morning sitting with Androw as the chieftain adjudicated disputes among the villagers. Liam spent most of the time observing, but there were a handful of matters where his presence as the earl's delegate was fortuitous. That afternoon, Elene and he slipped away to fish again. They spent the time talking about the places Liam had traveled and the battles in which he'd already fought. He feared sharing the tales would bore or scare Elene, but she asked insightful questions about tactics and what happened to his home when he and his father rode out.

Both nights, Liam accompanied Elene to the loch. He gave her privacy, holding onto his honor by his fingernails and not peeking while she bathed. He considered himself eligible for sainthood. When she finished, they would lie beside one another and point out constellations, sharing the stories they'd learned as children. They made up wild tales about dragons and serpents slithering across the night sky, chased by St. Michael and St. George. They confessed what they'd thought being an adult would be like when they were children. Both agreed there wasn't nearly the freedom they'd expected. Through their conversations, they both learned things about the other that were never said. Elene learned that family and duty drove Liam just as much as it did her. They both were loyal to a fault, and it was likely born of a similar stubbornness. They enjoyed one another's dry sense of humor, finding they both tended toward self-deprecation while making keen observations about mankind.

They shared kisses during those nights where they shared Liam's plaid, but neither pushed for more. Liam and Elene understood that their time together was brief and pursuing more would only leave them both heartsore. But neither denied their mutual attraction or how they enjoyed the feel of their bodies pressed together, the hunger it created for more. Keeping limits on their passion offered them the chance to foster a friendship. It allowed them to realize they enjoyed each other's company beyond the physical. They lingered outside the village for as long as they dared before Liam escorted Elene back. He opted to drag his exhausted body to the loch in the early mornings rather than returning each night. Their late-night talks left them fatigued, but neither regretted it.

On the third day after their first tryst, Liam watched Elene as he finished saddling his horse, *Urram*. She stood near her croft, shading her eyes against the midmorning sun. Liam looked for her in the mead hall as he sat with his host to break his fast, but she never arrived. When he didn't see her brother or sister, he realized she likely made that meal at home. She appeared and smiled at him as he stepped out of the hall. He moved to walk toward her, but Dermot waylaid him with questions about their impending journey to several nearby villages. They would be away for at least three days, and he'd already discussed their plans with his second-in-command. His heart sank when Elene changed course.

It was Liam's turn to make a detour when he finally freed himself from Dermot and tried to make his way inconspicuously to the well, where Elene stopped when she could no longer walk to Liam. However, Katryne bounded over to her older sister and pulled her back toward their croft. With no time left, it forced Liam to ready his horse and prepare to leave without speaking to her. Everything felt unresolved, and Liam sensed Elene felt as adrift as he did. He didn't want to ride away without speaking to her, especially since he learned that morning that Gunter was due to return to Skaill in three days. It was far sooner than Elene predicted, but fishermen had spotted Norse longboats the evening before. They said they recognized the sails.

Running out of time and frustrated, Liam abandoned Urram's side and strode to Elene. Standing to block the sun from her eyes, he feasted his eyes on her, recalling how she'd tasted and felt the night before. Her eyes roamed over him, memorizing all she could see and remembering the shivers that ran along her spine while his teeth tugged on her earlobe.

"I won't go to the loch alone. I promise."

"Elene, I didn't mean for you to give up something you love doing. Is there no one who can go with you?"

"He'll be away." Elene watched hurt flash in Liam's eyes before she winked. She watched his shoulders lower in a movement she was certain he didn't realize. "I thought about what you said the first night. I've always known the risk I take. I just hadn't a reason not to take it before the last three nights."

Liam nodded, suddenly at a loss for words. He didn't know if Elene implied she believed they had a future. He knew what he wanted with her while he was in Skaill, but he wasn't certain he was ready to make a lifelong commitment. And since he wasn't sure, he wouldn't act out what he'd fantasized about restlessly all night. Elene watched the unease return as Liam struggled to respond. She could have kicked herself for scaring him away.

"I don't want to leave," Liam admitted, finally finding his voice again. "I want to stay, but I must conduct my grandfather's business before I can consider aught else. I have a duty to him. But I'll be back in three days. I heard—"

"I know. That's what Katryne came to tell me. She heard some of the other children talking about Gunter's return. My mother is—she told Katryne and Johan that they needed to find somewhere else to sleep while Gunter is here. She's never been—discreet. It worries me why she wants them away but said naught about me sleeping somewhere else."

Liam glanced back over his shoulder at where his men waited, watching him. Some appeared annoyed while others were positively nosey. He turned back to Elene. "I will be back in two and a half days. I'll be here

when he arrives because I must for the sake of politics."
He knew he contradicted what he'd just said, but he
needed a reason to return sooner. "I also don't want
you here and afraid of your own mother and him.
Elene, I don't have a solution. I can't make any
promises. But I also won't turn my back on you. Even if
we hadn't... You deserve someone to take up your
cause."

"Thank you. Don't rush because of me. I told you,
he won't do aught while we're still here. I worry
about what he will say." Elene cringed. "I worry about
what my mother will say. But I don't fear him
harming me."

"I do. I heard more about him during the morning
meal. I fear he'll shove you on his ship and sail away if I
don't return before he can."

"If he marries my mother, no one will have a say but
him. It won't matter what you fear. Liam, you said you
don't have a solution. That's because there isn't one. I
don't expect aught from you. That wasn't what I meant
or why I..." Elene grew flustered, ridiculously nervous
to admit that she'd wanted their kisses, even though it
had been obvious she did.

"And even if we hadn't kissed, I would still worry
about you. Elene, I told you I would worry about any of
my cousins put in a position where they couldn't defend themselves. I worry what he will do to your
brother and sister. I've been raised to protect and defend those who can't do it for themselves. That's what a
laird does. But there's something about you. Something
that a man like him will do his best to extinguish. It's
the very thing that draws me to you, and we've known
each other a few days."

"Whatever this is," Elene flicked her fingers between
them, "makes me trust you when I trust no one."

"I will do my best never to betray that trust." Liam

grasped her fingers and gave them a quick squeeze. "I will be back before he arrives."

The couple gazed at one another, both wishing for another kiss, but knowing it was impossible where they stood. A nod was the best they could offer one another. Liam spun on his heel, his plaid swishing against the back of his thighs. Elene watched him mount his steed, tempted to wave when he looked at her. Without a word, Liam nudged Urram forward, leading the other Highlanders to the east, away from Elene and the people of Skaill. She watched until he faded from sight, dreading going back into her croft. She looked toward the bay, praying a storm materialized that would delay Gunter's arrival. She prayed a great serpent would pull him to his death in the sea's great depths. With a sigh, she accepted that there was little precedent of her prayers being answered.

The next two days passed in a muddy and windy blur for Liam. Uncooperative weather prevented him from traveling as far as he'd planned. The few villages he'd reached varied their reception from disdain to down-right hostility. It shocked him that even places where he'd once visited were disinclined to welcome him. He assured all and sundry that nothing would change now that his grandfather assumed control of the local government. It tempted him to promise that their lives would improve, but it was one he couldn't guarantee, so he refrained.

Liam understood it was apprehension rather than dislike, but it made the journey even more miserable. It was with a sigh of relief that he and his men returned to Skaill, sodden, hungry, and disillusioned. Their reception surprised his men as much as it had him, since

Laird Liam selected every warrior on the voyage from the Sinclair guard because they'd traveled to Orkney before. Only Dermot was a Mackay. The others were men who Liam had known for his entire life. His Mackay and Sinclair family visited one another often, and Liam fostered with the Sinclairs. While Skaill's villagers hadn't been effusive, they hadn't been rude.

As Liam passed through the gates, his eyes darted to where his Highland birlinns, or *longa*, remained anchored in the bay. Reassured that nothing was amiss, he looked around the village. There were few people braving the elements, but he suspected there would be one. He spied Elene draping burlap over early-blooming vegetables in the dirt patch beside her croft. There'd been an unexpected frost the night before, so she couldn't risk losing their meager harvest. Liam wondered if she realized her efforts were for naught if she and her family were leaving soon. That idea soured Liam further. He hadn't ceased thinking about their kisses and conversations. They filled his dreams, and they were the only redeeming moments of his trip. With only his men and Elene outside, it tempted him to visit her. But he feared people within their crofts would spy him. He didn't want to cause Elene trouble by stirring gossip.

When Elene spied the returning men, the noise drawing her attention, she barely turned her attention to them. Her disinterest made Liam wonder if she regretted their interludes. She didn't look at him. He thought she might spare him a glance, even if she was in the midst of her work. It stung to think that their kisses left her unaffected when he couldn't stop thinking about them. Forced to turn his attention to his horse, he led the animal to the stables. As he curried the enormous stallion, he told himself that it was of little consequence if Elene no longer shared his interest. He

49

reminded himself that he would return to Scotland in a fortnight, and then he would never see Elene again. It was even more likely she would leave for Norway before he departed for home. That thought only soured his temper further.

Disappointed and hurt, with remnants of his earlier frustration, Liam encouraged his men to seek hot food and shelter in the mead hall. He dismissed them to find sustenance, then to find dry clothes and cots in the village longhouse for unmarried men. He shoved the brush into his saddlebag with disgust and muttered an oath before he stepped out of the stall. He nearly jumped out of his skin when he found Elene standing to the right, her shawl draped over her head and her hand cinching it beneath her chin.

His doubts and anger vanished as they fell into one another's arms. It was an embrace, not a kiss, that they shared. There was an intimacy of its own kind as they held one another, drawing comfort and strength. The shawl slid from Elene's head, allowing Liam to stroke the thick, blonde locks. He kissed her temple over and over as she burrowed against his chest.

"I missed you," Liam admitted.

"I missed you too."

Both knew their interest had already surpassed lust. It felt far greater than that. They respected one another and admired the person they were discovering.

"How are you? Did aught happen while I was away?"

"He hasn't arrived. The storm was worse offshore, so it's delayed him. My mother has been in a fit since the first drop of rain. But it means naught has changed."

"Have you thought more about what you'll do?"

"It's nearly all I think about." Elene squeezed her eyes shut as she continued to lean against Liam's expansive chest. When his arms tightened around her, she suspected he knew what she meant and wasn't put off. Liam leaned back and tilted Elene's chin up. The kiss was just as soft as the first time their lips brushed together. Longing filled them both, but common sense told them to go no further. A deep and hungry kiss, like the ones they shared outside the village wall, would only lead to wanting more, and they both knew there could be no more with Gunter's imminent arrival. Drawn to one another like a moth to a flame, they both understood they would get singed. "How was your journey?"

Liam eased his hold and sighed. "Less fruitful than I hoped. I understand people's wariness, but I didn't expect their disdain. But truth be told, I suspect it's me. If it were my grandfather or Uncle Callum, I believe the reception would be different. I think they see me as little more than a messenger boy."

Elene bit her lip as she leaned back, then nodded. "I've heard people say as much. People wonder why neither Laird Sinclair nor Callum made the effort to come."

Liam's hands slid to Elene's waist, ending their embrace, but not their contact. "I was the one to suggest I represent them. I wanted to prove that I could."

"And you are. People don't know that's the reason."

"I'm not about to announce to everyone that I came because I want to show everyone I'm a man."

Elene's lips twitched before she swallowed, but she couldn't contain her smile. It was wicked as her eyes twinkled. She glanced down between them before her eyes met his once more.

"Lass," Liam muttered in Gaelic, forgetting himself. Elene giggled. The sound shot straight to Liam's groin, which his sporran mercifully hid.

"I need to go home before my mother wonders where I've gone."

"I need to find Androw, since I'm certain he knows we're back."

They were slow to step away, but once they broke their contact, Elene pulled the shawl over her head and hurried from the stables. Liam watched her disappear before he sloshed his way to Androw's home, assuming he was there rather than the mead hall.

"You survived and returned to tell the tale." Androw greeted Liam with a mug of warmed mead as his wife, Janet, set a trencher filled with a steaming pottage on the table. Liam gratefully accepted the refreshments offered. "Neither the weather nor the people have been on your side."

"You were right with your warning. I was poorly received, but I suspect it wasn't the message so much as the messenger. I think it would have been better had Grandfather or Uncle Callum come."

"But they didn't. Laird Sinclair trusts you."

"He does, and he gave me this opportunity. But perhaps I shouldn't have pushed so hard for this to be my turn. It might not serve him well after all."

"No. People won't remember who bore the message, but they'll remember Laird Sinclair as a fair leader. That's what matters. They already trust your family and him. As long as naught changes, then things will come right."

"I suppose. But I doubt having another group of Norse traders arriving any day will help."

"Actually, it should. Assuming you can keep Gunter from causing trouble. How you handle that will tell everyone what they should expect for trade in the future. If you can keep the Norse coming back despite losing control of the islands, then they will hail you a hero. If not…" Androw shrugged.

"Have they sailed any closer?"

"Yes. They should make landfall in a couple hours, just in time for the evening meal."

Liam nodded but opted to take a long draw from his mead rather than say more about Gunter. When he finished eating, he retired to the chamber Janet showed him the day he arrived. He gladly accepted the steaming bath that awaited him. He donned a fresh leine and clean plaid. As he wrapped the yards of wool around his waist, he equated it to girding his loins rather than merely donning his clothes. He stepped out of Androw's home as calls went up that the Norse rowed their curraghs ashore. He watched as six small row boats approached filled with blond and redheaded men and women. As the newest arrivals waded ashore, none appeared affected by the inclement weather, whereas Liam was certain he resembled a drowned rat when he arrived.

Gunter was easy to spot, with his sparkling ruby brooch clasping his heavy fur cloak around his shoulders. Deep-blue tattoos covered the sides of his shaved head and neck. Coarse blond hair that barely disguised the tattoos on the broad expanse covered his bare chest beneath the cloak. An axe swung from his waist while he carried a sword strapped to his back. Liam watched the man approach, certain the Norse king's younger brother embodied every legend ever told of Norse conquerors.

When the Norseman and Highlander locked gazes, it convinced Liam that his earlier poor reception would seem like a grand fête compared to what he faced. Androw came to stand beside him while Janet remained under the awning of their home. Liam refused to look away first, so he spoke to Androw without turning to the Orcadian.

"I assume he speaks Norn."

"He does. It's closer to Norse than aught else. What

he doesn't know how to say in Norn, he can convey in Norse."

"He's trying to look for my grandfather without taking his eyes off me."

"I know. He's older than Callum, so he will treat you like an upstart whelp."

Liam grinned. "He's not wrong. I'm *Wee* Liam after all." As Gunter drew closer, it was clear Liam and he were matched in size. However, there was a cynicism that oozed from Gunter than the younger man lacked. As Liam watched him, he prayed he never became so jaded. But he acknowledged he hadn't traveled as far or likely fought in nearly as many battles as Gunter. Yet, he would guess his father and uncles were just as experienced as Gunter, but none carried an aura of entitlement and ennui that mixed with Gunter's arrogance.

"Who's this?" Gunter demanded, focusing on Androw, and ignoring Liam despite demanding to know who stood before him.

"I am Liam Mackay, Clan Mackay's tánaiste and Clan Sinclair's delegate. I represent my grandfather, Laird Liam Sinclair, the Earl of Sinclair *and* Orkney." Liam refused to be spoken about rather than spoken to. Rather than use his grandfather's new title, the Earl of Caithness, he would remind Gunter just how wide his grandfather's governance spread. His emerald gaze bore into Gunter's murky-brown eyes, daring him to contest the reminder that Gunter's brother no longer ruled the land upon which they stood. While the isles were now part of Scotland, in practice, they belonged to Clan Sinclair.

"Where is the earl?" Gunter looked around, exaggerating his search.

Liam looked to the sky before looking back at Gunter. "Likely in Dunbeath's lists with my uncles and cousins."

"Too old to sail?"

Liam grinned, then laughed. "The last time he was here, only six months ago, your brother's delegate confused him for my Uncle Tavish. He's hardly old."

Gunter grunted as he sized up Liam. Clearly unwilling to extend his arm to shake forearms, Liam decided to match Gunter's standoffishness with his own. He already had his feet planted hip-width apart, so he crossed his arms.

"He's a Sinclair all right," Androw guffawed. Liam had watched his grandfather and uncles adopt the same stance his entire life. His father embraced it once he married Mairghread, and the Sinclairs considered him a fifth brother. It was as natural to Liam as it was to his male relatives. It also made the already-impressive men positively intimidating. With his ebony hair and brows, the posture appealed to Liam's brooding appearance and temperament.

"I'm a Sinclair as much as I am my father's son—and heir." Liam's piercing gaze challenged Gunter, asserting his clan connections and his future as the Mackays' leader. He wouldn't allow Gunter to believe he was a messenger who would merely disappear once he completed the mission. With an arrogance that nearly matched Gunter's, Liam continued. "On behalf of my grandfather, the earl, I welcome you back to Orkney."

"Smug little turd," Gunter snapped. Liam shrugged one shoulder, appearing unmoved by Gunter's insult. The man's opinion changed nothing. Gunter's brother no longer controlled Orkney, which made Gunter the guest rather than Liam. Gunter turned toward Elene's croft and bellowed, "Inburgh! Woman!"

The door swung open, and Elene's mother tumbled forward, wobbly on her legs. She pushed hair from her face as she lifted her skirts to her calves and squished through the mud to meet Gunter. Liam observed the

Norseman's reaction to his supposed betrothed. Irritation and disgust morphed to lust as the woman pressed herself against him. Liam watched as Gunter glanced toward Elene and Inburgh's home before he pulled Inburgh in for a sloppy kiss. Liam didn't need to look to know Gunter spied Elene and kissed Inburgh for effect. It disgusted Liam.

When Gunter pressed Inburgh away, Liam watched the consternation flash across the man's eye, telling Liam that Elene no longer watched. Gunter's gaze swung to Liam, a scowl deeply etched across his face. The older man sensed Liam gloated in silence. He narrowed his eyes as he assessed Liam.

"Been sniffing around, have you?" Gunter sneered. He knew Liam observed him when he sought Elene. The woman had plagued him since he first spied her a year ago. First, he'd lusted for her as any healthy man would. But as he'd observed her, he'd come to appreciate her finer qualities, such as loyalty, diligence, and steadfastness. He'd wanted to learn more, share his life with her, but she'd turned him away. Pride continued to get the better of him where she was concerned, especially since his interest hadn't waned. "Even gotten a taste? No sweeter honey, is there?"

Liam refused to react.

"Stoic now? Is that how you think you look?" Gunter laughed. If he couldn't vent his frustration at Elene, he would accept Liam as a scapegoat. His anger at her rejection was a constant simmer because she wounded his self-esteem. But his longing and abused ego wouldn't dissipate, so his feelings manifested as a bully. "Or mayhap, you're jealous. Haven't tasted that honey yet after all. I promise you it's the finest."

Liam shifted his gaze to Inburgh, shocked that the woman ignored the obvious innuendos her betrothed made about her own daughter. The intoxicated woman stood with her eyes closed as she ran her hand over Gunter's bare abdomen. Liam wondered if Inburgh even listened, and if she did, he questioned whether she believed Gunter described her.

"Woman, I'm starved." Gunter's announcement elicited a giggle from Inburgh.

"I'm certain I have some honey," Inburgh purred. The sound grated on Liam's ears.

"Food first. Then we'll see if you can keep me up long enough to find that honey." Gunter wrapped his arm around Inburgh's waist, once more exchanging a revolting kiss. With their eyes closed, neither noticed Elene slip from the croft. Liam tilted his head toward the stables. Elene crept around the side of her home until she could enter the shadows and make her way to the community stables. Liam observed Gunter and Inburgh as they traipsed across the village center. Inburgh entered first, but Gunter's towering height enabled him to see Elene wasn't within the single room croft. He ducked back out, looked around, and boomed. "Where the fuck is she?"

"She went hunting," Androw responded. His answer surprised Liam, but he maintained his neutral expression. "I'm certain she's respecting your need for privacy."

Gunter slammed the door shut, leaving Androw, Liam, and Janet staring at the Isbisters' home. It was Janet who spoke first. "Bring her here when it gets too late for her to remain in the stables. She'll freeze, or he's likely to find her."

Liam nodded, offering his family friends an appreciative smile. He walked around the back of Androw's house and past the mead hall before doubling back to the stables, unwilling to make his destination obvious.

CHAPTER 5

L iam entered the musty building, scant light finding its way through the wooden roof's slats. He peeked in each stall until he came to his own horse. There stood Elene, with an apple in her outstretched palm as Urram munched on another. Elene stroked the massive head, and Liam was certain the beast sighed. He approached and listened to Elene murmur in Norn, complimenting the horse on his manners.

"He only speaks Gaelic, and I don't know about his manners. I may have named him Honor, but he hardly has any when it comes to letting others eat. Greedy would be a better name."

Elene chuckled. "Greedy, or Belget, is my horse's name. I suppose that's why Urram and I get along. I understand him."

"You're lucky he hasn't taken your fingers off. He's a walking stomach."

"Typical man," Elene muttered playfully.

I certainly hunger for something. Liam scowled but winked. The image his trusted steed and the woman he craved created warmed him in a way that made his heart swell. The softer emotion, however, did little to assuage his desire to kiss Elene once more. But as his eyes skimmed over her voluptuous frame, Gunter's words came back to him. He wished to taste more than just Elene's honey, but he questioned whether Gunter had already enjoyed the privilege.

He knew it wasn't his business with whom Elene spent her time or how she did. But the thought that Gunter was once Elene's lover, or at least a love interest, made him uncomfortable. In part, it was envy. But he recognized another part was a fear that he appeared more like a boy than a man when compared to the more-worldly warrior. It wasn't often that Liam's self-confidence flagged, but he knew the sensation from times when he feared he would never compare to his legendary family members.

"You've wandered away." Elene's voice permeated Liam's inner musings.

"There is much on my mind. I'm sorry. I didn't mean to be rude."

"We're both preoccupied." Elene stepped aside as Urram nodded and snorted when Liam stepped forward. The animal pressed his nose into Liam's shoulder joint, then rested it over Liam's shoulder. "He's a big softy."

"Shh. Don't let the other horses hear. He has a reputation for being disagreeable with others. You'll hurt his pride if you give away his secret. He's more like a lapdog than a warhorse with me."

"I would hardly underestimate him in battle. He looks like he'd be ferocious."

"He is. His bite and his hooves are deadly. But we've spent so much time together that he's more a loyal hound than just my ride."

"I wish I could say that about Belget. The beast dislikes even a hint of rain. He balks if the wind blows up his nose. And he'd rather spend his day grazing than working. He's an old man." Elene rolled her eyes.

"How old is he?"

"Five-and-ten."

"He deserves to spend his days in a pasture not behind a plow. He is old."

"I know, but he and Bess are our only animals. I can't get a new plow horse, so he and I make do together." Elene glanced at the doors. "I suppose I won't need a fresh horse. My uncle agreed to care for him once we leave."

Elene and Liam stood in silence, neither knowing what to say. Their attraction was undeniable, but so was the reality that Elene would board a ship and sail to Norway. Liam would board his own ship and sail in the opposite direction, to the Highlands.

"Do you have family anywhere else?" Liam asked as he considered the villages through which he passed and the ones he was yet to visit.

"On Sanday. My mother's people are there. My uncle here was my father's only brother. That's it for Rousay. His people were originally from the Mainland island."

"What about Shetland?"

Elene shook her head. "No. Sickness stole most of my family years ago. My father died and so did his parents, an aunt on my mother's side, and several of my cousins. My mother's people don't travel, so once my father died, I had little way to see them. My mother never looked back once she married my father, so I don't really know them."

They fell silent once more. While he was away, Liam considered offering to take Elene to any extended family she might have. But it clearly wasn't an option. Liam chided himself that she would have thought of that if it was already an option. As he watched her,

Liam was certain his family would accept Elene. She could find a home among the Sinclairs or the Mackays. But he couldn't arrive at Castle Dunbeath or Castle Varrich with an unmarried woman who'd spent days sailing with him and his men. And he couldn't ask her to marry him.

Liam understood they didn't know one another well enough to consider themselves a love match. While his parents might wish that he find such a wife, he also understood his clan needed to make an alliance among the Highlanders. He didn't have the luxury of choosing his mate simply by attraction. His brothers and sister might, though he doubted it. But he was certain he couldn't, since he was his father's heir. As he gazed at Elene, he wished he could say duty be damned. Despite all this, he still felt compelled to help her, even if it meant sending her away rather than taking her with him.

"When do you leave again?" Once more, Elene interrupted his thoughts. She knew what his plans were before the weather inconvenienced him. She wondered how they changed.

"If the weather improves, tomorrow. I'll be gone for a few days since I must visit the other isles." Liam couldn't meet Elene's gaze. Guilt that he was abandoning her nipped at him. His eyes locked with hers when she laid her hand in his forearm and squeezed.

"I don't expect you to fix this."

"That doesn't mean I don't wish that I could. If I weren't..." Liam knew he was making excuses. His father had fought to marry his mother, both proving himself to Laird Liam and the Sinclair brothers when he protected her from his stepbrother. Tristan hadn't given in when the path to marrying Mairghread proved complicated. However, the powerful Mackay-Sinclair alliance had already been arranged by the time his parents married. Even if they hadn't fallen in love, Tristan and Mairghread's marriage benefited both clans. Liam felt obligated to both sides of his family to make an advantageous match.

But as he looked at Elene, there was no one else he could imagine wanting. He was grateful Andrew had no marriageable daughters since he might have found himself betrothed to one to strengthen the Sinclairs' claim to governing Orkney. However, he knew that several of the chieftains he was yet to visit had daughters or sisters who might make him a suitable match. Before he arrived in Skaill, he'd wondered if he might find one of these women enticing as a future bride. Instead, he found a woman who was wholly unsuitable for a political match. Elene possessed no connections and likely had no dowry. And yet, that made her even more appealing to Liam. He knew he wanted Elene for the woman he was discovering, not for what she could bring to a union.

"I'm sorry. I'm not being good company," Liam admitted. He wouldn't say that his wandering thoughts were all about Elene, but he could apologize for not being attentive.

"I understand. I can't stay any longer. I must at least acknowledge Gunter's arrival, and I need to make sure Katryne and Johan are presentable."

"Must you go in there now? Or can you wait until your brother and sister can go with you?"

"I'm not going in there while it's just my mother and him." Elene shook her head. Liam saw the fear flash in Elene's eyes. He pulled her into his embrace, tucking her head against his chest. He'd spent their brief time together telling himself why he couldn't run away with Elene, why he couldn't claim her and carry her away. However, he couldn't stop himself from wanting to shield her from Gunter and the danger the Norseman presented.

"Do you know where Katryne and Johan are?"

"No. I thought they were in the croft, but I suspect they are at my uncle's. He's a widower, and his children are grown. But he gives them odd jobs to make them feel grown up. He also slips them sweets that I wouldn't let them have. He'll rot their teeth."

Elene stepped away from Liam and looked toward the doors once more. She no more wanted to leave the stables and the safety she felt with Liam than to have her teeth rot like she warned her siblings.

"If the rain ceases, would you like me to take you to the loch tonight?" Liam couldn't think of anything else to say, and it was the only reason he could devise to see her again that evening. He understood his suggestion would only leave him frustrated by the time he retired to his chamber in Androw's home, but he felt miserable for Elene. He wished to give her something that he knew she valued, since he felt like he had little more to offer.

"I'd like that very much, but I don't know how I can. Once I return to the croft, Gunter will pay too much attention for me to sneak out. I don't want to leave my brother and sister there alone. I don't trust his temper if he discovers I'm gone. And he will know where to look for me. I don't want him to—" Elene snapped her mouth shut.

"Don't want what, Elene? Has he done something to you before?"

"No. But I don't want you to get involved. I heard what he said to you. He will try to kill you if he thinks you and I... He won't believe naught has happened."

"What would he do to you if he believed something did happen?"

"After he kills you and before he kills me? He'd see

63

no reason not to take what he wants if he thinks I'm already spoiled."

Liam considered what Elene said. He'd wondered if she still a maiden before, and she confirmed it with her last comment. But Liam couldn't shake the sense that there was some type of intimacy between Gunter and her, and Androw said Gunter acted more like a jilted lover than a stepfather who didn't want his stepchild.

"Can your brother and sister, and even you, stay with your uncle this eve?"

"Mayhap. But I fear involving him, too. He's not like you. He's a farmer, not a warrior. He can't defend himself or Katryne and Johan like you could."

Liam noticed she didn't include herself in the people who might seek Liam's protection. "Do you trust me to keep Katryne and Johan safe? Do you trust me to keep you safe?"

"Yes." Elene's blue eyes bore into Liam's. Her answer was forthright and unwavering. It made Liam feel guiltier. He almost wished he hadn't asked.

"I'll take you to your uncle's. If Katryne and Johan are there, then we don't need to look further. If they aren't, I will help you look. Once you're all with your uncle, I'll sleep in the corner. I won't leave you alone with only your uncle."

"I don't know, Liam. If Gunter finds you there, it will enrage him far more than finding us with just my uncle. But I fear he would kill my uncle without a word of warning." Elene shook her head. "We can't stay there. We need to go home."

"And if your mother is too drunk to care? What if Katryne and Johan hear or see something?"

Elene's gaze hardened. "They will never see aught. I'll make sure of that."

"There shouldn't be aught for them to see." Liam knew they were going around in circles.

"I managed him before. I will do it again. And if I can't, then that's what fate willed." Elene turned away, but Liam grabbed her arm and yanked back. He was careful not to hurt her, but he also wasn't prepared to let her walk away. When he saw lust spark in her eyes, he pulled her against him.

"Is that what you want? A man like that?"

"No. And you are not that type. You would never force me." *You wouldn't need to.*

"You sound as though you would accept him."

"I would accept ending my life before I let him touch me."

"No." Liam's mouth crashed against hers. The thought of Elene's life ending by anyone's hand sent a surge of emotion that tangled fear and rage to the point of boiling over. Elene opened to him, accepting his questing tongue into her mouth, sucking on him. Liam maneuvered them into a stall, where he pressed Elene against the wall, his hands resting on the wall beside her shoulders. She grasped his hips and urged them toward her, spinning his sporran out of the way as he obliged.

"Touch me. Please." Elene's hoarse whisper held all the longing Liam felt. His right hand trailed over her throat and across her chest, his knuckles grazing her bare skin. His fingers dipped into her cleavage before he cupped her breast. Elene arched her back as she pressed her palms against the wall beside her thighs. She felt the cool air on her shoulder, then her breast as her sleeve slid down her arm. With her eyes closed, she didn't expect the feel of Liam's tongue rasping over her nipple, then his warm breath on the puckered flesh before he took it into his mouth. She'd never imagined a sensation the like of Liam suckling her breast. Her hand tangled in his ebony waves. When she reached between them, Liam grasped her wrist and moved her hand aside.

"I want to touch you just as much as I think you want me to touch you. Naught matters more to me right now than bringing you pleasure. Let me. Please."

Elene stared into his emerald orbs before she nodded, stunned that he expected nothing—would ask for nothing—in return. She couldn't imagine any man being so content to go without. Liam's mouth returned to her breast, and she didn't bother to contain her soft moan. Liam reacted with increased pressure as his hand massaged her other breast.

A clap of thunder startled them, then they heard the stables' doors slam shut. Liam yanked Elene's sleeve onto her shoulder before he spun around, shielding her from whomever approached.

"Elene?" A girl's hushed voice floated to them. Elene hurried to right her gown before she tapped Liam's shoulder. He looked back at her, then stepped aside. She rushed forward, running a hand over her hair.

"Kat?" Elene emerged from the stall, but sensed Liam hung back. She understood his discretion and appreciated it. When she spied her brother standing by the door, she waved him forward. "Have you been home?"

"Yes. They're..." Katryne's cheeks flushed. "We heard them, so we didn't go inside."

"I'm hungry," Johan announced.

"We'll go to the mead hall. It should be time for the evening meal soon. We will eat there."

"Is the Highlander coming?" Katryne whispered. Elene froze. "We saw him come in here, then you came in. We haven't seen him come out."

"I don't know if Liam would like to come with us or if Androw and Janet expect him."

Elene's comment reminded Liam of what Janet said

earlier. It had slipped his mind, but he stepped forward. "I forgot Janet said I was to take you to their croft. I'll walk you all there."

Elene nodded as she ushered her siblings in front of her and out of the stables. Four sets of eyes swung to the Isbister croft, a collective breath held until they saw nothing amiss. They stayed in the buildings' shadows as they skirted puddles until Elene led them to the back door of Androw's home. As the village chieftain, his home was far larger than most, holding several rooms. There was a door at the rear of the building that connected to the kitchen. Janet hurried them in and pointed to seats in front of the hearth as she bustled around the kitchen, ladling bowls of steaming pottage.

"I told him you went hunting," Androw announced as he joined them before the roaring fire.

"What am I going to do when I bring naught home?" Elene looked between Androw and Janet, but it was Liam who answered.

"It's raining. Tell him the animals were hiding. If that won't work, I'll hunt now. There are several hours before it gets dark." Liam watched Elene debate his offer, but he caught Androw's slight nod toward the door. Before she could answer, Liam crossed the main chamber and entered the room where his belongings stood at the bed's footboard. He gathered his bow and quiver before he headed to the back door, but Elene met him there.

"I don't want you to get soaked. You're barely dry now, and you've been in the rain for days. I'll tell him they were all hiding."

"It's but a sprinkle." Liam's words bore no weight as another clap of thunder rattled the roof. "The Highlands aren't much different from here. I've been out in far worse."

"But—"

"Shh. If not for your sake, then to keep Katryne and Johan from worrying and to keep them out of his sights." Liam squeezed her hand, his body turned to keep the others from seeing. "I shouldn't be gone long."

Liam didn't wait for Elene to respond, slipping out of the door and along the village center until he reached the postern gate. He nodded to the guard, raising his weapon as he passed through the portal. He wasted no time drawing an arrow from the quiver he'd slung over his shoulder. He nocked an arrow, holding his bow parallel to the ground and inching forward on silent feet. He traversed the land, taking him past the loch and toward a meadow. In the distance, he spied a herd of red deer. Continuing to creep on soundless feet, a skill honed from years of practice, Liam drew closer. When he was certain he could hit a large stag, he raised his bow. He brought the arrow to eye level, drew a deep breath, waited a heartbeat, then released the arrow as he exhaled. The arrow zoomed through the air and buried its tip into the animal's broad chest. The stag staggered backward several steps as the other animals fled. It was only a moment later that the male deer crashed to the ground.

Liam hurried to retrieve his kill. It wasn't long before Liam hefted the stag over his shoulders, easily the weight of a heavy adult man. He stumbled a step, remembering the first time he was strong enough to hoist his father onto his back and carry him across the training field. At four-and-ten, he'd grown as tall as Tristan and made his first attempt to carry the massive warrior, but it wasn't until he was six-and-ten that he had the breadth of shoulders and strength in his legs to manage the feat.

Now he gained his footing, blaming the mud for his misstep. He knew he had to find smaller prey if Gunter was to believe Elene was the one who hunted, but his catch pleased him as an offering of thanksgiving to Androw and Janet for their hospitality. He hurried back to the village wall, leaving the animal behind Androw's house, and gesturing to the chieftain through the window to come outside.

Liam hurried back to the meadow, looking for rabbits or fowl. It wasn't long before he had a brace of rabbits and three stoats. He'd quickly made a slinger, realizing he didn't know if Elene hunted with a bow and arrow. He assumed she did, but she wouldn't be able to explain arrow wounds in her catches if Gunter saw her weapon still in the croft. He used the stone thrower to nab the smaller prey. Once finished hunting, he used the rope that launched the stones to tie the animals together.

He was nearly through the rear gate when Gunter materialized from a shadow and stepped onto Liam's path. The sneering Norseman stood with his arms crossed, more tattoos visible as his fur cloak fell away and hung down his back. He sized Liam up, casting a dismissive look as though he studied a disappointing child rather than a potential rival.

"Out playing with rocks?"

Liam shrugged with nonchalance, internally annoyed that Gunter discovered him hunting. He didn't appreciate Gunter foiling his plan, nor did he appreciate the older man taunting him. He made to step around the man, but Gunter blocked his way.

"The stag wasn't enough?" Gunter cast a speculative gaze over Liam before looking past his shoulder. "She isn't hunting, is she? You're trying to make it look as though she did, but here I've found you and not her."

"She had no luck. The animals were hiding earlier. They came out to eat since the thunder ceased, and it's not raining." Liam adopted a bored expression, as though his reasons were too obvious to need stating.

69

"She shall lead you around by the cock, but it matters not. She'll be boarding my ship." Gunter's cocked eyebrow did little to make the poor innuendo better. Once again, Liam refused to take the bait. He stood silently. He would wait out Gunter, and he would see if Gunter shared anything of use. Liam sensed he wasn't the type who was patient enough to leverage the silence to his advantage. As Liam suspected, Gunter shifted and spoke, needing to fill the void. "She is naught but a tease. But a Norseman will cure her of that."

"Mayhap one will, but the way you talk, it won't be you. She rejected you, and now you wish to get even. I never imagined a man with such duties as you have would care about a woman on a tiny island in the middle of nowhere."

"You know Orkney is hardly in the middle of nowhere. And she is hardly just any woman."

"She's the woman you want but doesn't want you. Mayhap if you were nicer…"

"You mean, a weak little man who trails after her like a pup wishing for scraps." Gunter's smug appearance made Liam want to laugh. The man tried too hard to hide his feelings and appeared a fool for it.

"I'm not in love with a woman who won't love me back." Liam wished he'd stopped while he was ahead. The moment the words passed his lips, he regretted them. The fury in Gunter's gaze told him he'd struck the most sensitive nerve. Gunter's bullish attitude was a guise for how he really felt, and Liam had the lack of forethought to point it out. The Norseman's curled fists and posture warned that he prepared to attack. "I will leave before that can happen."

Gunter grinned, thinking Liam admitted his own weakness. He took a menacing step forward, his hands resting on his belt near his knives. Liam watched each move, prepared to reach for his own knife, knowing he could throw one at Gunter far faster than he could load and shoot an arrow. "You'd do well to sail away before you make a greater fool of yourself. Before I remind you who's been on this island longer."

Liam nodded, scrambling to use the moment to his advantage and diffuse the looming fist fight. "Your brother was gracious to offer Orkney and Shetland as a compromise. My grandfather isn't interested in changing anyone's way of life here or in Norway. Just the opposite. He wants to ensure little changes for the Orcadians or Shetlanders."

Gunter grew contemplative, the shift to politics changing his mood. Liam watched the arrogance war with the realization that Gunter needed diplomacy, not veiled threats. "The people care not who calls Orkney theirs so long as they have what they need. They know where to turn."

"And a people who are well provided for are a content people. My grandfather understands that. He is not the man who found fault with the Norse. You've met him several times. You know he holds you and your people in high regard."

"Yet he didn't bother to show his face. He didn't even send his son. He sent a boy."

Liam chafed at the insult, which nettled his insecurity. But he refused to allow Gunter to know he'd hit a nerve with Liam. He refused to relent and give the Norseman the upper hand. "My grandfather and uncle understand your brother wants the best for Orkney and Shetland. Since no one will stand in the way of my grandfather governing these islands on behalf of King David, I offered to come in his stead. I've been here so many times, it feels like a third home. Only Varrich and Dunbeath are more familiar to me."

Gunter narrowed his eyes, realizing that a war of words wouldn't defeat Liam. He ran his gaze over

Liam, from his boots to his eyes. Liam knew Gunter was estimating how many knives Liam carried, particularly how many Gunter couldn't see. When the older man shifted his weight back to his heels, Liam felt confident their conversation wouldn't come to blows.

"Tell her she's expected home. Those rabbits and stoats won't cook themselves."

Liam watched Gunter turn away. He wondered what his grandfather and father would have said about the exchange. He'd misstepped more than once, but he'd used his mind rather than his might to maneuver Gunter. He hoped they would be proud. He didn't for a moment think Elene was any safer than she'd been before Gunter stepped foot on land. But at least he didn't fear trade evaporating between Orkney and Scotland's clans, either Highlander or Lowlander. He counted that as a win.

CHAPTER 6

awn greeted Liam with clear rose and lavender hues. While he appreciated a reprieve from the inclement weather, his mind rebelled at leaving Elene. Once he returned to the village, he accompanied Elene and her siblings back to their croft. He listened as she opened the door, Gunter merely grunting, then laughing, as she carried inside Liam's catches. But he heard nothing more once the door closed. There were no raised voices, banging furniture, screams, or fleeing women and children. He lingered outside the door for an hour before he abandoned his post to settle against the croft's back wall. He wouldn't announce his intention to guard Elene and her siblings by making his presence obvious. There were too many villagers and Norse moving around to remain inconspicuous. All the same, he refused to leave them.

He'd dozed throughout the night. He'd drawn a knife when someone approached, but he'd sheathed it when he recognized Elene carrying a blanket for him. They said nothing when she draped it over him and sneaked back into her croft. As the sun rose, it forced him to abandon his post to prepare to ride out with his men. They'd loaded a wagon the night before, bringing

73

more bushels of seed from the ship while Liam hunted. He felt ashamed that the men worked while he conducted a personal mission that he'd told none of them about. When he saw Dermot, his friend smiled and shook his head.

"We all heard him. We kenned ye wouldnae leave her on her own. If nae for her, then for the lass and lad. Besides, we've been eating their food three meals a day. It's just as well that ye hunted."

Dermot's comments assuaged Liam's guilt, but it did little to make him feel better about leaving Elene behind. He'd barely slept, only in part because he was attentive to his surroundings, vigilant against Gunter leaving the croft or any of his people sneaking up on Liam. But he struggled to settle his mind because of his unease about Elene's safety. He feared he would return in three days, and she would be halfway to Norway. He searched for her once he saddled Urram. He looked for her in the village before he wandered toward her croft and looked at the fields where he thought she might toil. When he found her in neither place, he stepped into the mead hall. Gunter and his fellow Norse sailors crowded the gathering hall. Inburgh draped herself over him, possessive in her brief moments of lucidity. Liam easily recognized the mockery in the Norse eyes as they watched their leader's betrothed.

However, he didn't spy Elene. He glanced at Androw and Janet, who watched him. They both shook their heads. He searched among the crowd for Katryne and Johan, but he didn't see them either. He wondered if Elene took them away to avoid Inburgh and Gunter. He tried to set aside his disappointment, telling himself that Elene caring for her siblings far exceeded the importance of seeing her before he rode out. As he considered the situation, he acknowledged he respected Elene for her dedication and duty to her family. They were qualities that formed the basis of his own values and character.

With regret, he mounted Urram and guided his mount through the gate. He scanned the surrounding area, looking toward the coast, then the meadow, in a last attempt to find Elene. But no one moved beyond the village wall. As the village faded into the background, Liam turned his attention to leading his men as they pushed their horses to cover more ground. He rode at the front of the entourage. Dermot brought up the rear with men surrounding the wagon as it jostled over the rough path that was little more than a deer track rather than a road.

"We deliver this grain seed, then we meet with Dillon and Henry." Liam looked over his shoulder. "They'll bring the curraghs south. From there, we row across to Mainland."

"What of the wagon?" Cadence, a younger Sinclair warrior, asked.

"We should be able to leave it in the village. We will sail back for it. It's not ideal, but we can't double back. We need to make up for the lost time." Liam wasn't fond of leaving anything in the safekeeping of villagers he wasn't sure would welcome him. But it made little sense to ride across Rousay to only ride back, then sail south to the strip of Mainland Orkney where they would trade next.

Rousay was barely four miles long, so it took little time to travel to the village they'd missed during their last tour. It was the farthest from Skaill, so they'd abandoned their intended stop, knowing it wouldn't take long to finish their rounds once the weather settled. They entered Traversöe Tuick, and Liam scanned the crowded space where villagers moved from building to building. It was easy to spy the chieftain as he approached. Liam dismounted and held out his hand as a

CELESTE BARCLAY

man close to his age greeted him. It was the first warm welcome he received besides greeting Androw. Liam wondered if their similar age bespoke the man's willingness to acknowledge Liam as a leader.

"Good day." Njál Spence grasped Liam's extended forearm in a warrior handshake. "We expected you sooner."

"We planned to be here sooner, but the rutted roads threatened to knock the wheels off our wagon."

Njál frowned but nodded. "It's been a wee damp." Liam wondered if the man possessed a dry humor or merely accepted Orcadian weather for what it was: wet and cold all year. "Come inside. Your men arrived only five minutes ago with your curraghs. They're already in the mead hall warming themselves."

Liam gratefully accepted his host's invitation and followed the man toward the village's meeting hall. But before he entered, he recalled his father sent a cask of whisky specifically for Njál. The chieftain's father and Tristan had been close, and the former chieftain had passed away only two months ago. It was both a gift of condolence and congratulations. Liam gestured his men to continue inside before he turned back to the wagon.

As Liam approached, the tarp shifted on the wagon. He drew his sword and inched closer, wondering if was man or beast that lurked beneath the tarpaulin. He positioned himself at the foot of the wagon on the left side and grasped the end of the covering. Sword poised in his right hand, prepared to drive it through any threat, he reached across with his left and whisked the material back. Shock, then anger burst forth as his green eyes met Elene's blue ones.

"Get down now," Liam snapped. His gaze darted around them before he grasped Elene's arm and steered them toward the village stables.

. . .

The uneven road had jarred Elene with each rumbling roll of the wagon wheels. She'd wedged herself between barrels and sacks, gripping a sack and pressing her feet against a barrel to keep from being tossed from side to side. She'd breathed a silent sigh when they came to a stop. She listened to Liam greet the man she knew was the chieftain. She'd remained as still as a corpse until she heard the men's voices drift away. She peeked out of the corner, relieved she was close to the shore. If she could slide free of the wagon, she would dash to the rowboats.

She knew the crew had loaded empty barrels onto the curraghs the night before, intending to receive ale from Mainland in exchange for the sacks of barley and wheat seeds she'd hid beside. She'd heard that the filled whisky barrels on the wagon would remain here with Njál. She just needed to make it to an empty one and fit herself inside before anyone noticed.

Elene shifted, freeing herself from the tight confines of her hiding place, tucked back where she hoped no one would spy her if they looked under the tarp. She cursed as her shoulder bumped the cover and caused a ripple. She pushed herself forward on her belly, prepared to look out again to ensure no one was nearby. Instead, she froze as someone suddenly ripped the tarpaulin back, and the end of a sword pointed at her nose. Her eyes traveled along the length of the sword, then the sword wielder's arm until it met a furious glare. She'd already suspected who she would greet, but she hadn't expected the reaction her appearance caused. When Liam barked an order, she scrambled to comply, shocked when he grasped her arm and dragged her to the stables.

"Liam—"

"Hush." The hissed word barely reached her as she looked over her shoulder to find Liam's back to her as he scanned their surroundings before they ducked into the stables. He hurried them to the farthest stall before whirling Elene around.

"Why are you so angry?" Elene's whisper seemed to echo in the silent building. There were only a couple horses munching on hay, so most of the building was empty. Liam assumed the animals were in the fields with the farmers.

"Angry? I'm bluidy furious."

Elene's eyes narrowed as she pulled her arm away, her own temper boiling over. "Forget you saw me. I'll be on my way." She shifted to step past Liam, but his massive frame remained like a stone monolith. "Move."

Liam laughed, but it was mirthless. "Where are you going to go? This bluidy island is four miles long. Njál will march you right back home."

"I didn't intend for Njál—or anyone else," Elene tacked on the last part of her comment when her gaze met Liam's, "to find me."

Liam's eyes widened. "The empty barrels."

Elene's head dipped forward, shocked that Liam deduced her plan within moments. She cocked an eyebrow in challenge. "Yes."

Liam sheathed his sword and took a step closer, further caging Elene between him and the stable wall. "Do you have any idea why I'm livid?"

"Frankly, no. I'll figure things out on my own now that you smuggling me is out of the question."

"Me smuggling? You'd be a bluidy stowaway. On a bluidy curragh!" Liam inhaled, his left hand curling into a fist. "Imagine it was a villager who found you? Someone either sent to get something from the wagon or spotted you trying to get in the barrel. The entire village would already know you're here. You're a free woman, no one's serf, but you're also unmarried and traveling with a group of men. It would destroy your reputation before you could take a breath. I'd be honor-bound to return you to Skaill, where they would force me to turn you over to your mother, which means Gunter. What would he do to you if he faced the humiliation of knowing you ran from him? What the hell were you going to do once you got to Mainland? Did you assume that when I found you, which I would since I'd be opening each barrel, that you would just walk away?"

Liam drilled Elene with one question after another, not giving her the chance to answer one before he fired the next one. Her frustration and fear, added to her agitation that someone would find them in the stable, made her anger match Liam's.

"As you pointed out, I am unmarried. That means you're not my husband. I'm also not a serf, so you are not my laird. Move." Elene once more made to move past Liam, but his hand shot out and pressed against the wall by her shoulder. She glared at him.

"Promise you will finish talking to me, and I will lower my arm. I know I'm crowding you. I'm doing it to keep our voices from carrying, but I'm also doing it to keep you here. I loathe making you feel trapped. I just don't trust you."

"You are doing all the talking and assuming I wish to do all the listening. I don't."

Their fury as they glared at one another sparked another elemental emotion. Neither knew who moved first, but their mouths crashed together. Elene's hands cupped Liam's jaw as his right arm snaked around her waist, and his left hand grasped her bottom. She reached between them with an irritable grunt as she tried to push Liam's sporran out of the way. He pressed his hips back until it shifted, then thrust them forward.

79

Elene's moan encouraged him to rock his rod against her mound. The hand that moved his sporran now grasped his buttocks. She marveled at the granite beneath her hand.

Their anger eased, but fear still thrummed through them both, pouring forth as lust. It was a need for Liam to know Elene was safe, and a need for her to know Liam could keep her safe. Their kiss stretched across minutes as their pelvises moved together, thrusting against one another. Liam gathered a handful of Elene's skirts and lifted, but he paused, giving her a chance to reject him. Instead, she fumbled and covered his hand with hers, drawing it higher until his bare palm cupped her bottom. She reached around him, yanking his plaid until her hand met his muscular buttocks.

Their frustration lay not only in being unable to press themselves closer, but in knowing the situation remained unresolved. However, neither had the words, or even the thoughts, to offer a solution. Rather, their need for one another combusted. Neither wanted to argue. Neither wanted the other to walk away. With no other way to communicate their swirling emotions, obliging their physical desire felt like the only option.

Liam drew his mouth away first before he nuzzled his nose behind her ear, smelling her fresh lavender scent. "I want to be inside you. I want to make love to you." Liam would sort out later why he'd said that, since he'd considered none of his previous interludes as lovemaking. "But I want to keep you safe. God, what if someone else found you?"

Liam returned his mouth to hers, their kiss once more exploding. Elene heard the desperation and fear in Liam's voice. It shook with his last sentence. She sensed it through his anger, but the catch in his voice made her realize the depth of his worry. It softened her anger. The tone of their kiss shifted, no longer a duel to dominate. It eased, becoming tender, filled with longing.

Elene drew away, brushing her cheek against Liam's bristly stubble. He hadn't shaved that morning. She kept her voice low, her warm breath sending an erotic shiver down Liam's spine. "I didn't think anyone could keep me safe but me. You didn't offer a solution. I didn't even know if you'd be back in time to offer one if you thought of it. I can't get on that dragon boat. If I do, I will never be free."

Liam's hand slid over Elene's hip until the side of his index finger slipped along her folds. It was Elene's turn to shiver. She widened her stance, inviting him to explore more. He dipped the tip of his finger between her petals, discovering her barrier. Part of him wanted to groan in disappointment that she was a maiden. He'd never considered she wouldn't be a virgin, but it felt monumentally inconvenient at the moment. He couldn't take what wasn't his to have, but he wanted to join their bodies more than he wanted his next breath. His thumb sought the pearl within its shell. Aroused and plumb, he circled it, eliciting a moan, and Elene's fingers bit into his backside.

"This solves naught. I know that," Liam murmured. "Not now and not once we stop. But I don't want to let go. I don't know if I ever want to let go. I need this. I need to know I can keep you safe right now, and I can give you pleasure amid this uncertainty."

"God, how I crave your touch. My body won't turn you away, but neither will my mind. I feel safe right now. I only feel safe when I'm with you. And the pleasure." Elene moaned as her core tightened, and she felt her release building. "It's unlike aught I could ever bring myself, even when I imagine it's you."

"You picture me when you touch yourself?" It was the most erotic notion Liam had ever heard.

"Yes," Elene moaned as her climax crested over her.

"I've thought of you every time I wrap my hand around my cock, every time I've wished it was your hand or your cunny."

Elene dug her nails into Liam's shoulders, which she now gripped to keep her steady. The thought that he desired her so strongly only increased the effects of his ongoing ministrations. A second release washed over her, making her knees shake. Liam's powerful arm around her waist was all that kept her from sagging to the ground, her body spent. As her mind cleared, she felt Liam's arousal still pressing against her. She moved to slide her hand beneath his *breacan feile*, but Liam grasped her hand. He shook his head.

"It might kill me to turn you down, but this wasn't about me or for me."

"I want this to be about us. I want to give you what you just gave me. You're always giving. Why can't you just take for once?"

"Because I never want you to question whether I'm with you just to get what I want."

Elene blinked several times, unsure how to respond at first. "I never thought that you were. That doubt never dawned on me. Why must you make me care for you even more when you said yourself that there's no solution to this?"

Liam released Elene's skirts and placed both hands on his waist, taking one step back. They needed to talk, not argue. And he wanted it to be a conversation between equals, not one where he imposed upon her.

"My anger—it was fear, and it was hurt. It shocked me to find you there, but you'd hidden. You hadn't trusted me. You hadn't sought my help. You put me in a position where I wouldn't have been able to shield you if someone found you. I don't know." Liam shook his head. "It felt like you lied and betrayed me, used me.

And it felt like I was a failure because you didn't believe I could help."

"I didn't think anyone could help me. It wasn't that I didn't think you would try. I just didn't think there was aught to do other than run away. You leaving Skaill, leaving the island, seemed like my only chance. I didn't ask you because I didn't want to face you turning me away. I didn't ask because I didn't want to put you in a situation where you would have to turn me down. I didn't want to make you feel trapped into helping. But I also knew it was too dangerous to set off on my own and too dangerous to trust anyone else. I trust you completely. I knew if you found me—" Elene's gaze flashed to the ceiling, "—when you found me, I would put you in a horrible position, but I wouldn't be in peril."

"But you are. You can't go back. You can't stay here. I've been in here with you for so long I'm shocked no one has come searching."

"If you can get me to Mainland, then I can figure something out. I'll say I'm a widow and couldn't manage my farm. Or I'll make my way to Scotland. I can speak Scots well enough, so I could go to the Lowlands."

"Do you have money for all this?"

Elene nodded. She touched the side of her gown Liam hadn't felt. He heard coins shift. "I've been saving every bit I can since shortly after I met Gunter."

Liam didn't care for either of those ideas, but he didn't have a better long-term solution. He chided himself because he knew that wasn't true. He knew what the solution was. He could marry Elene and bring her back to Castle Varrich with him. But he didn't want a marriage borne of convenience. His parents were a love match, and they'd promised all their children they could have the same. He wasn't prepared to call his feelings toward Elene love. He didn't want to act in haste and repent at leisure. He didn't want Elene to marry him out of desperation, either. He didn't want to spend his life married to a woman who regretted an impetuous decision. And a small part of him niggled that duty to his clan required him to marry a woman who brought a powerful alliance to his people.

He sighed. "I won't send you back alone. I can't take you back because I must fulfill my duties to my family. But neither do I want you hiding or setting off alone." He tilted his head back and sighed again. As he looked back at her, seeing her anxiousness, he thought of one possibility. One that didn't seem so horrible after all. "If you travel with us, then you must be part of someone's family. No one will believe you're anyone's sister, so you must be someone's wife." Liam watched Elene's expression as he poured forth his suggestion. She didn't reel back, but he wondered how she would react when he spoke aloud his conclusion. "The only person who would merit bringing his wife on a journey like this is the leader. Me."

Elene's cheeks heated. The idea of pretending to be Liam's wife was wholly appealing, since she wasn't averse to the idea of being his wife in truth. She wasn't ready to commit to a lifetime with him, but she could admit she'd never met another man with whom she'd considered wanting a home. As her gaze swept over Liam, absorbing the commanding presence, his handsome visage, and his powerful body, she couldn't think of a reason she wouldn't want to be seen with him or have people believe they were married. In fact, the notion that the women he'd meet would envy her gave her a wicked sense of satisfaction. She knew that was shallow and hardly what should concern her, but she couldn't help it.

"Lass," Liam muttered in Gaelic before switching

back to Norn. "If you keep looking at me like that, we shall end up kissing rather than talking."

Elene tilted her head slightly and cocked an eyebrow before smirking. "If people thought I was your wife, there'd be no harm in more of that kissing."

Liam stepped forward again as he pulled on her waist to bring her closer. He rested his forehead against hers, the tips of their noses touching. "This charade isn't without risk, and I don't know how long we can carry it off, but if it gives me permission to kiss you whenever the mood strikes, and you don't push me away, then I shall take it."

"I can't imagine pushing you away." Elene lifted her chin enough for their lips to brush again. The kiss was soft, the earlier passion missing. But there was a tenderness to it in which they both reveled. As they gazed at one another, something passed between them that neither wanted to speak aloud. But the connection deepened, and neither was sure they could ever walk away.

"We must tell my men what's happening. We can't afford for any of them to misspeak and give away that you're not truly my wife." Liam glanced over his shoulder, still surprised no one interrupted them. "Elene, if we can continue this ruse long enough to get you to my birlinns, then I will take you to Scotland. If you wish to live in the Highlands or the Lowlands, then I will take you where you want. If you want to make your home among the Sinclairs, I am certain you can." Liam paused, unsure if he should share the next thought. He worried it would sound like he rejected her if he didn't, but he also worried about her interpretation if he did. "If you wish to live among the Mackays, I know neither my mother nor father would oppose."

Elene watched as Liam struggled to decide whether he should share his final thought. She knew he worried he would hurt her feelings if he didn't invite her to his home. At the same time, she knew he feared she would read too much into his offer to take her to Castle Varrich.

"I don't know where I want to settle, but if we can travel to Scotland and I can find somewhere to call home, then I won't complain where." It was Elene's turn to glance toward the door. "How will you get me aboard the curragh now? Njál didn't see me arrive with you, so he will question how I came to be with you."

"I have a pair of breeks and a spare leine. I detest wearing the damn things, but I have them just in case whenever I leave the Highlands. You don those along with my cloak. We get you onto a curragh as quickly as we can and seat you with the oars to make it appear like you can't help carry the sacks. Keep your head down, even look like you're examining something with the oar. We'll leave as soon as we can load everything. I'll explain to my men in Gaelic."

Elene nodded once before Liam hurried to the stable door. He looked around, spying no one before he rushed to Urram's side. He pulled his spare clothes and cloak from the saddlebag before dashing back into the stables. He handed the clothes to Elene and spun around. He squeezed his eyes closed but peeked from one as he heard her clothes moving. He could only see the wall ahead of him, so he clenched both closed again. The temptation nipped at him, having already been so close to her naked body once. He inhaled deeply as he attempted to calm his sudden spike in lust. He nearly jumped out of his skin when Elene touched the back of his arm.

"I'm ready. What about these?" She held up her clothes, folded into a small bundle.

"I'll stash them in my saddlebag on the way to the wagon. Stand on the far side near the horses, so you're harder to see. Then we'll get you settled into the curragh once the others are there. We can't have you sitting alone where anyone can question you. Come. We need to hurry now." They moved together, trying to appear casual. Elene wore the hood over her blonde hair. Once she stood between the draft horses, Liam looked around, grabbed the gift cask of whisky, and made his way to the mead hall. With every step, he prayed their plan worked.

CHAPTER 7

*L*iam looked around the mead hall, easily spotting his men. Njál sat with a group of his own men but turned toward him as Liam squeezed between the benches to reach the other Highlanders. The Sinclairs and Dermot looked at Liam questioningly, but none spoke when Liam slashed them a quick, quelling glance.

"I wondered if you'd wandered into the sea," Njál teased.

"Yes, well, nature called." Liam grinned and shrugged. "Too many oatcakes. It took a while."

Njál chuckled and returned Liam's shrug. "Your men have eaten and drunk, so I suppose we can unload the wagon."

"We need to be off before the tide changes. My father sends his condolences and congratulations." Liam handed over the cask before he looked at his men, surprised to realize none had unloaded anything in his absence. When they filed out, Dermot leaned close to Liam.

"I stepped back out when ye returned to the wagon. I saw Elene."

Liam kept his gaze forward, but his heart lurched.

"Is that why nay one came searching for me? Why nay one unloaded the wagon?"

"Aye." Dermot waited for Liam to further explain, but when he glanced at his friend, he realized Liam was staring at the front of the wagon. Liam increased his pace and canted his head toward the wagon.

"She's coming with us. I need ye to help me shield her from any of the villagers seeing her." Liam scanned his men, who walked around them. Adopting a commanding voice, hoping it sounded like he ordered his men in Gaelic to unload the wagon, Liam said, "Elene is coming with us. Nay one says aught aboot her until we are away. Keep her protected and be quick with the sacks and barrels."

"They already kenned she's here. I warned them nae to say aught if they saw her. We'll all do as ye say, but do ye ken what ye're doing?"

"Ye bluidy well better hope I do." Liam stepped between the wagon's horses, his back to them but facing Elene. Dermot stepped behind her. When she made to look over her shoulder, Liam's hand brushed hers. She read his expression and kept still. He spoke to her in Norn, keeping his voice low. "Stay between us until we can get you on the boat. I need to talk to Dermot as though you aren't here, or people will wonder why we're standing around."

Elene nodded, then kept her head down. They shielded her smaller frame from view, but she wished she weren't so tall. Her heart pounded as she waited for someone to ask why she hid.

Liam directed his comments to Dermot, but he knew his men could hear. In Gaelic, he explained, "Once we load the curraghs, I want Elene seated with oars. Put Cadence in the other one. I need there to be a reason she isn't working. It'll look odd if only one rower is seated. Right now, she'll be facing away from the shore. I told her to look like she's examining the oars. I'll climb in and take her place before we turn them around. When I do and we push off, I'll have her lay in the hull until we're out of sight."

Liam looked around and noticed that everything they intended to leave in this village was already unloaded, and locals were carrying them away. He pointed to a sack as he grabbed one. Dermot hefted it onto his shoulder while Liam did the same. They made their way to the farther rowboat, the extra load aiding their large bodies as they blocked Elene from anyone's view from behind or the sides. She moved with ease once she climbed into the rowboat.

The bobbing affected her not at all, and Liam reminded himself that she grew up in a fishing village. She seated herself at the oars, and it was obvious she was familiar with the position. She followed Liam's instructions, pulling in one oar, and leaning forward as if she examined the handle. Keeping her head down, the hood continued to cover her blonde braid. Her heart raced, and she squeezed her eyes shut. She didn't open them even as she pushed out the oar she held and drew in the other. She felt the rowboat bob as the men added sacks and barrels. She'd noticed there was a bench for an additional rower, since the boats were larger than she'd expected.

A whinny distracted her from her fear, making her look between the curraghs. There was a platform with raised sides and ropes on the front and back. When Elene spied it tied between the rowboats earlier, she assumed it was for extra barrels that didn't fit in the rowboats. But she realized it was more of a barge for the horses. She watched, fascinated, as the men loaded the horses onto the floating platform. She marveled at how much sturdier it was than it appeared. She'd feared it would sink under the weight of the first two horses, but all of them fit. When the last horse boarded the barge, a Sinclair secured the front rope again. The men clamored into the curraghs.

Liam's hand on her shoulder as a man passed her to sit between the other set of oars signaled her to drop onto the hull of the boat. She drew the cloak around her and virtually disappeared once men sat on the other benches. The tension between her shoulders and clenched jaw made her body ache, but she wouldn't relax until she knew no one would stop them. She felt the curragh move into the surf, then the oars on the port side turn them, so the stern met the waves. The spray that misted her fingers as she clenched the cloak drawn around her was perishing.

"Elene, you can sit up," Liam stated. "Move onto a bench; there's room."

Elene sat up, looking around her. She looked at the bench behind her, opposite of where Liam sat rowing. She kept her head covered but took a seat, glad to un-curl her body from the fetal position. She flexed her fingers, alternating hands. She shifted her gaze from Liam to the surrounding men, then to those on the other curragh. However, the horses made it veritably impossible to see those men. She looked over Liam's shoulder and watched the land shrink as the distance grew.

"I really left Rousay," Elene whispered.

"You did." Liam's smile encouraged her as her heart finally slowed from its hammering pace. "We sail to Tingwall on the eastern shore to deliver seed. From there, we sail to Kirkwall to deliver the whisky and re-ceive the ale. Henry and Dillon will remain with the boats and stay in the village. They both have family there. We'll ride to Dingieshowe. I expect to stay there for three or four days. I am to meet several chieftains at their *thing*. If I visit their public assembly, then I can represent my grandfather to more leaders."

Elene shivered in mock fear. "Legend says the ancients burned a witch alive in Dingieshowe, and her head still appears in the sand. They also say that the great Norseman pirate Sweyn Asleifsson used to visit his uncle in Tingwall. Helgi was a chieftain." Elene grew serious, and this time the apprehension was real. "You can see the isles of Wyre, Egilsay, and Rousay from there."

"I know, but we'll be much too small for anyone to know who's who." Liam had already considered how short the distance was between the islands. He worried Tingwall would be the first place Gunter looked. He'd thought to spend the full day and a night in the village, but now he planned to keep their visit short and reach Kirkwall before nightfall. He would order Henry and Dillon to stow the curraghs farther along the Peedie Sea's coast. They could ride back to see their families in Kirkwall. He considered the merits of leaving Kirkwall and making camp somewhere away from the shore on the way to Dingieshowe. He would have to see what they accomplished that day.

Liam relayed the new plan to his men, who looked in Elene's direction, knowing she was the cause for the change in itinerary. Liam watched their expressions and saw no hostility, just curiosity. He gave thanks that no one begrudged Elene's presence. At least not yet. He hoped explaining her circumstances would ease any resentment or dissention before it began.

"I'm sure you've all heard Elene's situation with Gunter. Having met the man, I believe Elene's fears are legitimate. As Highlanders, as Christians, and as Sinclairs, we are duty bound to keep any person from being sold into slavery. Elene travels with us under the pretense that she's my wife. While I speak Norn almost like it's my first tongue, there may be times when she can interpret for me while I meet the chieftains at the *thing*. I see it as a blessing in disguise that she's with us." Liam continued to watch his men. He saw the notes of surprise when he mentioned they would pretend Elene was his wife. A couple of men shot him smirks. It was clear none of the men believed it would be a hardship for Liam. "We must treat her with the same dignity and deference we do Lady Siùsan, my mother, and all my aunts. Remember, in their eyes, she is the future Lady Mackay."

Liam hoped that reminder would keep any of the men from smirking in front of Elene. He knew she couldn't understand what they said amongst them-selves, but she was astute. She would perceive any questionable comments, and he didn't want her to catch any mocking miens. He prayed he didn't miss-peak among the Orcadians and giveaway their ruse. It was only a matter of minutes before they would arrive.

"Elene, if you were my wife, you'd deserve the title 'Lady,' so that is how I will introduce you. I want people to believe we married for some time ago, so if ques-tioned by any Norsemen, they won't think we just met. I haven't been to Kirkwall in two years, so no one knows whether I've visited other parts. We can't say we've been married longer than that because the chief-tain knows I was unwed then, but everywhere else we can say at least five years."

"There's a village on the way to Kirkwall called Is-bister. My father's people were from there before some settled in Skaill, and it's how we got our name. I still have family there, and when my father used to take me fishing, we would stay for a night or two. I know this coast well and several of the villages. If anyone asks questions, I should be able to answer."

The curraghs nudged the sandy shore, and a couple

horses whinnied. Liam helped Elene avoid soaking the hem of her skirts. It gave him the excuse to lift her into his arms and carry her to the grass beyond the moist sand. He enjoyed the feel of her arms locked around his neck and how her head rested against his shoulder. He regretted having to put her down. He sensed she felt the same since she was slow to release him and didn't pull away when her feet settled on the ground. His hands rested on her waist as their eyes met. Elene found reassurance in Liam's steady gaze. She offered a subtle nod before they turned toward the village and the approaching people. While the Sinclair men and Dermot led the horses to graze, Liam slid his arm around Elene's waist.

Once they stood before the village's chieftain and council, Liam withdrew his arm and laced his fingers with Elene. She leaned against him, suddenly nervous about pretending to be a noblewoman. No one would expect her to have been one from birth if she came from the hamlet of Isbister, but they would expect her to know how to act like one since supposedly they married years ago. She opted to remain quiet.

"Liam Sinclair!" A bear of a man clasped Liam's forearm and thudded his hand against Liam's back.

"Mawnus Leith!" Liam returned the embrace before leaning away. "Grandfather said you'd become the new chieftain six moons ago, but I can't believe the lad I used to build sand pies with is now chieftain."

"Yes, well, Johne wasn't fit anymore." Mawnus tapped his temple. "So the council elected me."

When Mawnus's attention turned to Elene, Liam beamed. "Mawnus, this is my wife, Lady Elene." Liam stopped before sharing Elene's surname. He recalled she would now be a Mackay if they'd married.

"Wife? When did that happen?" Mawnus didn't hide

his surprise. "I didn't imagine you'd settled down already. I know I don't intend to do so anytime soon."

Liam looked down into Elene's upturned face, and his admiration was genuine. "Five years ago."

"Five? Do you have a passel of bairns waiting for you to return?"

Liam froze, and he saw the nervousness enter Elene's eyes. "We haven't been so blessed yet, but then I enjoy not sharing my wife's attention." The only falsehood in the statement was calling Elene his wife.

"Not living *up* to the task?" Mawnus waggled his brows.

Liam scowled at Mawnus, displeased at how his childhood friend embarrassed Elene by discussing their supposed intimacies in front of her. "There are precautions to take. As I said, I'm not ready to share Lady Elene's attention. There are plenty of years for bairns in the lifetime to come." He squeezed her hand before looking back at his men. They nearly finished unloading the grain sacks.

"Will you come with me to the mead hall and share the midday meal?" Mawnus changed the topic, noting he would do well not to further insult the grandson of the Earl of Caithness. Once Liam and Elene sat at the high table and a servant placed a trencher between them, Liam read the decree to Mawnus, who couldn't do it himself. The chieftain nodded as he watched his villagers gather. When Mawnus introduced Liam, it was with more finesse and subtlety than Androw had used.

"It is an honor for me to represent my grandfather and all the Sinclairs as I tour Orkney. You know my family, both the Sinclairs and the Mackays, have ties to these islands since the days of the early Norse settlers." Liam caught himself before he called them invaders. He doubted that would be appreciated. "We have traded with you alongside our Norse counterparts, and we look forward to continuing as we have. My grandfather doesn't wish to change that. Rather than paying your taxes to the Norse crown, you now pay it to the Scottish. Your daily lives shouldn't change."

"Until the Norse no longer come," a man called out.

"The Norse settled on Orkney because their homeland isn't as good for farming as the land here. That hasn't changed. They need the trade, so they will continue to come. King David and King Haakon Haakonsson agreed business would continue as it has for generations. It benefits both countries and the people of Orkney." Liam prayed his words allayed their fears, but he understood that only time would prove it to the Orcadians.

Mawnus raised his mead horn and proclaimed, "Hail King David."

While the villagers' enthusiasm didn't match Mawnus's, there wasn't a tone of resentment. Liam counted this as a success. But only a moment later, his heart sank.

"Lady Elene, you wear Orcadian clothes, and you have an Orcadian name. From which isle do you hail?" Mawnus only spoke Norn, which meant he was certain Elene understood.

Elene smiled warmly, even as her left knee bounced in anxiousness. Liam's broad palm rested upon her thigh, the heat soothing her, and its presence giving her confidence. "This one, Chieftain. My father's people hail from Isbister. I find my Orcadian clothing more comfortable for the climate here, so I wear them when I'm not at home at Varrich."

"Are you an Isbister?" Mawnus pressed.

"I was. I'm a Mackay." Elene kept her tone light but resolute, and her expression serene as she looked past Liam to see Mawnus. As Liam listened to Mawnus and

Elene talk, he realized he needed to do something more to prove her pretend role. He knew she wore no ring, which was unusual for a married noblewoman. He considered what he could do.

"God graced me when I visited here and met Elene all those years ago. We had time to grow fond of one another before my family and I returned to Varrich. My father arranged the marriage with Elene's. We wedded before we sailed home." It surprised Liam how easily the lies fell from his lips. "Speaking of sailing. We can only stay briefly. They expect us in Kirkwall. We cannot miss the tide, or it will be a battle to get the curraghs along the coast."

"Such a short visit, my friend!" Mawnus frowned.

"The poor weather delayed us. We must make up for the lost time, so we are keeping each stop brief. I hate to appear rude, but you know how quickly summer passes into autumn in the north Atlantic. I don't wish to make the crossing once the winds pick up." Liam believed his excuses were reasonable. When Mawnus nodded, Liam hoped that was the end of the discussion. He moved it to what he hoped was safer: how the village elected Mawnus as chieftain.

Once the meal finished, Liam and the men loaded the horses back onto the barge, while Elene took her seat in the curragh. It surprised her when Liam sat beside her. She wondered if it was merely for appearances, since Mawnus watched them. But when he drew her against his side, adjusted her hood, and rubbed her arm, she realized that he'd done it to help keep her warm against the headwind. The spray wasn't as bad as when they pushed off from the Rousay coast, but it was still like icicles pricking the skin. Huddled in Liam's cloak, she worried he would freeze. When she peered out from beneath the hood, she realized he and the other Highlanders had all pulled the extra lengths of

97

wool from their *breacan feiles* over their heads and
shoulders. It buffered the wind and water.

As they approached Kirkwall an hour later, Liam
pulled a *sgian dubh* from his boot. The short but
wickedly sharp knife cut through the end of the sash
over his shoulder to where it met his belt. The sound of
rending fabric made Elene twist to watch. Her eyes
widened in surprise, but she remained quiet as she
watched Liam put away his knife and adjust the extra
length back into place.

"Put this across your left shoulder and tuck it into
your belt on your right hip. I don't have a pin to give
you," Liam instructed. Elene fumbled under the massive sealskin-lined cloak, but she arranged the sash as
Liam said. "I realized when we sat with Mawnus that
you neither wear my ring nor my clan colors. I don't
have a ring I can give you, but you can wear my colors."

"But you ruined your *breacan feile*."

"No. It still sits at the right length, and there's still
plenty of material to cross my shoulder." Liam
skimmed his eyes over Elene's lap, up her torso, to her
shoulder. He lowered his voice. "I enjoy seeing you in
my colors."

Liam knew his men could see them, so he settled for
feathering a kiss on Elene's temple. He would have
much preferred one of their explosive kisses, or even
one of their tender brushes of their lips. But he settled
for what wouldn't embarrass her. When they reached
Kirkwall, the men hurried to unload the barrels of
whisky and all but two horses. As the group moved
along the shore and climbed the hill to reach the village, Henry and Dillon rowed away to find a place to
hide the curraghs. The two warriors would supervise
filling the barrels with ale before they left the next
morning.

Their visit in Kirkwall was much like their stop in

Tingwall. But rather than share a meal, they settled for bread and cheese with mugs of ale. Liam claimed they were newlyweds of eighteen months. He figured that gave him the excuse to keep his arm around Elene as they sat together in the chieftain's home. She rested her head against the crook of his shoulder, grateful that he was so tall that she didn't have to tilt her head to reach.

As the men talked, Elene found the croft's warmth and her full belly were lulling her to sleep. She'd taken the blanket to Liam a couple of hours after everyone settled for the night. She'd done so, not just because she felt guilty that he sat in the brisk night air to guard her, but she wanted to learn how lightly he slept. She discovered he woke easily. Frustration filled her as she crept back to the croft's door. She was certain he heard it close, but she never stepped inside.

Instead, she crept past the front of two crofts before ducking into the shadows. She froze when she thought she heard a night guard approach. When the man merely looked in her direction and carried on, it relieved her to know no one spotted her. She wasted no time making her way to the stables, where she slid under the tarp of the waiting wagon. She curled up and hid behind the sacks of seeds and barrels as best she could. She prayed no one checked too far back before they set off. She hadn't slept at all, too frightened someone would discover her and sound the alarm. Then the road had been far too bumpy to rest.

Elene didn't realize how much time passed until Liam squeezed her waist and kissed the top of her head. He whispered, "It's time to speak to the villagers, *leannan*. If you're too tired, you can rest here before the fire. I will fetch you when it's time to leave."

"No. I don't want to appear weak or lazy. You brought me along as your wife. I represent your clan, so I should stand beside you." Elene rose and was unprepared for Liam to tunnel his fingers into her hair and pull her against his body. His kiss was fierce and consuming. She opened her mouth to him, welcoming the flash of his tongue before they pulled apart. She looked at him questioningly.

"You make me so proud." He pressed another brief kiss to her lips before they joined the chieftain and Dermot outside.

Liam repeated his announcement almost verbatim to what he'd said in Tingwall, including his response to the same complaint. He and his family spent the most time in Kirkwall since there was a bevy of Sinclairs in the village. His pronouncement that his grandfather now governed the islands on behalf of King David elicited the warmest reaction he had yet to receive. He counted it a minor victory. He would face the most scrutiny the next day when they arrived in Dingieshowe, and he met with chieftains at the *thing*. As a public assembly, villagers from across the islands could attend along with their leaders. He wondered if they would encounter any Norse traders there. He'd counted themselves fortunate that they didn't run into any in Tingwall or Kirkwall.

"You ride with me, Elene," Liam explained as they approached the horses. There wasn't one for Elene, and even if there were, Liam felt better keeping her close. At least until she mounted in front of him. He gritted his teeth as her backside pressed against his hardening manhood. His arms rested beneath her breasts as he held the reins. She shifted and released an annoyed sound. She reached behind her and shifted his sporran.

"That can't be comfy for you, and I can't ride several hours with the buckle pressing into my back."

"Elene—"

"Do you think it's any easier for me with your arms around me?" Elene shifted again, her lower back rubbing the tip of Liam's cock while the swollen length rested in the division between her buttocks. Liam groaned. He gathered the reins in one hand and slipped his other beneath her cloak. He cupped her breast and brushed his thumb over her puckered nipple. Then he slid his hand along her ribs and drew it across her mons. His fingers pressed beneath her mound, the heel of his hand resting against her pleasure button. He spurred Urram and allowed the horse's rocking gait, coupled with the pressure from his hand, to arouse Elene further.

"I shall give you relief, *leannan*."

Elene's hands gripped Liam's forearm as she struggled not to moan. It was a unique feeling, but the sensation made her core ache. No man had ever stirred the reaction that Liam did when he looked at her, let alone when he touched her. It was mere minutes before her fingers bit into his forearms and her belly tightened while her core pulsated.

"St. Columba's bones," Elene hissed. "There is naught more I want than to kiss you right now." Her body craved more, frustrated that what it believed should have been a prelude to more was the main event. Liam urged her to turn, so both her legs hung over Urram's right flank. He knew he could draw his sword from his back and swing wide without decapitating Elene.

"Lean against me, *leannan*. You can sleep the entire way. I can only imagine what time you rose to be in the wagon before any of us stirred. It surprises me I didn't hear or see you since I barely slept either."

Elene tried and failed to stifle her yawn. "I never went back into my home after I brought you the blanket. I feared you might not sleep much or are a light sleeper, so I made you think I went back inside. I hid in the wagon all night."

"Without a blanket or a cloak? You could have frozen." It horrified Liam that she'd left herself so vulnerable. The stables shut out the night's wind, but it had been the coldest since he arrived. The stables trapped that frigid air, and she had nothing to protect her but the tarp.

"It truly wasn't that bad. I hid behind and beneath the sacks. Their weight helped keep me warm." Elene kissed Liam's neck, touched that he worried so much. "You keep calling me *leannan*. What does it mean?"

Liam knew she would eventually ask since he didn't think she knew the Gaelic endearment, but he was still embarrassed to say it aloud. He felt a fool for using it since their relationship was a fraud, and they would part ways once he was certain she was safe. But it felt right to the very marrow in his bones.

"It means sweetheart," Liam answered. Elene nestled closer, burrowing against his chest. Liam looked down and found her eyes closed and her hand resting on his sternum. He murmured, "Sleep."

A nod and a sigh were all he received in response. As Elene's breathing slowed, and her body sagged against him, he recalled the story of how his parents met. Laird Liam Sinclair and Laird Tristan Mackay arranged for Mairghread Sinclair to marry Tristan's younger stepbrother, Alan, to end the clans' feud. Tristan arranged the marriage, hoping to avoid the matrimonial noose and hoping it would reform his wayward stepbrother. The moment Mairghread and Tristan met, magnetism drew them together as though an invisible thread bound them. It took only a night for Alan to ruin the pending betrothal and nearly get himself killed after he insulted and threatened Mairghread. Laird Sinclair intended to return to Dunbeath with his five children and happily continue the feud. It was

Mairghread who convinced her father and four brothers to remain.

Liam remembered his parents sharing how they'd stood together on the battlements early the morning after Alan's disastrous behavior. They'd admitted their attraction, and Tristan asked Mairghread to remain at Castle Varrich so he could court her. It took much longer to convince her father that they were a sound match. But everyone knew from the start that the couple was besotted with one another. His parents claimed it was love at first sight. Watching them after two decades of marriage, Liam believed it was likely lust at first sight. But he knew it took only days before genuine feelings blossomed between the couple.

As he peered at Elene's sleeping face, he wondered if God had granted him such an opportunity. His esteem grew each day as he got to know Elene better. There was no doubt that they were attracted to one another, but he found he enjoyed merely being in her company. Their couple of nights stargazing had been two of the best memories he had. He couldn't think of anything that had felt more natural than lying beside her and talking. The only thing that came close was the feel of his sword in his hand. He'd held one every day since Tristan gave him his first wooden sword at five years old. Holding Elene as she slept, knowing she depended on him and trusted him enough to lower her guard, made something change within Liam. He was certain his heart swelled, but he felt worthy in a way he'd hoped representing his grandfather would create. He didn't want to imagine the feeling ending when he left Orkney and parted ways with Elene. He wondered if he would ever feel this way about another woman, the woman he would eventually marry.

CHAPTER 8

"*H*ow long are ye going to keep pretending?" Dermot asked as he and Liam collected firewood. Liam looked over his shoulder toward the camp they pitched halfway to Dingieshowe.

"I dinna ken. As long as it takes to get her away from Gunter and keep her from going back to Skaill."

"Ye ken we have to go back to Skaill, dinna ye?"

"Of course I do. I may be enamored, but I havenae forgotten everything else aboot this voyage. Our ships are there, and Androw expects us to return within a sennight." Liam considered that while they rode south of Kirkwall. They'd traveled two hours before they stopped for the night. Elene woke after only a half an hour, but she looked more rested. They'd spoken little while riding, both watching the surrounding landscape. It gave Liam more time to plan now that he had an unexpected member of their party. "When we arrive back at Skaill, we'll do it in the dark. We'll bring the curraghs straight to the birlinns. That way, people believe we're securing them and the barge. Elene will lie in the hull of our curragh while it's hoisted and battened down. We'll all come ashore in Alfred's curragh. She will have

104

to remain hiding in the curragh until we can set sail in the morning."

"She'll freeze. And what aboot food and water for the lass?"

"We fill the waterskins before we leave Kirkwall and make extra bannocks that morning. We have enough oats. There's dried beef aboard the birlinn, and I'm certain we can get pickled herring in Kirkwall. Elene will need spare plaids to bed down with, but it should keep her warm."

"Ye'd best pray the weather holds."

"I ken. I dinna like the idea of leaving her alone all night. If ye're willing, I'd ask ye to stay aboard. As captain, I can make reasonable excuses for ye to be checking the ship before we depart." Liam locked eyes with Dermot, the warning clear.

"I willna touch her or try to seduce her. She's yer woman." Dermot threw up one hand while the other arm carried twigs and branches.

"See that ye dinna. Ye have a way with women."

"Dinna I ken it." Dermot grinned and waggled his eyebrows. But he grew serious, looking around at the men near them also gathering wood. His cheeks flushed. "I'm mending ma ways."

"Ye think Hildie will have ye?" Liam named a young woman he knew Dermot had fancied for years, but she'd never shown interest.

"Aye. I talked to her before we left. I told her the whole truth." Dermot's good looks and charming disposition drew women to him easily, but he'd been just as careful as Liam in his partners. People assumed he had far more prowess than he did. He'd confessed his bravado to Hildie, fearing she might choose someone else during his mission.

"Wise. She's a good lass."

"Just as yer Elene is."

"Wheest. She isnae ma aught."

"But ye'd like her to be."

"It's too soon to tell. And I have to think aboot the clan before I can think aboot asking for any woman's hand."

"That's a pile a shite. Ye ken that, and I ken that. Yer mother and father wish all of ye to have the same ful-filling marriage they do. They dinna care if ye marry a princess or a peasant as long as ye choose a woman who can help ye lead. We're prosperous enough without a bride's dowry. None of yer aunts came with a dowry nor alliances, and ye ken yer father and mother welcomed them just the same, as did yer grandfather."

"That's easy for ye to say. The duty doesnae rest on yer shoulders."

"If I have the courage to tell Hildie I'd be muddling along with her on a wedding night, then ye can find the courage to admit she's who ye want."

"Who I want isnae the same as who I need."

"Keep following the lass like a lost puppy, and ye'll find ye need her to keep from pining yerself sick." Dermot cocked an eyebrow before stepping back into the camp. The two men dumped their loads beside the fire ring. Elene stepped forward to build a blaze. Liam handed her his flint and squatted beside her to help stack the branches and twigs.

"Is everything all right? You and Dermot seemed to have a heated conversation."

"We've been friends since we were in raggies. We tease one another aboot almost everything. It was naught serious, except for the part where I shared what I think we must do when we return to Skaill."

"Return?" Elene shook her head and rose, but Liam caught her hand before she could step away.

"Let's finish building the fire, then I'll explain." It was only a couple minutes later that cheery flames snapped and popped in the evening air. Liam entwined his fingers with Elene's and guided her to the edge of the camp where they could speak privately, but their distance didn't expose them to unwelcome strangers. "We have to go back for the birlinns. We'll time it so that it's dark when we arrive. We'll secure the curragh and barge to my ship, then the men and I will go ashore in the other one. Dermot will stay aboard my birlinn and make it appear as though he's inspecting it before we sail. We'll set sail for Dunbeath with the morning tide."

Elene nodded, but her expression reflected her doubt. She feared coming within spitting distance of her home. It seemed foolish to tempt fate. She considered another possibility. "My family will hide me in Isbister. Can you return to Skaill, gather your ships, and come back for me there? If that's too inconvenient, I can walk from Isbister to Snusgar. It's only a few hours."

"You are not walking across the island alone." Liam saw the merit in Elene's suggestion. He'd prefer not to get her anywhere near Skaill and anyone who might discover her return. But he wouldn't leave her alone and unguarded to walk the twelve miles across the island. "Are you really close enough with this family to trust them to help you?"

"Of course. The only reason I didn't want to go to them is because I didn't want Gunter following me there. My father's aunts are still alive. His cousins are the ones who let us stay with them when we visited. There are at least four homes I can pick from. My father's parents, brother, and one uncle moved to Rousay. The rest remained on Mainland. Since this would be temporary, I'm not so scared to involve them."

"Do you have a relative who could take you to Snusgar? I worry about you going alone. You'd be a target even without Norsemen likely searching for you."

"One of my cousins can. They have family on their other side who live in Snusgar."

"That's the best place for us to sail to, but it's a large settlement, which means Gunter might search there."

"We're assuming he's looking. He's likely to give up once he knows I'm not on Rousay. With your boats still in our harbor, he'll believe you haven't smuggled me to Mainland yet. If you return without me, it will utterly confuse him. I'm scared, though, that he might force his way onto your ships once you return. He would find me."

"That's true. Can you and your cousin make camp outside Snusgar and come into the village when we drop anchor? I can say I came to buy—mmm, smoked char." Liam shrugged, saying the first thing that came to mind. Arctic char was a favorite of his, but his home wasn't far enough north for him to fish for it in the Kyle of Tongue.

"Then that's what we'll plan for now. But I worry your family is going to wonder about delays."

"They will, but they'll assume weather, or something, came up that I needed to sort out on my grandfather's behalf. Once they meet you, they'll understand."

The couple had no more time to talk. Men returned from hunting, and Elene wanted to help prepare their evening meal. She was determined to do what she could, so the men wouldn't resent her. She drew a knife from her boot that Liam hadn't realized she carried. She noted his surprise with a smile and a shrug. She set about skinning the catches and placing the rabbits and squirrels on the spit a Sinclair constructed. She remained by the fire, turning the meat to roast it evenly. By the time she finished, half the men had already bathed in the nearby stream. The other half hurried to take their turn as the meat cooled. The men teased and chatted while they sipped whisky after they tossed the bones into the fire.

Elene wondered what she would do for a bedroll, since she hadn't been able to pack one. She jumped when Liam tapped her shoulder and drew her closer to the fire. He laid out his and handed her an extra plaid.

"What about you?"

"The fire will keep me warm enough." He gave her a loose, one-armed embrace. "I'll be all right. I'll sleep close to it."

But it dismayed Elene when she realized Liam intended to sleep a respectful distance from her—on the opposite side from the fire. She realized he did it so no intruder could reach her first. She watched him prop his head against his saddle after once more pulling the extra length of wool over his shoulders and head. He lay with his back to her, so he could watch anyone's approach from that side. Elene could tell he hadn't fallen asleep, even after she heard snores from the other men. She rolled toward the fire and stretched to grab a long stick that remained in the pile the guards would use throughout the night to stoke the flames. She turned back to Liam and stretched once more, poking him in the back.

Liam rolled toward Elene, ready to draw a dirk before he realized it was she who prodded him. She glanced over her shoulder, then lifted the plaid she used as a blanket. The invitation was obvious. Liam inched closer, so he could whisper without his voice carrying. "I can't. The men on guard will see me, and the others will too when they get up to take their turn at watch."

Liam knew the disappointment on Elene's face matched what he felt. He longed to wrap her in his arms and nestle her against him. They'd laid together

watching the night sky, so he already knew how perfectly they could cuddle together. He'd pictured them
sharing his bed in his Castle Varrich chamber. However, when the wind blew his plaid around his thighs,
he was certain his bollocks would shrink. But he knew
the other men felt it, and he would use it as an excuse
for why he needed to sleep closer to Elene. He knew
none of the men would believe it, but it would save face
for Elene. He inched over.

"I must stay on top of the plaid, but I can hold you
while we sleep," Liam explained as he placed his sword
behind him but within reach. He slid his arm beneath
Elene as she wiggled closer. Her contented sigh shot
straight to his groin. He'd brought her to release earlier
on horseback, but his unspent lust still strummed
through him.

"Would that we were alone," Elene whispered. "If
only you could share this blanket properly."

*If we share a blanket, we'll be handfasted before the sun
rises.* Liam nodded as he adjusted the spare plaid
around Elene before he adjusted his own around his
shoulders. He kissed her forehead, the back of his fingers stroking her cheek. It wasn't long before their eyes
grew heavy, and they were both asleep. But Elene's eyes
snapped open the moment Liam pulled away when it
was his turn at watch. She didn't fall back asleep until
he returned an hour later. She realized, despite the surrounding men, she didn't feel at ease until he returned.
She trusted the men because Liam trusted them, but
only he kept the fear from overwhelming her.

Morning came all too soon for the Sinclair party.
Elene made bannocks with the oats she asked for. She
assumed it would be like the bannocks she made with
beremeal. She was careful not to burn them, unsure if
they would cook as quickly over the open fire as the
beremeal ones she made at home. They were back in

the saddle as the sun rose over the horizon. It was only two more hours to Dingieshowe. Seated in front of Liam on Urram's back, she listened to the men whistle.

Liam could see the side of Elene's mouth turned up, so he knew she smiled while she listened. When there was a pause between tunes, he hummed. He felt Elene jump when his rich baritone rumbled behind her. He chuckled and squeezed the arm wrapped around her waist. He chose a ballad that he'd heard since he was a child. It was a song about two lovers separated by a sea. The woman prayed to God to reunite them, but it was the fae who answered. They agreed to turn her into a selkie, a sea creature that shed its skin to become human. But if anyone ever found her seal-like skin, it would force her to make her life among the marine animals when she sank to the depths of the sea. It was her lover who found it, not knowing the arrangement she'd made. The one person she longed to be with was the person who forced her away.

After humming a few bars, Liam sang. He'd loved to make music as a child, and he often sang alongside Tristan and his brothers. The four men had deep, resonating voices that could fill Castle Varrich's Great Hall. When she grew old enough, Ainsley would join them, her contrasting soprano sounding like tinkling bells. Only Mairghread refused to sing, claiming she sounded like a magpie among doves. Liam knew his mother loved to sing, but she hadn't been blessed with the gift of singing well. Still, she spent hours singing to her children when they were little. She need only sing a couple of lines of any song, and Liam calmed. Even at two-and-twenty, hearing his mother sing made him wish he could crawl onto her lap like he'd done for half his life.

He knew Elene couldn't understand the Gaelic words, but he hoped she understood he was serenading her. He infused all the emotion he could into the song: the longing while the lovers were apart, the joy when the fae granted the woman's wish, and the melancholy once the selkie returned to the sea. Elene rode astride, so when she leaned her head against his chest and crossed her arms around his arm that kept her snug on the saddle, he knew she understood. She linked her fingers with his, hidden beneath her cloak. Her other hand stroked his forearm.

She wasn't certain Liam meant to be romantic, but to hear him unabashedly sing to her such a heartfelt song in front of his men made her feel cherished. He'd offered his protection the first night at the loch. It was the first time she'd felt safe since her father died. He'd given her the gift of hope when he agreed to help her. Now he gave her the gift of feeling cherished. She didn't know how he understood just what she needed, what she never received from anyone else, but she refused to take any of it for granted.

When the song ended, the group rode in silence. Elene sat in awe of Liam's talent and the sentiments she felt from a song she didn't understand. None of the men wished to ruin the moment, and none knew what to say after such a moving rendition of a song they all knew. Several exchanged glances. All the Sinclair warriors but Cadence remembered Liam's birth and the pride their laird felt when he welcomed his first grandchild. They remembered the toddler who chased his father and uncles, begging to ride on their shoulders, fisting their hair like it were reins to a stallion. They remembered the holidays when the Mackays joined the Sinclairs, and the journeys they'd taken to accompany their laird and his family when they visited the Mackays. And they remembered the lad who grew into a man while fostering with his Sinclair family. For them, all but one of whom were old enough to be Liam's father, it was as though they watched their own son falling in love.

It was summiting the rise that overlooked Dingieshowe that shattered the reverie. Beyond the village, moored along its coast, sat three Norse longboats. The group reined in and looked down at the bustling village. It was clearly prosperous, with a market and several central buildings that were likely grain stores, along with their mead hall.

"We don't know that it's him," Liam said to Elene as her body went rigid.

"I don't need to get close enough to see the prows. He must know that you planned to speak before the *thing*. He's here to cause trouble, regardless of whether he thinks I'm with you."

"I know you're likely right, but no one panics until we know that there's a reason to." Liam turned to his men to give orders, switching to Gaelic. "Dermot, Alfred, Colin, Benjamin, and Samuel, ye ride into the village with me. Albert, Michail, and Cadence, stay with Elene until we ken who's here. If it's safe, I'll send someone for ye. If it isnae, I want ye to stay off the road. There arenae many trees to hide among but do what ye can to keep out of sight."

Liam swung down from the saddle and lifted Elene off his steed's back. She stood facing Liam, but she turned her head toward the water. They could see the boats bobbing on the waves, but they were too far to make out any details of the people moving around the village. They could see farmers tending their crops beyond the village wall, and they could see smaller fishing boats floating alongside the longboats. The scene would have been idyllic if it weren't for the likely threat.

Liam handed his reins to Dermot before guiding Elene to a patch of tall grass yards from the road. The men he assigned to guard Elene followed at a discreet distance. "I'll try to find a way into the village for you before nightfall. If I can't, then I will come to you."

"What if someone finds us sneaking around? You're better staying there."

"I'm supposed to be here for three or four days. I can't leave you or the men out here that long. There has to be a way to get you into the village and somewhere safe. Do you know anyone here?"

Elene shook her head.

"Be careful, *leannan*. I would trust these men with my mother and my sister, so I know you're safe with them. Even with three guards, be alert. Never stray past where they can see you. You're tall, but not as tall as them. You'll be able to see them from a greater distance than they can see you."

"I won't. Be careful if Gunter is there. I trust him not a bit. Even if he doesn't find me with you, he'll blame you. He'll use it to pick a fight with you and to cause trouble for your grandfather. He doesn't like competition, and he's quick to back men into corners by questioning their honor."

Liam and Elene exchanged a brief and chaste embrace before Liam nodded to the men he tasked with guarding Elene. He mounted and nudged Urram forward as he watched Elene. She waved before she disappeared within the tall grass. He knew she sat, but his heart still thumped the moment she left his sight. He turned back and led his men into the village. He turned his focus to the business to which he came to tend. If he appeared like a bumbling fool, he would lose their respect for his grandfather, and he would draw too much attention. As they passed through the gate and into the village, Liam no longer doubted Gunter was there. The man stood outside the mead hall, hands on his hips, sneering.

CHAPTER 9

$\mathcal{L}$iam reined in Urram as his men did the same with their mounts. He'd considered what he would say the entire way down the hill, but he'd failed to devise anything productive. He'd only thought of snide comments that would antagonize Gunter. It would hardly give him the upper hand to prepare for appearing in the public assembly. Instead, he met Gunter's gaze and held it, daring Gunter to look away first. The silent battle continued until Gunter capitulated. He made excuses, though.

Gunter pointed toward the mead hall. "Shall we see how warm your welcome is here? Mayhap you'll need extra mead, since I've heard your other receptions have been rather frosty."

Liam withdrew a flask from his saddle bag and shook it. "Mayhap you'd like some Highland whisky. I can see you need that thick cloak because your chest is as smooth as a bairn's arse." His comment elicited chuckles from the people who gathered despite the smattering of blond curls that covered the skin. He continued before Gunter could reply. "Ninian! It's good to see you."

A middle-aged man with a shock of white hair am-bled forward, looking back and forth between Liam and Gunter while grinning. He proffered his arm to Liam and grasped the younger man's forearm in a warrior handshake. He tugged Liam forward and embraced him, whispering in Liam's ear, "He's already causing trouble. Claims you stole his woman. I hope you haven't. But you are your father's son, so I'm guessing you did."

The two men stepped apart. Ninian Sinclair traded frequently along Scotland's eastern shore and had learned Scots and Gaelic over the years, so Liam switched to the former, knowing not even his men would understand. "You can only steal a possession, and that's how he sees her. She's a person. She belongs to no one."

"That's not how he sees it."

"He intends to sell her." Liam's comment garnered the response he expected.

"Fuck. He's a slave trader?"

"He is where it concerns her."

"Is she with you?"

"Do you see her?" Liam twisted to look behind each shoulder.

"I don't think I want to know after all. Watch yourself, lad." Three men, the same age as Ninian, interrupted their conversation.

"Bernard, Hugh, Mans!" Liam greeted, switching smoothly back to Norn. "It's good to see you. Bernard, what happened to your hair, old man?"

A potbellied man with deep creases around his eyes and mouth chuckled. "The wind blew it away."

"And he's too fat to chase it," the man next to him supplied. "Speaking of growing old, I thought you were Laird Mackay for a moment. You might be larger than your father."

"Almost, Hugh. I certainly eat enough that I should be. Mans, how are Meg and your lads?"

"Growing just as fast as you and your brothers did, and my Meg is a blessed saint with those nine running around."

"Nine? Christ on the cross, it was only five the last time I saw you."

"You haven't seen me in six years," Mans grinned.

"I suppose your lads aren't the only things still growing," Liam guffawed.

"Cheeky, lad. Shall we see how well that sword swings in the lists tomorrow?"

"Always hard and at the ready, I bet," Ninian teased.

"At least I know it's reliable." Liam shifted, pretending to look at Ninian's back, where there was no sword sheathed like the Norse and Highlanders.

"I was polishing it earlier and left it at home." Everyone laughed, knowing Ninian and his wife only had one child, but it wasn't from a lack of trying.

"You chatter like old women," Gunter interrupted. The four men were closer in age to Gunter than Liam, and turned to glare at the Norseman.

"Liam is family," Hugh stated before turning his back on Gunter. It was true, even if distantly and several times removed. The four men were chieftains of their own villages but were second and third cousins. They all bore the surname Sinclair.

"Let's move inside. The wind makes my joints ache," Ninian complained jovially. The Highlanders formed a wall behind Liam and the Orcadians, forcing Gunter and his warriors to trail behind. Liam desperately wanted to look toward the hillside, praying Elene was well. But he would do nothing that made Gunter suspicious.

Liam, Dermot, and the Sinclairs entered the mead hall to cheers of welcome and good tidings. As he waved, he canted his head to see how Gunter responded to the warm welcome. A woman with rosy cheeks and gray hair tied in a bun bustled forward.

"Meg." Liam smiled as he leaned nearly in half to embrace the woman.

"My, what a braw mon you've become. I know everyone says you have the look of your father, but there's something in those eyes that reminds me of your grandfather. It doesn't surprise me Laird Sinclair sent you on his behalf. You remind me of him when he was a young man, just before he met your grandmother, may her soul rest in peace."

"My brother—" Gunter began, but Bernard interrupted.

"There's time for that tomorrow. No politics this eve. We shall feast and welcome our Sinclair relatives." Bernard pointed to the far end of the raised high table. "There is space for you and your second-in-command."

Liam's men found seats at a lower table, nodding to those around them since they spoke proficient Norn, but the villagers spoke no Gaelic. Dermot sat beside Liam, placing the men between Hugh and Ninian. It wasn't long before women placed heaping trenchers before them. Liam had a wave of guilt that Elene and his other men wouldn't be eating so well that night.

"I will try to sneak them food later. I'll see what I can squirrel away in ma sporran," Dermot offered.

"Thank ye. I dinna ken if they'll dare a fire this eve. I worry they'll all be too cold. I ken what ye all thought aboot last night. But she genuinely was too cold. I came back from watch, and she was frigid."

The meal progressed with good cheer between the Orcadians and Highlanders, but the Norsemen scowled throughout. Liam knew Gunter stewed and would snarl by morning. He also understood the message the chieftains sent to both the Norsemen and their own villagers. The Sinclairs of Orkney stood alongside the Sinclairs of the Highlands. Any discussion of politics the next day or after would be pro forma. The chieftains already sided with Liam and the new Earl of Caithness. Gunter might have his chance to speak, but it would be of little consequence. From his murderous glare, Liam knew he understood the situation.

"Ninian will host us," Liam whispered to Dermot as they ate. "He just told me, ye and the men are to come to his home, too. He warned us all to sleep with one eye open. He doesnae trust Gunter nae to attack."

"I wasna eager to bed down in the stables or a barracks. Far too easy for them to get us. What aboot the others?"

"Ye ken they secure the gates here, and they dinna open them for anyone. This settlement's nearly as secure as Varrich or Dunbeath, despite the walls being made of standing tree trunks rather than stones. I amnae worried that they'll claim they're headed to their longboats then search for Elene. I fear one or two of them going over the wall."

"I thought the same." The two men grew quiet as the meal progressed, then as they watched people move aside the tables and benches. As the music began, the Norse gathered to pass their mead horns and join in the dancing. The Sinclair men moved to the side, sipping whisky from their flasks. Dermot prepared to join them as a man slipped behind him and made his way to Ninian. The older man looked at Liam while his guard whispered to him. Liam wondered what the guard said since Ninian nodded, but his expression told Liam not to ask questions. He whispered something back to the man before the guard left.

Ninian kept his voice low. Speaking in Gaelic this time, he explained. "Ma guards didna approach, but they spied three Highlanders and a woman who looks

119

suspiciously Orcadian. They were aboot three miles past the wall, atop the hill. Did ye lose some of yer warriors?"

"Ye ken I didna. And ye can guess who's with them. Gunter and Elene have some type of past that's made him vindictive toward her. He's supposedly betrothed to her mother. I told ye, he's threatened to drag Elene back to Norway then sell her as a bed slave."

"The buggering hell he will. He may be King Haakon's brother, but we are nay longer Norwegian. He's a foreigner now, and he willna commit such a crime in Scotland. He can keep to his pagan ways, but we are good Christians here. We dinna allow any slave trading, and that includes forcing anyone into slavery."

"Now ye understand why she's with us. She couldnae stay on Rousay and be safe."

"Aye, but ye've brought her to the mouth of the dragon. Ye need to get her away from here. He has his own scouting parties. It might take them longer than it did ma men, but they will find her. They'll kill yer men and take her. Once they sail away, ye willna catch them, and ye willna ken where to follow. He could go anywhere in Norway. Nay one will turn away the king's brother."

"I ken. We didna expect to find him here."

"We didna expect him to arrive, but once he accused ye of stealing his woman, we all kenned he came to make trouble beyond just politics. We need his trade, but nae at the expense of condoning such a sin as selling a person. Besides, I canna imagine—actually, I take that back. I can imagine what yer grandfather would do if he learned we abetted such a crime. Family or nae, he'd rain holy hell down on us. We dinna need the Sinclairs sailing here with the Mackays and Sutherlands adding to the fleet."

"Ye ken ma grandfather willna abide any woman

being mistreated. I heard the stories aboot ma Grandmama Kyla and how her father mistreated her. The Sinclair lairds have protected the women of our clan for generations, but ma grandfather is especially unyielding after what's happened to ma grandmother, ma mother, and ma aunts Siùsan and Brighde."

"I ken. Even if yer grandfather wasna now the Earl of Sinclair *and* Orkney, I'd nae take on the women in yer family. I'd have a dirk in ma throat before I kenned where to look. It'd come from yer mother or Lady Siùsan. Ladies Deirdre and Brighde could fire an arrow through ma heart from halfway across the isle. And yer Aunt Ceit would have already spied on me and reported to yer other aunts." Ninian shook his head. "Yer father and uncles are like a pack of pups compared to those she-wolves."

"They're a wee protective."

"Ye dinna say." Ninian shifted his gaze to the Norsemen before looking back at Liam. "I told ma mon to bring the lass and yer men to ma home. Sonneta will feed them. If she needs to, she'll ken to hide them in the cellar. We canna retire too soon, or Gunter will find rumors to start."

"Are ye sure that's wise? I dinna want ye in the middle."

"It put me in the middle the moment ye brought the lass within sight of Dingieshowe. But Gunter made it ma business when he thought he might capture the lass here. I'm nae having it."

"Thank ye, ma friend. Will ye tell the others?"

"Nae if I can help it. The fewer people who ken, the safer we'll all be."

"She has family in Isbister. We planned to travel there next, but I will send her and ma three men tomorrow."

Ninian shook his head. "Part of the reason I'm

bringing her inside the walls is because Gunter sent out two hunting parties yesterday. I thought it was to offer us meat for all they will eat while here. Deer and boar arenae what I think he's hunting. Until he leaves, the lass and nay one with her are safe outside this village. Even if he discovers she's here, there are too many chieftains who would cut off trade with Norway and find better arrangements with the Scottish. The chieftains fear losing what they already ken, but nae as much as they will fear the Almighty striking them down if I must remind them how Christ taught against slavery."

"Ye're a good mon, Ninian. I'm sorry to put ye and yer family in danger."

"Haud yer wheest, lad. This is the safest place ye could come while still in Orkney. There are more people here than usual, which brings its own risk, but ye also have more leaders from across the isles than ye could meet anywhere else. If Gunter missteps, he'll ruin his brother's plans throughout Orkney and Shetland. Hopefully, he has the sense to ken one woman isnae worth that to him."

"Mayhap. But I think Elene scorned him. I think this is aboot revenge."

"I figured as much. Even brutal men like Gunter dinna condone that pagan practice. It had to be something more than just business."

"I dinna ken all of it, but aye, it's more than just business." Liam watched as the Norsemen and women filed out of the mead hall. "Where are they sleeping?"

"They pitched tents in the far northern corner of the village."

"Thank the Lord for small blessings. I'm glad yer home is at the south end. Will they be with Sonneta yet?"

"I pray so. The gates lock soon, and they dinna need

to be creeping in while the Norse are crossing the village center. Come." Ninian rose and led Liam to the door. He signaled to Dermot and the Sinclair warriors, who followed the Orcadian. They arrived at Ninian's door just as it closed. Ninian opened it but jumped back, bumping into Liam. Three swords and a deadly knife pointed at him.

Liam placed his hand on Ninian's shoulder and nodded to his men. They sheathed their swords, but Elene didn't return her dirk to her boot. She waited until Liam eased past the older man and opened his arms to her. She fell into his embrace, her knife clattering to the floor. Liam guided her backwards, moving them farther into the croft and allowing the others to enter.

"I think he saw me," Elene whispered.

"We need to get you in the cellar," Sonneta instructed. The woman had flaxen hair, even lighter than Elene's, tied in a bun at her nape, and her blue eyes sparkled with intelligence. She wiped her hands on an apron tied around her waist before pointing to a cowhide stretched across the floor beside the family's table. Ninian threw back a corner and lifted a trap door. Liam looked into the darkness, knowing that many Orcadians followed the Norse tradition of digging pits to store food. The Norse would place massive lumps of ice cut from fjords to preserve food in the summer months. He didn't have time to wonder what the Orcadians did without ice readily available.

Liam offered Elene his hand as she sat on the edge and swung her feet. She couldn't feel the floor, but she knew it wouldn't be deeper than her height. Elene dropped and crouched, feeling around in the dark. She found barrels that she assumed contained ale and pickled fish, maybe even root vegetables. She shifted them and wiggled behind before scooting them back to hide her. She waited to see if the men who'd been in the meadow with her would climb down.

"They can stay," Ninian stated. "We'll say they came later because a horse threw its shoe. They knew to come here from past visits."

"It took three of them to deal with one horse's loose shoe?" Elene asked. She thought it a flimsy excuse.

"We'll say they scouted," Liam decided. "If Gunter has his own people outside the walls, then it shouldn't surprise him if I did the same."

Liam lowered the trapdoor and drew the cowhide over it, once more hiding it. He wondered how many people Ninian hid, or what he hid, that he kept this cellar a secret. He knew from being a child that they had a separate one dug two yards from the back of their home. Instead of questioning the man, he pulled a stool onto the rug and gestured for his men to take the other ones. It left Ninian and Sonneta with the only two chairs. The woman hurried to pass around mugs of mead while the men settled. They were barely in their places before someone hammered on the door.

Ninian glanced around before moving to the door. He opened it, and it surprised no one to spy Gunter on the other side. He tried to push past Ninian, but the aging man stood to his full height, throwing his shoulders back. While not a regular warrior, he'd been a farmer since he was old enough to pick weeds. Years of toil gave Ninian strength and a breadth of shoulders that barred Gunter from passing without permission. A glare pinned the Norseman in place.

"No Norseman has the right to enter any Orcadian home without invitation. We are not Norse anymore," Ninian reminded.

"I'm still a king's brother."

"Of a land that doesn't rule here. What do you want?"

"I want Elene Isbister. I know she's here."

"No one by that name's here," Ninian responded, his feigned confusion convincing.

"I saw her," Gunter argued. "She was coming down the hill as I crossed the village."

"You saw a woman coming down a hill near a village where many women and girls live. That hardly surprises me."

"A woman walking with three Highlanders. Did your people take to wearing blankets?"

"That was my cousin, Cristen," Michail spoke up. "She was gathering medicinals when we arrived. Albert and Cadence stayed behind with me, and we waited until she finished before we walked back with her." Michail knew his cousin would defend any story Michail told. She knew he would only lie to save someone. They'd grown up together at Dunbeath before she moved to Dingieshowe with her Orcadian husband. They'd been as close as siblings since his parents raised her after illness killed her parents.

"Cousin?" Gunter sneered.

"Shall I fetch her?" Michail offered.

"Send someone," Gunter ordered Ninian. The chieftain merely cocked an eyebrow. "You play a dangerous game, old man."

Ninian once more straightened his back. "It is not I who shall lose. This village hasn't needed to trade with your people in generations. We don't need to now. We've continued out of tradition. We are Orcadians who bow to the Scottish King David. Your brother has no control, which means we do not have to welcome you. The Earl of Caithness is King David's godfather. The king will take particular exception to trouble toward his godfather's grandson. The king and Liam were raised like cousins. If you didn't know that, you'd do well to remember it now."

Gunter's gaze shifted to Liam, who continued to sip his mead as though there weren't a confrontation brewing merely a yard in front of him. Liam shrugged one shoulder. "My mother and uncles and their Sutherland cousins were all the old king's and queen's godchildren. We've kept it in the family, I suppose." Liam took another draw from his mug before swirling the contents, blithely sharing that the five Sinclair siblings and their three Sutherland cousins were all King Robert the Bruce's and Queen Elizabeth de Burgh's godchildren.

"That's why the king gave your doddering grandfather the earldom," Gunter mocked.

Liam turned his head ever so slightly before lifting his gaze to Gunter, puffing a disdainful breath. "I told you before, the last time my grandfather was here a few months ago, someone confused him for my Uncle Tavish. He received the earldom because he's the Sinclair. A Norse surname isn't the most common one in Orkney. Sinclair is. This has always been our land." Liam gave another one shoulder shrug. "You just borrowed it."

Gunter lunged forward, but Liam was quicker. He was on his feet with his sword drawn, the tip beneath Gunter's chin before the Norseman reached back for his own weapon. Gunter leaned away, taking a step back as Liam approached. He didn't stop his pursuit until Gunter crossed the threshold. Liam slammed the door in his face and dropped the bar across it. Everyone else watched in stunned silence.

"That went well," Sonneta stated, as though there hadn't been a standoff in her home. She bustled around gathering blankets from a chest. She glanced down at the cowhide, then toward the door and shook her head. She handed a blanket to each Highlander. She moved to where she prepared the food and looked out the tiny window. Everyone waited until she nodded, watching Gunter cross the village in a huff.

Liam threw back the rug and yanked the trapdoor open. He reached a hand into the darkness, grabbing hold of Elene's wrist when he felt her hand. He extended his other arm and grasped her free one before he pulled her from the cellar. With her feet barely on the floor, he pulled her into his embrace, plucking a spiderweb from her hair. Elene wrapped her arms around Liam's waist and rested her head against his chest, deep shuddering breaths rattling her frame. When she felt composed once more, she nodded and drew away.

"Thank you," Elene said to everyone. Turning to Liam, she lowered her voice, despite knowing people could still hear her. "I will leave for Isbister the moment the gates open in the morning."

"You can't," Ninian responded before Liam could. "He didn't believe a word of our stories. He'll only redouble his search efforts. No one can see you until after Liam and his men leave. My son and I will get you to Isbister."

Elene stared at Ninian before turning back to Liam. "You told him where my people are from?"

"Elene, I've known Ninian since I was born. Sonneta is more like a grandmother to me than a family friend." He'd lost both his grandmothers long before his birth. Sonneta and his mother's aunt, Lady Amelia Sutherland, were the two women most like the maternal figure he lacked. "I trust no one on Mainland more than I do them. Besides, Gunter just said your name. Ninian and Sonneta would have recognized it and known your family is from that village."

"That's different from telling them," Elene muttered.

Liam tilted Elene's chin up and gazed into the shards of sapphire, realizing his conversation with

Ninian angered her. He leaned forward to whisper in her ear. "I'm sorry I betrayed your trust. I didn't do it on purpose. But I'm not sorry that I trust Ninian and Sonneta. I will do what I must to keep Gunter from finding you. We need help, or my men and I will wind up dead, and you'll be on a longboat to Norway."

Elene glanced at Ninian, who'd returned to his chair and chatted with Dermot. The Sinclairs moved near the hearth and rolled out the blankets. Elene watched Sonneta tidy her kitchen and the table in the center of the home. She nodded once she returned her gaze to Liam's.

"Do they know we're not married?" Elene murmured as she stretched to whisper into Liam's ear.

"Ninian hasn't asked, but he knows Gunter claims I stole you. He must have deduced that we aren't. But he won't question it now that he knows Gunter's intent."

"But if Gunter tells anyone else in the village that you stole me, then they will know we're lying about being married."

Liam clamped his mouth shut before he offered to handfast with Elene and solve the problem of their lacking marriage. If they pledged themselves in a trial marriage, either of them could repudiate it before it would expire after a year and a day. But that wasn't how Liam wanted to begin his married life, and he didn't intend to marry more than once. He wasn't ready to commit to Elene, and he wasn't certain she would accept except out of desperation. Once more, he didn't want to act in haste and repent at leisure.

Ninian and Sonneta approached, the older woman speaking first. "Elene, I don't know all the details, and it's best that I don't ask. But Ninian and our son, Steven, will take you to your family. Whenever Liam and his men leave, Gunter will follow. There is no doubt he will try to attack. If you are there, he will force you. One way or another." She gave Elene a speaking look. "Liam and his men can't defend themselves properly if they're also defending you. Traveling with them overland is likely to get them killed. Ninian and Steven can take you by curragh to Isbister faster than Liam and his men can ride. You may be there before they arrive."

Elene shook her head. "We can't go there. Gunter knows my family's name. Now that he's certain I'm on Mainland, he will go there. I can't endanger them. I've already done that to you." She turned to Liam. "Take me back to Rousay. It was bad enough when I endangered you and your men without asking. Now I've involved more people. I can take my father's fishing boat and sail to Sanday. From there, I will find a way to Shetland."

"And go closer to Norway? No." Liam crossed his arms and stood with his feet hip width apart.

"Give in, lass." Ninian shook his head. "When the Sinclair and Mackay men stand like that, naught is happening if they don't let it."

"Arrogant," Elene muttered.

"Determined," Liam countered.

"Morning will be here soon enough," Sonneta intervened. "We shall know what to do after a good sleep." She handed Elene a blanket but looked at Liam. He knew Sonneta was no one's fool. The grandmotherly figure warned him not to sleep too close to a woman who wasn't his wife. Liam took Elene's blanket and spread it before the hearth. The men had already made a semicircle near it, so Liam easily placed it in the center. No one would reach Elene without going through nine Highlanders. Liam laid his bedroll closest to the door. At Elene's questioning look, he darted his gaze to Sonneta and Ninian, who were retiring to the curtain enclosed bed they shared at the back of the home.

Elene looked around as the men settled, their backs to her, and their swords held protectively under their arms like a lover. She turned to look where Ninian and Sonneta disappeared before looking back once more at Liam. There was nothing she could do to sleep next to Liam that night. She wrapped the blanket Sonneta gave her around her shoulders, then added the spare plaid Liam lent her. Between the two heavy layers of wool, she felt comforted by the cocoon she created. She settled on her side and stared into the flames, but when she heard Liam stir, she twisted to see him. He'd set up his bedroll, but he sat on a stool with his sword across his lap. He offered her a reassuring smile as she realized he would be on watch that night. It bothered her that she'd intruded into someone's home and brought such danger that the men needed to sleep with their swords unsheathed and someone on guard.

As she turned back to stare into the fire, the undulating flames hypnotized her. Before her eyes drifted closed, she pondered her options. She could turn herself over to Gunter, which she refused to consider. She could return to Rousay, but that was the same as giving herself to the Norseman. She could go to Isbister and risk Gunter following. Or she could set out for Snusgar. She understood she couldn't expect Liam to put his life on hold, detain his men and keep them from their families, and delay his report to his grandfather. At best, she hoped he might stop in Snusgar, where she could board his birlinn. She wouldn't mind a life in the Highlands. She doubted it was that different from Orkney. Perhaps less pickled fish in winter.

Her heart ached knowing that regardless of where she went, her relationship with Liam would end. She knew her social status was far too low for Liam or his family to consider her acceptable. She knew without asking, Liam would never accept her—or any woman—

as his leman. She couldn't go to Varrich. She couldn't watch him eventually marry someone else, even if she found a mate for herself. She was heartsore at the idea of seeing him visit Dunbeath with a wife and children, but that notion was far more palatable than living outside his front door, likely serving his family in the Great Hall.

Elene thought she'd just closed her eyes when Liam shook her shoulder. She looked around and realized the fire was banked. The Highlanders were scrambling to their feet, one of them gathering her blankets before she'd gotten to her feet. Dermot threw back the cowhide and yanked open the trap. Liam guided Elene to the hole, where she jumped down without hesitation. Liam took the blankets from his warrior and passed them to her.

"Cadence heard him during his watch. He peeked outside; Gunter's coming." Liam closed the hatch before Elene could respond. Trapped once more in the dark, she heard the thunk of first the door, then the hide, put back in place. She tried to imagine what was happening, but she heard nothing after her hiding place was once more disguised. She heard no movement. She heard no voices. She didn't even hear her own breath it was so shallow. Like she had the first time, she creeped behind the barrels and burrowed under the blankets. Just when she thought they sounded the alarm for nothing, Elene heard the distinct sound of steel on steel.

CHAPTER 10

Cadence's alertness to a sound outside the croft had prepared Liam and his men. They were staggered throughout the one-room cottage, ready for the first Norseman to cross the threshold when the door burst open. Only a moment passed, a chance to ensure they slayed no one without cause, before they launched their counterattack. Sinclairs angled beside the door drove their swords into the first wave of Norse warriors. As their victims fell to the floor, another surge came from their enemy. Liam thrust his sword into a woman's belly as she raised her arm to swing her blade at his head.

Liam recalled how aghast he was when he first heard the tale of Lorna Mackay and how her relatives had slain Norsewomen when the pillagers raided Varrich all those centuries ago. He learned that Lorna's father trained her as a warrior, thinking to keep his only daughter occupied while he taught his sons to lead. When she left Varrich and went to Norway, she became a renowned shieldmaiden. She'd been no different from Freya Ivarsdóttir, Tyra Vigosdóttir, and Gressa Jorgensdóttir. But it was Freya's mother, Lena Tormudsdóttir, who'd been a legend long before the High-land sword wielding woman arrived.

Now Liam swung his sword indiscriminately, aiming for anyone who intended to kill him and harm Elene. He heard someone collide with the table, then a crash as the table hit the floor. In between opponents, he glanced back and found Albert and Michail fighting men from across the table. It gave him an idea. As his comrades defeated their enemy, Liam leaped over the table.

"Lift it," Liam commanded as he bent to grab the lip of the table. Albert and Michail obeyed, guessing Liam's plan. The three men brought the table to chest height and surged forward. Dermot was the first to join them, followed by Cadence. Alfred, Colin, Benjamin, and Samuel continued to fight until their opponents succumbed to the Highlanders. With nine Highlanders charging forth with the table as a battering ram, they forced the Norse outside. Angling themselves, they passed through the door and continued to knock down their enemies.

As they trampled their fallen opponents, the Sinclairs released the table from the back forward as each man drove his sword into a Norseman sprawled on the ground. Liam and Michail were the last two to drop the table and swing their swords. Liam split his attention between the woman he fought, the man approaching him from his right, and his search for Gunter, who he hadn't seen. Discharging the woman with his sword through her belly, he spun toward the man, swiping his blade across his ribs and nearly cleaving him in half.

Liam was about to wipe the sweat from his brow when he finally spied Gunter charging toward Ninian's croft. Racing forward and leaping onto the edge of the table, Liam used it as a springboard to propel his body toward Gunter. With the roar of a lion, he grasped his claymore in both hands and brought it high over his shoulder, his arms extended for his full wingspan. But at the last moment, a Norseman ran between Liam and Gunter. The force with which Liam swung his sword took the man's head from his body and slid through bone, muscle, and sinew, carving off a shoulder and ribs. It would have shocked Liam if he weren't so determined to catch Gunter.

His shoulder barreled into the dead man's body as it crumbled to the ground. He was nearly to Gunter when he watched in horror as a Norseman handed off a burning torch to the king's brother. Liam knew what Gunter planned to do. Getting inside to save Elene, Ninian, and Sonneta before it burned them alive became more important. As the flaming log landed on the croft's thatched roof, Liam burst into the building.

"Out!" He bellowed to Ninian and Sonneta, who were dashing to the trap door. "Go! I'll get her."

Ninian and Sonneta fled as Liam heard three more thuds on the roof, knowing more torches had landed to set the home ablaze. He dropped his sword as he unfurled the cowhide and yanked open the trapdoor. Fingers curled around the edge as Elene scrambled out. Liam grasped her under her arms and pulled her free. He grabbed his sword as the roof crumbled around them. Sparks filled the air, smoke blinding and choking them. Liam hoisted Elene over his shoulder as he bolted for the door. Leaping over the flames that were licking the floor in front of the door, he pitched forward. Rolling to protect Elene from his sword and from landing underneath him, the force knocked the wind from both of them.

Spluttering, Elene pulled herself on her elbows until she hovered over Liam, her ear next to his mouth. She felt no waft of air, so she nearly jumped out of her skin when lips pressed against her cheek. As she turned her head, steely arms wrapped around her and drew her onto a chiseled body. Their lips brushed together as Liam stroked hair back from her face. She cupped Liam's jaw as she pulled away, needing to see with her eyes what her body felt. He was hale. He hadn't succumbed to the battle or the fire.

"Are you all right?" Her parched throat rasped each word.

"Yes. You?" Liam coughed after choking out the two words. They looked around when waterskins were thrust in front of both of them. Dermot stood beside them, his face bloodied, but his body in one piece. Liam eased Elene to sit beside him before he rose to sit and accepted the waterskin Dermot offered him. They both guzzled, the cool liquid quenching their thirst and easing the stinging ash from the back of their throats.

"Yes," Elene whispered as she looked around. Liam belatedly realized it was likely the first battlefield Elene ever saw. He tried to pull her face toward her chest, shielding her from the death that spread around Ninian and Sonneta's home. But she wouldn't budge. She looked at each person lying dead in the wake of the Norse attack. She closed her eyes and said a prayer of thanksgiving that there were no plaids among the slain. She scanned the surrounding area, finding Ninian and Sonneta encircled by three Orcadian men and a woman.

"That's Bernard, Hugh, and Mans. The woman is Mans's wife, Meg," Liam explained. "They're chieftains from other villages on this island."

Elene nodded, her throat still too sore to strain with words. A howl forewarned the roof caving in, and a boom that rattled their bones sounded as the walls exploded, leaving nothing of the croft where they'd all slept only a short while ago. The sun was only just starting to rise when the attack happened, the dawn sky lightening from the night's blue canvas. Now, at sunrise, the sun inched above the horizon, and Elene could see the oars cut through the air before dipping back into the sea as their attackers fled.

At least Elene wanted to think it was fleeing. She wanted to think Gunter was a coward and unwilling to accept the consequences of his failed attack. But she looked at the smoldering ruins of the home where she'd hidden twice. Then she looked at the couple who'd opened their door to her and lost everything in exchange. Gunter wasn't a coward. He was conniving and one step ahead of them. She knew where he was headed.

"He's going for my mother and my brother and sister. He's going to take them away." Elene looked out to sea once more, certain to her marrow that Johan and Katryne were no longer as safe as she'd tried to convince herself they were. Gunter had no need of stepchildren, not with his own bastards. She doubted he intended to keep a concubine, whose children others would expect him to house, feed, and clothe. He would sell or murder Johan and Katryne. "Then he will kill them. I doubt they will make it to land. If they do, it's only so he can do to them what he threatened to do to me."

Elene turned her attention to Liam. Her heart raced when she curled into the cellar the second time. She'd nearly screamed when the table overturned. The smoke that immediately filled the croft convinced her she would die. She was certain she would never see Liam again, that he was already dead. Hearing his voice through the trapdoor as he ordered Ninian and Sonneta out made her heart feel as though it stopped. Now it pounded in her ears and behind her ribs with conviction to reach her siblings first.

"I'm going home." She turned a challenging mien to Liam, daring him to stop her.

"We'll get them, I swear." Liam turned to the Orcadians, who approached.

"I'm sending my fastest rider to Tankerness," Mans announced. "He can be there in half an hour, which is faster than Gunter can reach there, even with all the oars in the water. The tide and wind are against him. All of my fishing boats can be in the water before Gunter reaches there. They'll form a blockade he will struggle to navigate around. It won't stop him, but it will slow him."

"If you ride hard, you can be in Kirkwall in just over two hours. Get your curraghs and get back to Skaill," Ninian stated. Liam didn't know what to say. He'd brought a fugitive to his friend's home, and he'd endangered everyone under Ninian's roof. Now Ninian and his family lost everything, when all they'd ever offered the Mackays and Sinclairs was hospitality. "If it were Sonneta, or any of our wives, your family would have risked the same. We will rebuild. We can do that far easier than you can find another woman you love."

Liam was aware that Elene could hear Ninian. He didn't know what to call his feelings toward her, but he knew he wouldn't stop until she and her siblings were safe at Dunbeath or Varrich. It didn't lessen his guilt, but he appreciated everyone's understanding.

"You can't dilly-dally any longer," Bernard stated as Meg ran to the group, a basket swinging from her arm. She'd packed loaves of bread along with cheese, shoved in into the basket every which way. She handed it to Liam as Mans stepped forward.

"You can't ride double. Take Meg's gelding. He's as

fast any of your horses. Wild woman that she is refuses to ride a more sedate mount."

"He'll keep up, then lead the way once he spies his home. I can ride with Mans on the way home. You need to go. Now." Meg urged them toward the village stables.

Men from the village had already saddled the horses and brought them from the stables. Elene, Liam, and the men mounted and charged out of Dingieshowe. Liam and Elene looked back, Liam with remorse and Elene with resolve. She would protect her siblings, and she would mete out justice for Ninian and Sonneta. As she looked at the road ahead, nothing had ever filled her with such hatred and determination. She and Gunter could both play with fire, and he made his ships out of wood.

Liam glanced at Elene several times as they galloped, but he finally kept his eyes forward when she glared at him and pushed her horse to lead the group. He doubted she was angry with him, but he'd annoyed her when the situation already made her overwrought. He couldn't blame her. He worried about Elene, but he'd belittled her by not having more faith that she could keep up. She had ridden little more than a plow horse her entire life, but she showed a natural ability as she controlled the powerful gelding. Mans hadn't overstated the animal's strength and endurance. Liam suspected she would have figured out how to ride a dragon with the determination that radiated from her set jaw and her eyes, which spat sparks of conviction that could have melted ice. He'd never seen a more arresting and irresistible woman.

As they clattered into Kirkwall, kicking up a dirt

storm, Liam released a piercing whistle. It was only minutes later that Henry and Dillon dashed out of crofts on opposite sides of the village. They gave quick embraces to their families before the men ran to meet the arriving party.

"Get yer mounts. I'll explain on the way to curraghs. We ride now." Liam swung Urram toward the trough outside the stables. The others followed, allowing their horses to nudge one another as their noses pressed forward, and they drank their fill. Once Dillon and Henry mounted, Liam ordered Dillon to lead them to the rowboats. "Gunter burned Ninian's croft while Elene was inside. Nearly killed her, Ninian, and Sonneta. He didna fight in the battle he started. He ran to his ships and sailed away instead of facing me. We sail straight to Skaill."

Within fifteen minutes, they had the horses loaded onto the barge. Elene wished their weight didn't slow them, but she knew they stood no chance to get ahead of Gunter if they hadn't been able to ride to Kirkwall. She watched as two men sat on each oarsman's bench. With four men rowing each curragh instead of only two each, they cut through the wave break and were into the sea with ease. Elene picked at her nails, a nervous habit she'd had since she was a child. She fought the temptation to bite them and chew on her cuticles. Instead, she tore them nearly to the quick; the cuticles bled on several fingers. When she could do no more damage to her ravaged fingertips, she curled her hands around the edge of the bench upon which she sat. She caught herself before she shifted her weight from one side of her buttocks to the other.

She nearly demanded the men explain why they stopped after half an hour. But it became obvious the men were switching positions. The current forced the starboard oarsmen to work much harder. She knew that if they didn't rotate, the men would grow too exhausted to keep going. Guilt nipped at her that she couldn't take her turn. She was experienced, but she was far too weak compared to the battle-hewn bodies the warriors possessed. Liam offered reassuring smiles between deep inhales. She watched as his muscles rippled beneath his leine. Were she not so terrified that they wouldn't reach her siblings in time, she would have fully appreciated the raw masculinity Liam showed. She wasn't immune to it. She found watching him eased some of her tension. His calm leadership and his physical strength alike gave her more confidence.

As they entered the strait between Mainland and Rousay, Elene strained to spy Gunter's fleet, but there was nothing in sight. She wondered if that meant the fishermen blockade worked or if the Norseman was already at Skaill. As they rounded the northern tip of Rousay, Elene trembled, terrified she would find Gunter loading her family onto his longboat before they could stop him. But as the harbor came into view, there were no dragon boats moored there. Elene whipped her gaze to Liam, who she could tell saw what she did.

"Dermot will get you onboard my ship while we load the horses. Then I'll take the curragh with two of my men to shore. I'm not speaking to anyone I don't have to. If Androw stops me, I'll tell him Gunter assumed you were with us and burned the croft. He's smart enough not to ask if you were. If he doesn't ask, then I don't have to lie."

"I don't know if they'd come with you without me. And what about my mother? She won't let them go without alerting the entire village."

"Do your people side with her or you?" Liam cocked an eyebrow.

140

"They're still her children," Elene responded without actually answering.

"And who raised them? Do your people really want children to suffer Gunter? Suffer his family and what they might do to two innocents? Do they trust your mother?" Liam knew he'd made his point just as the curraghs reached the Highlanders' birlinns, which they'd moved away from the docks. Dermot tossed a rope onto his ship's deck and scaled the side with ease. He tossed a ladder over the side before moving swiftly to remove a part of the rail. He lowered a wide plank to the barge. It was hardly ideal loading the horses in the open water rather than at a dock, but they'd done it before when they'd sailed places with no permanent structure attached to the shore. The men moved with silent cooperation, each already knowing his task. It took only ten minutes before horses were loaded onto both boats, with empty barrels stored on Dermot's vessel.

Elene kept the hood to Liam's cloak over her head as she laid on the curragh's hull. The ramp was broad enough for two men to pass side-by-side. When Dermot returned to the curragh, Liam led, with Elene walking behind his right shoulder. Dermot followed, shielding Elene as best he could from anyone who might watch on the shore. Once aboard, the men shifted to hide Elene from behind. Liam quietly told Elene where to move to hide behind the barrels they'd meant to fill in Kirkwall. Certain they safely tucked her away, he ordered Albert and Henry to accompany him to shore.

It was nearly midmorning, and people were moving around the village by the time he arrived. Liam's mind buzzed with ideas of how to find Johan and Katryne, convince them to come with him, and to get them aboard the ship without having the villagers chase him with shovels and swords. He scanned the village center, seeing children playing, but none were Elene's siblings. His gaze darted to the coastline, praying he might spy them fishing, but it was to no avail. As he drew closer to the villagers, he forced himself to inhale several deep breaths to slow his heart rate and to keep his hands from shaking. He felt a jitteriness that he'd never experienced before, not even when he and his own siblings tried to get away with mischief or when he'd ridden into battle. He'd known fear many times, and a twinge of it still accompanied him into fights. He understood that it kept him alert and therefore alive. But this was different. Never had he been so fearful of failure, of disappointing someone.

"Back already?" Androw asked as he fell into step with Liam. He'd seen his family friend approach, but he'd kept his long stride as he moved toward Elene's family croft. He hoped it appeared like he was eager for a reunion with her.

"Aye. We finished our business faster than I expected." That was the truth. He hadn't expected someone to burn down the home in which he stayed. He hadn't expected to race back to Skaill with a fugitive in his midst. He'd expected to come back to Skaill, say a heart-wrenching goodbye to Elene, then sail back to Dunbeath.

"Gunter was in a right lather when he realized Elene left with you."

"She didn't leave with me." *She left without telling me she was coming along.*

"That isn't how anyone saw it."

"Everyone saw us leave. They saw she didn't ride out with us."

"Mayhap she waited for you near the loch." Androw shrugged. "But she disappeared at the same time you left."

"And Ninian and Sonneta Sinclair lost their home for that assumption." Liam turned a hard stare at Androw, anger threatening to boil over. His fear receded only slightly, but rage and a desire for vengeance filled the space.

"What?" Androw stopped short.

"Gunter believed we hid Elene. He set their croft ablaze after sending his people in to attack. My men and I pushed the battle outside, and Gunter himself tossed the first torch onto the thatching. He cared not who was still inside. He fled to his ships. I'm certain he's on his way here to punish Elene through her family. The lass told me she believed he wouldn't hurt them since they're still young. After he willfully tried to burn people alive, I won't put aught past him. I fear he will sell them like he planned to sell Elene."

"You're here to take them."

"Since that sounded like a statement rather than a question, I shan't give an answer."

"It's good that you came. Whether Elene is with you, or you know where she is, you need to get Katryne and Johan far from here. Inburgh has been worse than ever before. She beat Katryne when she discovered Elene fled. Inburgh was so drunk that she thought the young lass was Elene when Elene was a child. She chased the girl home, screaming Elene's name, and barricaded the door. I had to take an axe to it, but Katryne already had a swollen eye, cracked lip, and now has bruises on her arms and ribs. Johan tried to step between them to protect his sister. Inburgh swung a rolling pin at his head. The lad was agile and ducked. He had the wherewithal to push Katryne away too, or the lass would have taken it to her throat."

"They didn't stay with her, did they?"

"Of course not," Androw snapped, insulted that Liam would ask. "They've been with Janet and me. Inburgh sobered enough to know the difference between her daughters, but she's shown no remorse. She hasn't been to visit or to demand they return. Everyone thinks she's glad to be done with them. She won't notice that they're gone."

"What will everyone say? I can't wait until nightfall. As it stands, I'm likely to pass Gunter's ships as I sail west. He's as likely to attack me at sea as he is on land."

"We know. The council and I met the day after Katryne's beating. We were going to send them to Isbister if you weren't willing to take them with you. We considered what would happen if you encountered Gunter on the open water. He has far more boats and far more warriors than you. He would slaughter you and take your goods, then sink your birlinns. You need to sail east and go around the southern tip of Rousay, past Egilsay, then around the southern tip of Shapinsay. You'll pass Dingieshowe if you need to stop again. Otherwise, go directly to South Ronaldsay. You can hide for a couple days until Gunter's swept through here. From there, you can finally sail to Dunbeath."

"Where are they?"

"In my croft. Janet has food ready for you."

"Do I need to sneak them to my boat?"

"No one but Inburgh would stop you. I haven't seen her in a day. She could have drunk herself to death, and I wouldn't know."

As though Androw's words summoned her, Inburgh lurched through her door and stumbled. She picked up her skirts and hurtled herself toward the two men as they passed the village well. Liam glanced at it, remembering that he'd first seen Elene as she argued with her mother beside the well. It felt like so much longer than a sennight ago. Elene felt like a friend he'd had since childhood. He'd told her stories only his siblings knew. He trusted her as much as he did any member of his family, and he respected her just as much. Liam looked back as Inburgh brandished a knife.

"You took my whoring daughter. You will not take my other two," Inburgh shouted. Liam locked eyes with her and realized she was far more lucid than he expected. He wasn't certain whether that made her more dangerous than an intoxicated woman with a blade. He would prefer not to face either. "Gunter expects us ready to sail when he arrives. His son and daughter and his new bride."

"You've married already?" Liam's brow furrowed.

"They haven't, but in her mind, they have," Androw whispered. "She's not been right in the head since her husband died. She's a complete bampot now."

"Inburgh, I—"

"It's Lady Inburgh to you now, you son of a whore. I'm a prince's wife."

Liam inhaled, struggling to grip his tattered patience. "Lady Inburgh, I took no one, and I'm here to take no one. I returned for my ships and to bid my friend and his wife farewell."

"You lie!" Inburgh lunged. Androw grasped one arm while Liam squeezed the wrist of her knife-wielding hand. The dirk dropped to the ground as Inburgh wailed like an animal. People stopped to stare, but soon turned their back on the trio. The situation screamed to Liam, despite no one speaking. It was clear to Liam that the village cared not what happened to the woman; no one would come to her aid. He wondered if that extended to her children.

"I sentence you to two days in the stocks, Inburgh. You attacked a nobleman." Androw shook the woman, who mumbled incoherent threats. He turned to Liam and tilted his head toward his home. As Androw dragged Inburgh to the public-shaming post, Liam recognized two village councilmen hurrying forward to

145

help Androw. Liam supposed it was a blessing in disguise. She could no longer oppose the children leaving with him. He hadn't lied. He hadn't come to take Johan and Katryne. He believed they would choose to follow, so they could be with Elene.

He knocked once, and Janet pulled the door open as he prepared to knock again. He stepped inside to find the children staring out the window at the scene in the village center. Liam observed their expressions. Neither child's expression reflected that they watched their mother being dragged, then forced to place her head and arms through the wooden holes before Androw locked the blocks together. He knew they'd noticed him, but neither turned to him until there was nothing left to see.

"Is Elene all right?" Katryne asked, her voice trembling.

"Yes. She's safe, but she misses you both terribly."

"We miss her," Johan whispered. "Why did she leave us behind? It was so much worse than before."

Liam approached and squatted, bringing him eye level to the children. "She truly thought you would be safe, even if you went to Norway. She feared staying would only endanger you more. But we all know that isn't the case now. She desperately wants you to come with her."

"Where's she going?" Katryne asked.

"I'm not sure, but it'll be somewhere in Scotland."

"We don't speak Scots well," Johan pointed out.

"But you know Norn. Plenty of words come from Scots. It's how I learned it so easily as a child. It'll be easy for you to learn Scots, just like it was for me to learn Norn."

"What if she wants to live among your people? None of us speak Gaelic." Katryne appeared on the verge of tears. Speaking about her sister and their future elicited a far different reaction than observing their mother's punishment.

"Gaelic will be harder to learn, but not impossible. If she chooses Dunbeath, there are plenty of children in the village and in my family who can help teach you."

"Don't they only speak Gaelic?" Johan's lip trembled. Liam placed his hand on the boy's shoulder.

"My cousins speak Scots and Gaelic. My uncles, aunts, and grandfather all speak Norn. There are plenty who will help you."

"But they're noble. We're just peasants," Katryne pointed out.

"You're my friends," Liam smiled. "I will ask my family to help, and they will. They know you're important to me."

"Elene is, not us," Katryne corrected.

"You are. You're Elene's brother and sister, which makes you important to me. But I like you both in your own right. You're brave, loyal, funny, hardworking. Shall I go on? I can. There is a lot that I admire about you both that has naught to do with my friendship with your sister."

Katryne cocked an eyebrow; the twelve-year-old understood there was more than mere friendship between the pair. But ten-year-old Johan nodded his head enthusiastically. Janet came to stand beside them, a burlap bag overflowing with food. Liam graciously accepted, proffering a kiss on Janet's cheek and a one-armed embrace. Janet opened her arms, and the children didn't hesitate. Liam wondered which of his aunts would take them under her wing. He suspected they would take turns.

But as the thought entered his mind, another jostled for its own place. It was his mother who he envisioned helping to care for them. He realized it was Varrich that he saw in the background of his musings, not Dunbeath. He reminded himself that it wasn't his decision. Elene would choose where they would make their home. However, it suddenly felt urgent that she know she was just as welcome at Varrich as she would be at Dunbeath. He wasn't sure how to communicate it, but he knew he had several days of hide-and-seek from Gunter to figure it out.

CÉLESTE BARCLAY

CHAPTER 11

*E*lene wanted to pace. She wanted to peer over the rail and look toward land. She wanted to swim ashore and demand to know what was taking so long. She'd watched Liam walking away, then recognized Androw when he joined Liam. Her heart dropped to her toes when she watched in horror as her mother approached the men. She could only imagine what Inburgh said, the accusations she lobbed. She'd been beside herself when she watched Androw drag her mother to the stocks. Her mother had humiliated her many times over the years, but knowing Liam watched her mother being dragged away—for whatever she said to him—was beyond the pale.

As her horror morphed to anger, she searched the village center and along the coast for any hint of her siblings' whereabouts, but she saw nothing. She watched Liam change course, assuming he'd likely approached her home in hopes that Katryne and Johan were there. She realized he headed to Androw and Janet's croft. She wished to tell him he was wasting time, that he needed to search in the fields or at the loch, but she breathed a sigh of relief when Liam looked toward the ships and nodded. Her hands fisted in frustration when Liam entered the croft, and she could no longer see what he did.

"He'll bring them soon enough," Dermot said in broken Norn. "He'd sooner die than disappoint you."

"Thank you. I know he's trying. I'm scared and impatient." Elene kept her sentences simple, hoping Dermot could understand. When he nodded and offered her a sympathetic smile, she knew he had. He offered her dried beef and cheese, along with a waterskin. She was still tucked away, but she had a clear line of sight to Androw's home. She nearly burst into tears when she watched Liam leave Androw and Janet's home with a sack in one arm and Katryne in the other. Elene's brow furrowed as she wondered why he carried her sister. Katryne waved to Janet, who stood in the doorway. Elene waited for someone to sound the alarm, for her mother to caterwaul from the stocks. But no one seemed to bat an eyelash as Liam led the children to the curragh or when they stepped in. She watched Androw help Albert shove the rowboat into the surf as Henry took up the oars.

She eased away from her hiding place, her head still covered by the cloak's broad hood. She glanced out to sea in all directions, but she saw no sign of any boats approaching. She was nervously shifting her weight when the curragh bumped the birlinn's hull. Dermot tossed a rope ladder over the side. When Johan's head popped up level to the deck, she dashed forward and pulled him into her embrace. She waited for Katryne, but when her sister didn't appear, she looked over the side.

"Dear God! Katryne!" Elene's voice croaked as she took in the sight of her sister's battered face. She leaned forward to take her from Liam's outstretched arms, but Cadence eased her aside. The young warrior lifted the girl with ease and carried her to a corner where the bulkhead buffered the wind. Elene opened the cloak and her arms, inviting her siblings to sit with her once she arranged herself in the corner. They both sagged against her, as though they were too exhausted to keep themselves upright. Elene looked at both children, finding their eyes closed. She stroked their hair and kissed both of their heads before shifting her focus to Liam. She read the concern in his eyes, and her heart melted to see he worried for her siblings as much as he did her. He hadn't exaggerated when he said Johan and Katryne were important to him.

Liam nodded to Elene once he saw her brother and sister settled against her. He fetched his bedroll and Dermot's, taking the spare plaids and wrapping them around the three Isbisters. He cupped Elene's cheek in his massive hand. She closed her eyes and leaned against it, releasing a shuddering sigh. When she flickered her eyes open, there were fat tears threatening to fall. Kneeling on one knee, he leaned forward and kissed her forehead. He would have done more, but there were far too many people watching.

"We're setting sail now. Androw told me they expect Gunter's return. He said we should sail east, then south, while Gunter likely searches Rousay and Mainland again. We can hide near South Ronaldsay until it's safe to cross to Dunbeath. It'll take a few days to be sure he hasn't followed us, but I doubt he will sail in between the islands. He's more likely to sail home and cry to his brother, insisting that King Haakon intervene."

"That'll just make problems for your family. The Earl of Caithness won't want to deal with three runaways as his first issue as the new overseer of these islands."

"This is exactly the type of issue he would make his priority. My grandfather will never condone, never turn a blind eye, to mistreated people. My father taught me that those who are strong have a duty to protect those who are not. It's why we train warriors and why we value being part of a clan. Life is too harsh without help and protection. I fostered under my grandfather. He taught me how to defend those who cannot defend themselves. He wouldn't easily forgive me if I ignored your plight, regardless of what you mean to me." Liam snapped his mouth shut. He prayed Elene wouldn't pounce on his words. Instead, she gazed into his eyes and nodded.

"Thank you, Liam. You're the only person I've felt safe with since my father died. I don't know what it is, but no one else—not the men in my village or even your men—makes me feel like I can trust them as much as I've already come to trust you. I wish I could offer you something in return. I feel like all I've done is take."

"Elene," Liam whispered, fairly certain both Katryne and Johan were already asleep. "Part of what drives me is honor and duty, but that's not all of it. I came on this mission wanting to prove to others than I'm man enough to lead. Being with you makes me see the man I really want to be. Someone others can depend upon. Someone people trust. Someone who sees a wrong and refuses to leave until it's righted. I want to see you happy and safe wherever you wish to go. I'll do aught that I can to make that happen."

"I—I don't know where that should be." Elene looked down, her cheeks heating as tears once more burned behind her lids. Liam nudged her chin up and pressed a soft kiss to her lips.

"I don't have all the answers right now, but I know I'm not ready to say goodbye." Liam's emerald orbs sparkled as he gazed into Elene's sapphire ones. He hoped she understood what he couldn't say aloud. When she nodded and lifted her chin to offer him a kiss, he thought he might float away.

"Let's get to Scotland, then we'll figure out what comes next. But I would like to make our home at Dunbeath—or Varrich." Elene waited, her abdomen clenched.

"You'd like both places," Liam hedged. "Though I will always think Varrich is the better."

"Liam!" Dermot's call drew their attention toward the ship's captain. He gestured Liam over, forcing him to leave Elene where she sat with her sleeping siblings. He watched as she leaned her cheek against Johan's head and closed her eyes. He hoped she would at least rest, if not fall asleep. "We need to sail further out to make sure we dinna run aground. But it means making us more visible until we round the island."

"There's naught for it. We have to take that risk, since ripping our hulls open willna get us home sooner. We stay as close as we dare until we are on the east side of the island. Then we can sail even farther from the coast in case Gunter somehow crosses the island by land. I trust ye and Alfred."

Dermot nodded as he looked over his shoulder at Alfred, who was at the helm of the other birlinn. "How are they? The lass looks in a bad way."

"She's a brave little thing. Her mother was too drunk to notice she wasna berating Elene. Somehow the woman thought she was yelling at a younger version of Elene while accusing her of things she believes the adult Elene did. She beat Katryne, then tried to hit Johan in the head with a rolling pin when he stepped between them. He ducked and pushed Katryne out of the way. Androw took an axe to the door and rescued them. He and Janet took them in until we arrived. Inburgh came at me with a dirk. That's what wound her up in the stocks. It was the excuse Androw needed to get her out of the way. She never said a dickeybird as she watched the three of us walk to the curragh. I dinna ken if she doesnae care or if she's biding her time until Gunter returns. I ken some parents mistreat their children, but it is so far from how I grew up that it's hard to believe until I see something like this."

"That's because Laird Mackay and Laird Sinclair would string a mon up by his bollocks, and he'd have a woman in the stocks for a moon of Sundays, if anyone in either clan thought to hurt their child. But our clan and the Sinclairs are unusual."

"In just aboot every way. The only other ones like us are the Sutherlands," Liam mused.

"Aye. But the MacLeods of Lewis and the Camerons are like us now that Lady Maude married into the Mac-Leods, and Lady Blair married into the Camerons. Their husbands are like yer da, grandda, and yer great-uncle Laird Sutherland."

"They are. It's what's unusual that makes our alliances so strong," Liam pointed out.

"Aye, and we're all better for it. They'll be safe at Dunbeath." Dermot cast a speculative look at Liam before turning his attention back to the sea.

"Varrich." Liam waited for Dermot to look at him once more. "I dinna ken how it will work out, but that's where I hope she'll go."

"Ye would never take her as yer leman. Do ye wish to see her married to another mon?"

"I've been thinking aboot what ye said. Ye're right. Nay one in ma family would care whether I married a princess or a pauper as long as we love each other, and she'll be a good partner when I one day lead."

"Are ye in love then?"

"I dinna ken. But I ken I dinna want to say goodbye. And I dinna think duty will force me to. I thought so at first, but I think I can serve ma clan and still have a wife I love."

"Have ye told her this yet?"

"When could I?" Liam glanced back at Elene, whose head drooped forward in her sleep. "There's still too much uncertainty for either of us to pledge love and devotion. We need to get to Scotland first, then we can see if we should plan a life together."

"Then ye should put yer arse on a bench and start rowing. The sooner we get somewhere safe to hide, the sooner ye can start planning."

"Aye, Captain." Liam grinned before calling the other men onboard to take up their oars. He watched Dermot signal to Alfred, and soon the oars from both boats were in the water.

Elene roused as she felt something shift against her side. She watched as Liam led Johan to the rail. She watched in amusement as Johan excitedly relieved himself over the side of the birlinn. She supposed it was a great novelty to a young boy. She watched as Liam said something and tossed up the front of his plaid. She couldn't see anything, which she considered both a blessing and a disappointment.

The duo laughed over something she didn't hear, but it lightened Elene's mood to see Johan enjoying time with a man who valued the child. Her brother and sister had few memories of their father, and Gunter hadn't been a welcome substitute. A surge of affection and longing coursed through her as she observed Liam. She had a powerful craving for them to form the family she'd once had. She wanted a life with Liam where they could care for her siblings and one day have their own children.

She chided herself for being ridiculous. They were attracted to one another, even fond of each other, but that wouldn't change their stations. It wouldn't change

CELESTE BARCLAY

Liam's obligations to his clans. She'd never imagined she would take such liberties with a man who wasn't her husband, and she knew she would be heartbroken when they went their separate ways. But she didn't regret the kisses and touches they shared. She suspected they were what would keep her company in the days ahead, when she struggled to begin life anew in a foreign land among strangers. She didn't doubt Liam would do what he could to help them adjust, but he wouldn't be their nursemaid forever.

Elene considered how Liam said that they would enjoy life at either Dunbeath or Varrich, and how he'd added that he liked Varrich better. She wanted to believe it was a subtle invitation, but she refused to get her hopes up lest she be made a fool. As she watched Liam lower his plaid and clap his hand on Johan's shoulder before they turned back toward Elene and Katryne, she wondered if she could live as a man's mistress, even if only for a while. She knew to her core Liam would never keep a leman once he married. Even if it were a political union and in name only, he would never be unfaithful. What would become of her as an unwed woman who'd bedded the laird's son? She would either end up as a tavern wench or the wife of a man desperate enough to accept a nobleman's castoff. There was no chance for further intimacies aboard the ship, and the responsible part of her knew there should be no more. But she still craved his touch, at the very least his kisses.

"Are you hungry?" Liam asked as Johan settled against Elene once more. The jovial child from a moment ago once more turned into a sleepy boy as he took comfort in his older sister's embrace. Elene suspected they'd barely slept since she left Katryne and Johan in their mother's care. Guilt plagued her that she'd been too naive to realize the danger in which she

156

left them, which only worsened when she admitted to herself that it hadn't been naivete but selfishness: she'd abandoned her younger siblings. Accepting the thought she'd harbored since she devised her plan to escape on Liam's wagon curdled her stomach. She shook her head.

"They will be when they wake," Elene kept her voice low. "Janet was kind to gift us so much food."

"I sensed she didn't agree with Androw when he said there was little they could do to help you. I think it relieved her that they came to her croft, where she could tend to them. She might have been the one to smuggle all three of you away."

"She was always the mother I wished I had," Elene confessed, praying neither of her siblings heard. Despite all their mother's sins, she didn't want to speak ill of her in front of Katryne and Johan. It felt wrong.

"I'll bring the sack over, and you can have what you like. It'll be awhile before we have aught that's fresh. We can't stop to fish right now, but we will when we find somewhere safe."

"Dunbeath is the only place that will be safe to stop."

"That may be, but we'll have to go ashore for more water. While we're anchored, a couple of the men will fish, and at least one will hunt. We'll cook what we can on land since that's not an option onboard the birlinns. Whatever we catch should last a day or two, then we have other reserves for the crossing. I wish I could offer you all something heartier."

"We'll manage just fine, Liam. You're already doing plenty for us. I don't want to endanger anyone by them going ashore unnecessarily. There's too much risk Gunter will find us, or someone will see us and tell him. He has a way of being very persuasive when he wants information."

"I know. We'll be careful. Do you need aught? A moment of privacy or a chance to stretch your legs? I can sit with them if you do."

"I'm all right for now. I'm enjoying having them beside me. It feels like ages since we sat like this, even though it's only been a couple of days."

"Then rest. There's no need for you to do aught but be with your brother and sister." Liam caught himself before offering to hold her while she rested. His arms ached to wrap around her, to offer her comfort when the strain was so obvious. He had no more answers to the unasked questions than he did when he discovered her on the wagon. But he hoped she understood he shared her burden willingly, that he would do everything he could to keep the three Isbister siblings away from harm.

"Liam?"

"Yes."

"Mayhap we can watch the stars together tonight."

Liam beamed. "I would love it. I've missed that with you."

"Me too." She wished the hours away. She knew they would have no privacy, and they wouldn't be able to lie beside one another, holding hands. But it was a pleasure they could share. She didn't think she could pass the time patiently, so it was just as well that she fell asleep for most of the afternoon.

Liam took his turn at the oars as he and his men pushed themselves to put distance between them and Skaill. Liam prayed Gunter didn't think along the same lines as them and sail the eastern coast to return to Skaill. It wouldn't surprise him if Gunter assumed they would try to evade him, then hunt them along this alternative route. As the passed the southern tip of

Rousay, he strained his eyes as he scanned the western horizon for longboats. There would be a brief time when they were exposed before they reached Egilsay. When no one materialized, Liam nodded to Dermot, who told the men to rest before signaling to Alfred.

Liam checked their freshwater barrels, alarmed that there was less than he recalled. They would have enough for the rest of the day, but the sun was warm, and the men exerted themselves as they rowed. There was a small freshwater lake on Egilsay, and they would have to stop to replenish their supply. It was nearly dusk, and there were few people who inhabited the island. He and three of his men could traverse the distance and fill waterskins with few people noticing. It would give the men time to rest, which they needed if they were to continue that night. He rued ordering them to row, but they must if the wind didn't pick up.

Liam signaled Alfred to come to the rail as Dermot and he walked to meet him. The birlinns sailed close together, making it easy for Liam to discuss his plan with his captains without his voice carrying too far.

"How is yer water supply?" Liam asked Alfred.

"After this past stretch, it's low."

"Same as ours," Liam responded. "We have to stop at Egilsay and go to the loch. If we dinna, we canna have the men keep rowing. We canna rely on the wind, and we canna linger. South Ronaldsay is the only isle with enough coves for us to hide. The sooner we get there, the sooner we can all breathe easy."

"Aye," Dermot interjected. "It doesnae feel like we shall have a change in the weather. Fair as it might be on land, it's a nuisance at sea."

"We can go ashore as soon as the sun sets and before it gets too dark to see one foot in front of the other." Liam glanced over his shoulder, then to Alfred's crew. "We swim. We canna get too close, and I dinna want anyone happening along and finding our curraghs. It'll take too long to get them in and out of the water, anyway. I dinna want to dally."

"In that case, take Benjamin, Dillon, and Cadence. They're the strongest swimmers beside the three of us," Alfred suggested.

"Do ye ken how to find the loch?" Dermot asked.

"I have an idea of where it is, but I havenae been here since I was a wean. There's naught here but some farms, so we didna have much reason for all of us to travel. Da, Grandda, and ma uncles would go on their own."

Elene tapped Liam on the back. She stepped forward as he turned to her. She hadn't understood what the men said except for the island's name and the word "loch." From their tone, she didn't think they knew where it was.

"Are you going to get water at the loch?" Elene inquired.

"That's our plan. After sunset, four of us will go ashore and find it."

"I know where it is. I used to fish there with my father in summer. For a long time, he had no sons to help him, so he had to rely on me."

"How do you get there?"

Elene grimaced. "I shouldn't have fallen asleep. We've come down the Rousay Sound. We should have sailed along the Westray Firth. The loch is on the other side of the island about a *miil* and *fjerdingsvei* from Whistlebare. It should only take a few minutes to get there, but you have to pass at least four farms."

Egilsay was a mile-and-a-quarter wide, so it wasn't a long walk. But Liam hadn't expected to hear there were so many homesteads to pass. He looked at Dermot and Alfred, but there was little they could do. They couldn't ignore their need for freshwater if they planned for the men to be at the oars throughout the night. Before he could share that their plans wouldn't change, Elene spoke.

"I can swim it. The people know me. Even if I'm soaking wet with waterskins, they won't question me. I can guarantee Gunter won't stop here. There are so few people that he won't bother. But if they see four Highlanders, it will raise the alarm."

"There are too many waterskins for you to carry them alone," Liam pointed out.

Elene's lips pursed and twisted to the side as she thought. "I'll go ashore with you and your men. Only one person can come with me to the loch. The others must hide."

"You're staying here and keeping out of sight." Liam watched as eyes as deep blue as the water in which they sailed turned toward him. Elene's left eye narrowed as she studied Liam, choosing her words with care, not wanting to argue in front of his men, even if they didn't comprehend.

"I understand why you wish that, but I'm the reason they had to row. I'm the one who knows the way. And I'm the one who can give a reasonable excuse. If anyone sees four Highlanders upon Egilsay, creeping in the dark, the entirety of Orkney will know by midmorning tomorrow. I'm dressed as an Orcadian, and I know the people. I can give just enough of the truth to be plausible without giving away everything. You need me."

"I need you to stay safe."

"And if they rounded up and bound you and your men because the farmers fear attack, how safe will any of us be?" Elene cocked an eyebrow. Liam's mind jumped to how Elene must look when she scolded her siblings, which only made him think about how she might look if she scolded their children.

"Fine. But it's against my better judgment."

"I know." Elene offered him a sympathetic smile, not envying Liam the weight of responsibility. She looked at the two captains but kept speaking to Liam in Norn. "The water grows shallow a long way from the shore. The swim will look long, but the ground comes up fast. We're already as close as I would sail."

Liam nodded before giving orders for the three men to join them as they rounded up as many waterskins as they could carry. Liam watched as Elene explained to Katryne and Johan what would happen. As she talked, she toed off her boots and peeled down her stockings. When she returned, she gathered her share of the waterskins, then pulled the back of her skirts between her legs and tucked them into the girdle around her waist. Dermot removed the section of rail that they used for loading the horses.

Liam was about to say he would go first to test the depths, but Elene was over the side before he could say anything. He marveled at how she leaped with her legs scissored and arms wide. As she entered the water, she brought her arms together as her legs closed. She kept her head above water and rolled onto her back before kicking. When all four men were swimming toward her, she rolled back onto her belly. She swam a hundred yards before she paused and tested the water's depth. Pleased to find her toes brushed sand, she turned to Liam.

"You can stand here. I still need to swim a few more feet." Elene continued swimming as the men switched to walking. It was only a moment later that she waded beside Liam. When they reached the shore, all of them wrung out their clothing as best they could. Elene put her finger to her lips as they began their walk across the island. Ten minutes later, Elene once more put her finger to her lips, this time pointing to smoke rising from a croft. She leaned toward Liam to whisper. "This is as far as they can come. They can hide in the tall grass. You and I go together."

Liam relayed Elene's instructions before they set off together. Elene and Liam skirted the crofts, and it wasn't long before they reached the loch. They exchanged a longing glance, both recalling their times together at the loch near Skaill. There was no opportunity to linger now. They'd barely finished filling their last waterskins when a voice carried to them.

"Who are you?" An angry man demanded. Elene spun around with a smile plastered to her face. She prayed she'd receive a better welcome once the man recognized her.

"It's me, Malcolm."

"Elene?" Malcolm furrowed his brow before pointing to Liam. "Who's that?"

"My husband, Liam."

"Husband? Last I heard, Gunter Haakonsson intended to take you and your family back to Norway. I didn't get the impression he would let you marry."

"It wasn't his decision to make." Elene shrugged.

"Does he know that?" Malcolm chuckled. Elene shrugged again, the cool air making her skin prickle. She kept to the shadows, hoping Malcolm wouldn't notice how their wet clothes stuck to their bodies. When she offered no response, Malcolm asked, "What're you doing here?"

"We were fishing for the sennight, and I was clumsy and knocked over our water barrel. I knew we were close to the loch, so here we are."

"This is why women are bad luck on boats. I warned your father." Malcolm tsked and offered Liam a sympathetic grin. Elene grimaced. She relaxed as Liam slid his hand into hers and squeezed her fingers.

"I get lonely without my wife," Liam grinned. Malcolm's gaze swung to Liam, shocked that the man clad in a *breacan feile* spoke Norn. Suspicion became obvious on Malcolm's face. Elene appreciated Liam's support, but she wished he'd stayed quiet. She pressed her nails into the back of his hand. He gave a quick flex of his fingers and added nothing more.

"We just finished filling our waterskins, so we will be on our way," Elene nodded.

"Join us for an ale."

Elene knew he didn't offer hospitality. He was nosy and a gossip, worse than any woman she knew. She wanted to share nothing that would spread across the Orkneys by the first wave of fishermen meeting on the water.

"We didn't plan to stop here, so we must be on our way. My father's family expects us, and we are already late."

"Why didn't you just get freshwater in Isbister?" Malcolm pressed.

"Because we need freshwater now?"

"Why?"

"I'm thirsty. Malcolm, the tide is about to change. We need to go. We have our water, so we will be on our way."

"Felicitations on your marriage. Where are you moving to?"

Elene grinned. "I'm making an Orcadian of my husband."

"He's already learned Norn. You must be a good teacher. He practically sounds like a local." Malcolm stared at Liam, assessing him.

"He wishes to fit in with our people."

"The Mackays already fit in." Elene and Liam froze. They'd fooled Malcolm not at all. "You must have traveled here often with Laird Mackay if you know Norn so well. What does he say about one of his warriors choosing to live on a small island rather than fighting for a powerful clan?"

Liam and Elene realized Malcolm didn't recognize Liam as the clan's tánaiste. As the Orcadian farmer stared at them, Liam wrapped his arm around Elene and looked down at her. Her beseeching eyes made him cautious, but the trust he saw made him feel as though he were a thousand feet tall.

"My laird knows how important Elene is to me. He understands why I choose to make a life with her. Laird Mackay loves Lady Mackay more than aught but his children. He knows what it is to choose a woman because she's the ideal helpmate. He doesn't question my decision."

Elene felt the truth in Liam's words as though he made a pledge to her rather than justify their appearance on Egilsay. Malcolm nodded and stepped aside, seemingly satisfied with the couple's explanation. Neither Liam nor Elene wasted time with their goodbyes as they hurried back to the path. Liam shook his head to his men as they walked past. The men remained hidden in the tall grass until Liam and Elene walked around a bend in the path. When the couple looked back, they could no longer see Malcolm. Liam released a soft bird call, and his men materialized from the shadows. The group hurried back to the shore, where they could see the birlinns bobbing high in the water. Liam's heart slowed, having feared he would discover his men battling angry Norse warriors. It wasn't long before Elene and the men were aboard their ships.

"We can't stop to fish or hunt until we make it to South Ronaldsay," Elene blurted. "We can't risk going anywhere on Mainland. Malcolm will have told everyone on Egilsay by now. The few fishermen who live on the island will tell all the men who sail past in the morning."

Liam relayed Elene's warning to the men, who exchanged uneasy looks. Liam feared they would resent Elene, but most looked at her, then her siblings, before taking their seats at the oars, unbidden by Liam or his captains. They were soon on their way, giving Mainland a wide berth as they rowed west. Finally, they pointed in the right direction to make their way to Dunbeath.

CHAPTER 12

The sun was a mere hint on the eastern horizon when Michail roused Alfred, who signaled Dermot and Liam. The warrior had the last shift of the night watch on his ship, and he'd spotted the Norse dragon boats as the sky lightened from the ebony of night to the royal blue of predawn. He could make out few details besides the bobbing shapes materializing and growing closer.

The two Highland birlinns had made progress to the open water between Egilsay and Shapinsay. It exposed them to the Norse fleet near Tingwall. As far as the Sinclairs and Mackays traveled to avoid detection, it left them vulnerable with no alternative route. The distance remaining to South Ronaldsay wasn't great, but the men faced at least another four hours of rowing. With only four rowers at a time on each birlinn, they couldn't outsail the Norse with their sixteen rowers per longboat.

"Mayhap they willna see us," Dermot suggested.

"We're east of them. If we've already spied them, the rising sun will make us obvious." Liam hurried to the rail to consult Alfred before all the men took their places at the oars. The best they could hope for was to make it to Shapinsay before the Norse reached them. They could use the island as a barrier while they sailed farther southwest. However, if Gunter guessed their route, they could cut off Liam and the others between Shapinsay and Mainland. If that were the case, there was little chance they could avoid being boarded. Liam's mind raced as he considered ways to hide Elene and her siblings. There was no cabin or hold on a birlinn, so there was nowhere for them to disappear into. Even if there were, Liam knew the Norse would search them.

"Liam, they see us," Elene whispered as she squatted behind him. "Before they get too close, put each of us in a barrel and toss them over the side. We'll float. It's still dark enough that they may not see us."

"And when they do, because they will, they will demand to know why we set them adrift. They'll guess you're in there."

"Tell them you refuse to give up your whisky and ale to them. You'd rather they float away than they take them."

"They'll merely scoop you up and take you, anyway."

"There is no other place for us to hide."

"Can Katryne and Johan swim? Can they tread water?"

"Yes." Elene glanced back at the children, who clung to one another.

"We wait until the very last minute, but you'll have to go into the water. Keep close to the birlinn and prepare to duck beneath the surface if anyone gets too close."

"No." Elene shook her head. "I might survive the cold, but they won't. They're too small. They'll freeze to death or drown when they don't have the strength to tread. The barrel will keep us each dryer for longer."

"The current will carry you away."

"We're likely to wind up on Mainland. If you..." Elene didn't want to finish her thought, and she flinched when Liam did.

"If we survive, I'll search for you."

"We don't have much more time." Elene watched the longboats loom larger with each moment they spent debating. "We have to go over the side before they see us do it."

Liam loathed the idea, but he knew it was far better than having them directly in the frigid North Sea. They would freeze. The swim had been short to Egilsay, and the night air held no breeze. The four swimmers were chilled to the bone by the time they returned to the bir-linns, but they hadn't risked hypothermia. It was more likely the Isbisters would succumb than survive if forced to tread water during a battle.

"Dermot," Liam called. "Take my oar. They're going over in barrels. I'll take the tiller as soon as they're in the water."

Dermot's eyes widened. Liam knew the suggestion shocked the other men, but no one gainsaid him. None could think of another solution as they continued to row. Liam rushed to open the empty barrels as Elene reassured her siblings that they would be far safer with her plan than anything else. Katryne's eyes watered with trepidation, but she nodded. Johan burst into tears and clung to Liam as he shook his head.

"Johan, your sisters won't go without you. If you don't get in, then Gunter will take all three of you. This is dangerous, and you must be brave. But we will all be so proud of you. This will be your first chance to be a man instead of a boy." Liam prayed his words empowered Johan rather than shame him into cooperating.

"A man like you?" Johan mumbled as he wiped his tears.

"I would do this without a second thought if it

would protect my brothers and sister. I know you are like me. You would do aught to protect your family. This is what you need to do now. I will fight for you on deck, but you must fight for your family by listening to Elene's idea."

Johan straightened, his shoulders going back as he inhaled a shuddering breath. It was obvious it still terrified the boy, but he resolved to put that fear aside to keep his sisters and him alive. "Put me in the first barrel and toss me in. If I float, then send my sisters with me."

"You have the courage of a lion," Liam grinned.

"What's that?"

"A very large cat from lands far away. The Romans once kept them as pets. They're fierce and loyal to their pack. They're so ferocious they scare people away." Liam didn't think it was the right time to explain the ancient people used the animals for entertainment and made them fight to the death.

"That sounds like you. But you're a Highlander."

"I am. I suppose my people share some of those qualities."

"You're a Highland lion," Katryne announced. She took her brother's hand and led him to where the crew stored the empty oak casks. Elene gestured to Liam that she would go first. Once the two sisters and their brothers hid, Liam lifted Elene into the air, then released her into the water. He leaned as far forward as he could, trying to lessen the impact. When the barrel didn't immediately sink into the sea's depths, he repeated his actions for Johan, then Katryne. He'd ensured the lids were tight enough not to allow in water, but they could each push them free if they needed.

He watched them bob in the current, the distance growing between the three large casks and the birlinn. The waves carried them toward Mainland. Liam prayed they remained afloat long enough for the Isbisters to make it to safety and that they didn't wind up in a crosscurrent. He trusted Elene would take them to safety once they made it ashore. With nothing more that he could do, Liam turned his attention to the approaching Norse. It was only a matter of minutes before he once more stared at Gunter.

"Highlander, you have what's mine. It was bad enough when you stole my woman, now you stole my children."

"They were never yours." Liam crossed his arms, flexing his chest, as he came to stand with his feet hip-width apart. It was the pose the men in his family were notorious for using. It intimidated most people, but Liam knew it would only prove his resolve. It would take far more for the Norseman to feel threatened.

"You know naught of my past with Elene. She refused me, and now she must live with what that choice brings."

"I'd guess your ego makes up for what you lack elsewhere. Having it tweaked must hurt as much as being kicked in the bollocks. You've doled out an equal dose of humiliation by taking up with her mother. Be done." Liam gave a dismissive expression, then made it appear as though he would turn his back to Gunter. He never would lest he get a sword through it.

"You risk much speaking this way when we so clearly outnumber you."

"I know you outnumber us. But I'm not worried. Kill me and my men, and your brother will find himself in more trouble than a few islands can fix. He's already *persona non grata* with King David. Remember, we now govern Orkney because your brother was too poor to pay a dowry and failed to beg funds from your jarls. Kill a man who King David treats like a beloved cousin, and my sovereign will not hesitate to make King Haakon's life even more miserable. It will be your death that satisfies King David. What then? We're both dead. Rather wasteful, and you're still the loser."

"I'll take my chances. Your king scares me not a wit."

"Then you're a daft man."

"I will have what is mine, Highlander."

"I am a Highlander. I'm one connected to every clan north of the Grampian Mountains. My family extends as far as the Hebrides. Even your Norse sailors don't compare to Hebridean seafarers. You shall have an army at your doorstep if you do aught to ruffle any more hairs on my head. As is, my grandfather shan't be happy to hear what happened on this journey. You underestimate just how powerful the Earl of Caithness is. My great-uncle is the Earl of Sutherland, who is the brother-by-marriage to the Earl of Ross. I have cousins who are lairds commanding armies of more than ten-score men. Your brother will not think me worth the trouble. Leave, and I shall forget this happened."

"I'll leave when I have what is mine," Gunter insisted as he brandished his sword.

"Come aboard and look for yourself. Though there's not much that you can't see. Our boats are the same shape. No hold. What you see is what we have." Liam backed away before gesturing for Gunter to come aboard. When the Norseman narrowed his eyes but took a step forward, Liam raised a hand. "But only with two of your people."

"I'll bring as many as I want."

"You still speak as though I must obey because your brother is sovereign of these lands. He isn't. My grandfather's godson is. Make your choice. Oblige me, and I oblige you. Refuse and you get naught."

"And if I kill you all, there will be no one to tell the tale of what became of you."

"Except for an irate set of chieftains who witnessed

you burn one of their crofts. Chieftains who share a surname with my grandfather, the earl."

Gunter made a guttural sound before pointing to two women, who preceded him onto the birlinn. The three Norse warriors swept across the deck, kicking empty barrels until they toppled. They strew the contents of food sacks and cut open seed sacks. But they huffed in frustration when they'd done all the damage they could, and they still found no fugitives. Liam watched passively, but his smug expression antagonized Gunter. The Norse prince struggled to keep control of his temper, once more embarrassed that the Highlander had the upper hand.

Liam held his breath that Gunter didn't notice the three barrels barely visible in the early morning light. He nearly groaned when Gunter stepped to the far rail and pointed toward the Isbisters.

"What are those?"

"I'd rather my whisky sink than wind up on your boat."

"You threw your whisky overboard? What will your dear grandfather say about that waste?"

"He'll say thank you. He wouldn't wish for you to have shite from him."

"What a fool," Gunter scoffed. He shook his head as he sneered but abandoned his search. He jumped back to his longboat. Liam expected him to cross to Alfred's boat, but Gunter gave the signal for his longboats to back away. "This isn't done, Highlander."

"I didn't think it was, *vikingr*," Liam grinned as he used the Old Norse term for the sea-roving pirates. It surprised Liam that Gunter didn't board the other birlinn. His heart dropped that he'd endangered the Isbister siblings needlessly. He wished he'd sent them to the other birlinn. But he reminded himself that had he not put them over the side, and had Gunter boarded

Alfred's ship, Elene, Katryne, and Johan would be in Gunter's net. As much as he wished to dash to the opposite rail and search for the barrels, he didn't. Instead, he waited as the Norsemen sailed between the two birlinns, knocking against the Highlanders' boats as if to cast one last jab at them.

"Where do you think they're going?" Alfred asked as the birlinns floated back together.

"I don't know. I'm certain he doesn't believe we let them go. My guess is back to Mainland, but further along the southern coast. I fear he intends to waylay us again. If we sail back north and go around the opposite tip, we could stop in Snusgar for water before we cross to Scotland. I don't want to add the extra distance on either side of the island, but we have little chance of avoiding him otherwise. I want to get back to Dunbeath as fast as we can. In the meantime, we have to get them before they freeze."

Elene jostled the sides of the barrel as the waves crested, then dropped into troughs. Fortunately, the water was calm. She didn't think they would survive if the swells were any larger. Water seeped into the barrel, but it was a slow. She didn't fear sinking, but she was wet and shivering. She could only imagine how Johan and Katryne fared. She'd ceased hearing Liam's baritone voice only moments after going over the side. She hadn't realized how comforting the sound was until it vanished. Where she'd felt confident only moments ago that he would rescue them, fear licked at her, tightening her belly, and making her heart race.

"Johan?" Elene called, unsure whether her voice would carry.

"I'm here," came the weak response. "It's so cold."

"I know, little one. It won't be much longer. Katryne?"

"I'm here. Elene, my barrel is sinking."

"How much water is in it?"

"I can barely keep my head above it. Help!"

Elene told herself not to panic. She pushed against the lid, but it wouldn't budge. There wasn't nearly enough room to turn so her feet were where her head was now. She pushed herself down into a tight squat before surging upward with her hands by her head. They, and the top of her head, slammed into the lid. It burst open, and water surged in. She knew she'd laid sideways, but she hadn't expected the wave that would try to submerge her. She swallowed a mouthful of briny water before she gathered her bearings. She gripped the edge of the barrel and pushed herself free. Her skirts tried to pull her to the bottom. She tore at them, gathering them to her waist. She frantically tucked them into her girdle as best she could. Her legs were free, so she kicked to the surface.

As her head emerged, she spun in a circle, taking in as much as she could. She spied Liam's boats in the distance. She noticed she and her siblings were farther from shore than she expected. The current pushed them out to sea rather than to beach. She found both barrels, but she was unsure which one contained Katryne.

"Katy, bang on your barrel, so I know which one is yours." Elene strained to hear over the sea's voice. It was as though a sea monster taunted her as she tried to catch even the slightest noise. A rapping staccato sounded. Of course, it was the barrel farther from her. She fought the freezing water threatening to drag her under. She fought her clothes' weight. She fought her fear. She wouldn't give up on her sister. Not after all they'd endured over the years, and not after what they risked by escaping. She reached the large cask and gripped the lip, trying to determine which end was the top and which was the bottom. "Katy, I'm here. Tap on the lid. I don't know which end is which."

"The left side." Katryne's weak voice was barely audible.

"I don't know which side is your left. Knock on the top." When Elene heard the clear sound, she swam around to the opposite side. "I need you to curl up as small as you can. When I tell you, put your hands palms up by the top of your head. Jump and push off the bottom. I'm going to pull. Water is going to rush in, so you have to take a big breath before you jump. Do you understand?"

"Yes. Please hurry. There's too much water."

Elene could tell. The barrel was sitting lower in the water by the moment. She grabbed the edge and brought her feet up and beneath her until they rested against the wood. "I'm going to count to three, then you jump as high and as hard as you can. You're going to bang your head, Katy, but use it to push the lid off. Are you ready?"

"Yes," Katryne's voice burbled against the water filling her soon-to-be tomb.

"One—two—three." Elene yanked as hard as she could. She used her feet for leverage as she threw her weight backward. She pushed away with her feet as her arms tugged. The lid flew off, knocking her back and slamming into her mouth and nose. Pain ripped through her face, but she released the lid and swam back. She caught the shoulder of Katryne's gown and pulled her sister into her arms. She held onto her with one arm as she swam to the third barrel. "Hang on, Katy. Johan?"

No sound met her. She tapped on the barrel once more, but there was still nothing. Fighting panic, she forced herself not to grow frantic. She ensured Katryne draped her arms over the top of the barrel before she moved to what she believed was the top. She tugged on the lip, but nothing budged.

"Katy, I need you to stay awake." Elene watched as her sister's eyes drooped closed. "When I get the lid off and pull Johan out, the barrel will fill like yours and sink. I need you to pay attention and swim. Can you do that?" Katryne had no choice. There was no way Elene could hold on to her sister while freeing her brother, and if Katryne clung to her, they would both go under.

"I can. Hurry and get Johan. I'm scared."

"I know. I am too, but we have to be brave together. Hold on." Elene felt her strength flagging as the cold seeped into her bones. She pried at the lid, but it wouldn't budge, even when she used the same tactic as she did with Katryne's. All it gained her was saltwater up her nose and down her throat. She felt around for the dirk in her boot, yanking it free. She'd nearly kicked the shoes off, but she knew she would need them once they were on land. They pulled at her like anchors, but she kept her legs circling as she tread water.

"Johan?"

Elene tapped on the lid of the barrel once more and listened. She heard a thud, so she knocked harder.

"Elene?" Johan's voice barely reached her ears, but she was certain she heard her name.

"Yes, little one. I'm going to use my blade to pry the lid free. Keep your head away from the top. Shrink as small as you can."

"I already am. It's so cold."

"I know, but you're doing so well. Is your barrel filling up?"

"No. But it's just so, so cold."

Elene pressed her knife into the miniscule crack between the lid and the barrel, but it wouldn't budge. She tried another spot, but it wouldn't give. The freezing water made the barrel contract, trapping the lid in place. She shifted to move near Katryne.

"I can't get the lid off, Johan. We're going to kick to shore. I'll smash the bluidy barrel if I have to. Come on, Katy. Help me now." Elene put the knife's handle between her teeth, not trusting herself to find the sheath in her boot. She grunted as she pushed against the barrel, kicking as hard as she could. She nudged her sister with her elbow and canted her head toward shore when Katryne turned glassy eyes toward her. She moved one arm to reach across Katryne's shoulders, bringing her sister closer. She pressed her hand over Katryne's, encouraging her to keep going.

"Liam," Katryne whispered. Elene looked at her, noticing that she stared past Elene. The older sister turned her head to follow Katryne's gaze. She nearly wept when she caught sight of the two birlinns cutting through the water toward them. She'd feared they would all drown before Liam was free of Gunter and could come for them. She watched as all oars sliced through the water, then the air, then the water again. She kept kicking, nudging Katryne again to tell her to keep fighting the waves. They couldn't wait for Liam and the Highlanders to reach them if they wanted to keep Johan alive.

Elene grunted as her knee slammed into sand and seashells, but it relieved her to feel land. She pulled her dirk from her mouth and handed it to Katryne, who scampered onto the shore. Elene knew she couldn't roll the barrel, lest she rattle her brother into unconsciousness. She pushed it up the sand, her knees bent, her feet sliding. But she finally drew it past the water's edge. She tried once more to pull the lid free, but the wood was still too tight to give way.

"Johan!" Elene called.

"I'm awake." Elene could have cried upon hearing the trembling voice, but she feared wasting the energy and that her tears might freeze her eyes shut. She looked around for anything she could use to the fracture the barrel's planks. She saw nothing of use. She considered jumping on top of it but feared crushing Johan if it splintered.

"Elene!"

She looked up, finding Liam, Cadence, Albert, and Dermot nearly to shore in the curragh. The four men fought the waves, their backs straining within their leines. Liam handed his oar to Cadence and jumped over the side, splashing his way up to the beach.

"Johan's trapped. I can't get it open. The wood shrank." Elene clung to Liam as he wrapped her in his arms, but the embrace was fleeting.

"Get them blankets," Liam ordered as he drew his sword. Elene gasped until she realized he intended to use the sword's pommel, not its blade. He reached above his head but paused. "Johan? Can you hear me? Tap where your head is."

A faint scratching sound came from his right. Liam shifted further left before driving his sword's hilt into the wood. The sound of splintering timber filled the air. He repeated the move thrice more, putting all his strength into cracking the barrel open. When he could see fabric between the boards, he dropped his sword and used his hands to pull the barrel apart. Elene joined him, yanking from the other side. The barrel burst open when Cadence and Albert added their muscles to the endeavor. Elene fell, landing hard on her backside, but she scrambled on her hands and knees to reach her brother.

"Enie," Johan whispered the name he'd used for his

oldest sister when he was too young to say Elene's full name.

"I'm here." Elene accepted a blanket from one man, she didn't know who, and wrapped it around Johan as she pulled him onto her lap. She looked up when she felt Katryne lean against her. Then a blanket enfolded all three of them. A solid wall was against her back, and she knew it was Liam who held them together.

"I'm here," Liam whispered in her ear, repeating the reassurance she'd given Johan only moments ago. She rested her head against his chest, finally feeling safe after the sheer terror she'd experienced while in the water.

CHAPTER 13

*L*iam looked around, still surprised that they'd wound up back on Mainland rather than Shapinsay. They'd been closer to the small island, but the sea had a different notion of where to carry the three barrels. His heart was in his throat from the moment Gunter boarded his boat until the moment he leaped out of the curragh. Every moment that he engaged with Gunter was time for the Isbisters to float away.

Once Gunter passed back to his boat, and his fleet was underway, Liam forced himself to wait until they were nearly out of sight before he ordered the birlinns toward the three barrels. It shocked him how fast the sea swept them. He'd seen them carried away from the coast, then he'd watched Elene's head burst above the surface. He watched in horror as she struggled with Katryne's barrel, then sank beneath the surface. But a heartbeat later, she emerged with her sister in her arms.

He'd ordered the curragh into the water as Elene helped Katryne to the third barrel. Rowing forced him to turn his back. He wished to look over his shoulder, but he knew it would interrupt their progress. He had to trust that he was drawing closer. When he heard Elene's voice on the wind, he'd finally given in and looked for her. He thought he might faint from relief when he saw her on the sand, but he quickly realized only Katryne was with her. He saw her struggling to move the last barrel up the beach. He'd passed his oar to one of his men and gone over the side and into the frigid water. It was like knife blades cutting his calves and thighs. He couldn't imagine how all three survived in the near frozen water of the North Sea. He thanked God that Elene had insisted on the barrels. If they'd listened to his plan, all three siblings would be dead like Elene feared.

As he held on to Elene, Katryne, and Johan, he knew he could love the two youngest Isbisters as much as he did his own brothers and sister. He wanted to. He looked down at Elene's closed eyes, the fine blue veins pronounced in her eyelids. Her body still trembled against him as she shivered. He would gladly trade places with her if it meant she survived and could make a life with him. He knew what he wanted—needed—with a certainty he'd never felt before. But as much as he longed to profess his feelings, he knew it was far from the right time.

"We need to get you back to the ships. We can't stay here, exposed, and you all need dry clothes."

"We don't have any," Katryne whimpered.

"I'm sure they'll give us plaids," Johan reassured as he reached blue-tinged fingers out to his sister, taking the hand she had curled beneath her chin. "We made it. We're safe now that we're with Liam."

Liam prayed he lived up to such expectations. He helped the three siblings to their feet as he looked around. Elene leaned away and glanced over his shoulders.

"I don't believe it," Elene murmured. "We're near Isbister. I recognize those rocks." She pointed past where Albert stood. "We can walk there in five minutes." She squinted down the coast. "Those are their fishing boats."

"Dermot, Cadence, go back to the birlinns. Bring them round and dock just beyond those boats. Then you and the men join us in the village." When his men nodded and trod back to the curragh, he turned toward Albert. It pleased him to see that the fatherly warrior already carried Katryne in one arm and lifted Johan in the other. Liam scooped Elene into his arms, her head resting against his shoulder as she curled against him. "Where do we go?"

Elene kept her eyes closed but pointed to the right of the rocks she'd recognized. She pulled her arm back in and tucked the plaid she still had closer to her chest. She murmured, "When you get to the village, the second croft to the right is my great-aunt's. Go there. She'll know me and know what to do."

"Elene, stay awake, *mo ghràidh*. You can't sleep until we have you dry and warm. I fear you'll drift off and not wake again."

"I'm so tired, Liam. I can't. Please let me sleep." Elene whimpered as Liam kissed her forehead.

"As soon as you're dry, you can sleep as long as you wish. But not yet. I'm scared you're going to die."

Elene's eyes fluttered open at the anguish in Liam's voice as much as the words he uttered. She saw the fear in his emerald orbs, and she felt him pick up their pace. He was nearly running by the time they reached the village.

"Her name is Ilka," Elene mumbled, her teeth chattering harder than they had when Liam first found her. He looked around as people came out of their homes and others stopped what they were doing in the village center. Liam led the way to the croft Elene told him about, Albert following close behind. Liam could hear the rumble of the older man's voice, then the higher pitch of the children's responses. They both sounded in better shape than their older sister. Liam looked down at Elene, whose eyes were now open but glassy.

"Elene?" An older woman flew through her open door, hiking up her skirts as she ran toward the newcomers. "Merciful angels, what's happened to you, child?"

"Auntie Ilka?" Elene rasped before coughing. Liam tightened his hold, fearing she was already falling ill.

"It's me, lass. What's happened?"

"Can we go inside?" Liam interrupted, surprising the woman with his native-sounding Norn. She looked him up and down before glancing at Albert, who still carried Johan and Katryne.

"Yes. There's time to explain later." Ilka led the way to her croft, holding the door open. Liam scanned their surroundings, noticing an area cordoned off with a curtain. He assumed it was Ilka's sleeping area. He carried Elene to it and eased her to her feet, but she sagged against him. He heard Albert following, then watched him lower Katryne and Johan to their feet. Where Elene looked near death, color had rushed back into the children's cheeks.

"Johan, Katryne, get out of your wet clothes," Ilka instructed as she handed breeks and tunics to them both. The children would swim in the clothes, but they were dry. The older woman dropped a stack of drying linens on the bed within the curtained area. She bustled past Liam and grabbed a wool dress from a peg beside the bedhead. "I'll help her."

Liam hesitated before letting Ilka take Elene from his arms. He considered telling the older woman that Elene was his wife and that he would tend to her. But he didn't know what Elene would want them to say to

184

her extended family, and he didn't think she would appreciate being nearly unconscious the first time Liam stripped her naked. He realized he intended to do just that for many years to come.

"Liam, stay," Elene whispered. "Husband."

Liam glanced down at Elene, then Ilka, the older woman watching the couple. Albert had already stepped back, giving the family and Liam privacy.

"*Mo ghràidh*, you need a hot bath. Your aunt will tend to you while I get buckets heated."

"No," Elene cried. She clung to his leine and shook her head. She burst into sobbing tears. "So scared I'll wake up from this and find it was a nightmare, and you're not here. Don't want to let go."

"I'll fetch the water," Albert called before the door clicked closed.

"I'll see to the tub. Get her out of those clothes, then bring her near the fire while you wait." Ilka didn't look back as she hurried to stoke the fire. Katryne and Johan hadn't dawdled and were already in dry clothes by the time Liam accepted he would tend to Elene.

"Liam, I know you saw me that night at the loch. I could see you as I got out of the water. I—I—wanted you to. But this isn't how I thought you'd see me bare for the first time up close. I thought I would care, but I don't. Please don't leave me. I'm so scared."

"Shh, my little warrior. I won't go anywhere you don't want." Liam lowered his voice. "I don't think your aunt believes we're married. Are you sure you wish for me to strip you? I can stand just beyond the curtain. You'll see my shadow."

Elene wiped away her tears as she looked into Liam's worried gaze. Even after such a near-death experience, he worried for her dignity as much as he worried about her person. How had she found such a perfect man? She'd never imagined one existed, let alone that she would meet him. But she stood before him now, and her heart filled with love. It was enough to finally put the cold at bay. She reached behind her to tug at her laces, but the salt-encrusted ribbons wouldn't move.

"I need your help. The laces are stuck. If you can get me free, I can peel it off on my own. I'll wrap the plaid," Elene dropped Liam's spare plaid on the bed, "around me and come out then. If I can get my feet warm..."

Liam turned Elene as she talked and fumbled with the knot. But it wouldn't budge, not even when he used the tip of his *sgian dubh* to loosen it. "Do you think your aunt has extra laces? Unless you bathe with your gown on, I can't get the ties undone with all the salt and sand."

"We'll figure it out. Someone is bound to. Cut them if you must." Elene shivered as she felt warm air brush against her back as Liam's dirk severed the ribbons. She shuddered, unprepared for the feel of his soft lips against her bare shoulder. He wrapped one arm around her waist as she felt him putting away his knife. The hand now free of the blade pulled the gown down her left shoulder. He kissed her neck as his arm tightened around her waist.

"I need to walk away, Elene. If I keep touching you, if I see more of you, I won't let go ever again."

"I don't want you to," Elene confessed, her emotions as bare as Liam's.

"As much as I want you, I need you to get warm and eat something hot. I fear you shall fall ill soon." Liam loosened his hold around her waist, but her hands gripped his forearm. She turned in his embrace. She cupped his face and raised onto her toes, finally feeling like she wouldn't turn into an icicle. She knew it was the heat from Liam's massive frame pressed against her as well as the heat stirring low in her belly, her arousal finally chasing away the chill.

"Thank you, Liam. Thank you for saving me, for saving my brother and sister. Thank you for being honorable when it's the last thing I want. I—" Elene stopped herself before she blurted out her feelings. This wasn't the moment, not the place, and not the time.

"We shall talk tonight." Liam pressed a soft kiss to her lips before stepping past her and into the croft's main room. He knew Ilka had heard at least parts of their conversation, despite how she pretended to ignore them. He stood outside the curtain, just as he promised. Johan and Katryne sat huddled together, chattering about their adventure, as only children could now that they were safe. He watched Albert arrive with buckets of water. "Elene, I'm going to help Albert with the buckets. I'm still here."

"All right." Elene emerged with Liam's plaid wrapped around her, her bare shoulder peeking from beneath the wool. Liam's already-turgid length twitched as his eyes devoured her. He knew what she looked like and felt like beneath the blanket. He wanted nothing more than to press her beneath him and sink into her. He would warm her as he made love to her.

Liam dragged himself away, but he kept his eyes on Elene until ensuring he didn't scorch his hands forced him to look at the buckets and fire. He helped Albert hang them on the swinging metal arm that held the containers over the flame. Next, he moved the tub before the fire. Once set up, he and Albert dumped the buckets into the wood and copper barrel. Liam had a moment's worry that Elene wouldn't want to step into another large cask, but she came and dipped her fingers in.

"Albert and I will step outside. I'll be just past the

door. My men will be here soon. I'm certain the chieftain will have questions." Liam offered Elene a reassuring smile. She stepped close to him, her forehead resting against his chest as he rubbed a hand over her back.

"Please tell them we're married," Elene whispered. "Others on the island believe we are. And I don't know whether any of them will force me back to my mother if they find out we aren't."

"If that's what you wish. But no one is taking you from me, and no one is forcing you to go anywhere you don't want."

"Thank you." Elene kissed his neck before stepping back. Liam nodded to Ilka, who unabashedly watched the couple. She'd shooed Johan and Katryne to the table and gave them bowls of pottage. Elene wouldn't linger in the bath, knowing her siblings needed to use the water while it was warm. Even though they had fresh clothes to warm them, they still needed to wash the seawater from them. She stepped into the tub and hurried to run the soap and linen over her body. As her hand passed along her netherlips, temptation nipped at her to relieve the ache Liam created, but she wouldn't dare do something so personal where others could see. She slid under the water, wetting her hair and shaking out some of the sand. When she emerged, she hurried to lather and scrub her locks.

Ilka stepped behind the tub just before Elene reached for the bucket of clean water. Elene leaned forward as Ilka gently poured the water over her head and down her back, washing the suds from the golden tresses.

"Thank you, Auntie Ilka. I know you're wondering why we're here, and why we're a soggy, bedraggled mess."

"The thought had crossed my mind. My guess is it

has something to do with that Norse trader your mother took up with." Ilka's astute eyes bore into Elene's as the younger woman looked over her shoulder at her great-aunt.

"It does. He threatened to sell me when I rejected him."

"And the Highlander? Who's he?"

"The Earl of Sinclair and Orkney's grandson. His name is Liam Mackay."

"You called him your husband, but he seems rather uncertain about that title."

"He's—I'm—" Elene stumbled over her words. "He's promised to take me to Scotland. He says Johan, Katryne, and I can start new lives among his people. But while we're still in Orkney, it seems best to say I'm traveling with my husband. Naught untoward has happened."

"Yet. The way the two of you look at one another is likely to send the entire village up in flames."

Elene flinched, causing Ilka's brow to furrow. "We were in Dingieshowe a few days ago. Gunter was there and saw me. Liam, the chieftain, and the man's wife hid me. When Gunter didn't get what he wanted, he lit their croft on fire and nearly burned Ninian, Sonneta, and me alive. They lost their home because of me."

"Ninian and Sonneta?" Ilka's face reflected her sadness. "They are good people. She's my second cousin once removed."

"I had no idea. She never said we're family. She knew my surname."

"I don't know why she didn't say aught, but it doesn't surprise me she helped you and your Highlander. Ninian has always been on good terms with the Mackays and Sinclairs, and you're my grandniece. Between those two things, they wouldn't consider turning you away. I will visit them and take them what I can."

Ilka held a drying linen up for Elene as she stepped out of the tub. Elene toweled herself dry before wrapping it around her hair. Ilka handed her the dry clothes, which Elene rushed to don. With a comb in hand, Elene worked the tangles from her hair as she listened to Ilka tell Katryne to take the next bath.

"It's clear you desire one another, but you're not married. The way he speaks to you, it's clear the man loves you. But you didn't say aught about being his wife once you're in Scotland."

"I don't know that he loves me, Auntie. But we're fond of one another."

"Fond," Ilka snorted. "If you say so. You love him as much as he loves you. I'm not so old that I can't see that."

"He's Clan Mackay's tánaiste, and I'm a farmer's daughter from a tiny northern isle. He doesn't strike me as a man to take a mistress. We are naught but a passing fancy to each other."

"You can tell yourself that lie to protect your heart, but we both know it isn't true."

"Whether I'm right or wrong matters little, until I know Katryne and Johan are safe in Scotland. That's what matters most. I don't trust Gunter not to abuse them or sell them like he threatened to do to me."

"The Norse don't have thralls anymore," Ilka argued.

"He's the king's brother. He can do as he pleases." Elene glanced at Katryne, who hummed to herself as she bathed. "He might sell them or kill them, but he won't keep them as his stepchildren now. And if he doesn't kill us all, then he'll most certainly sell me as a bed slave. Christian or not, he holds a grudge."

A knock cut their conversation short. Ilka opened the door a crack, protecting Katryne's privacy. Liam turned his back but spoke over his shoulder.

"Elene, the chieftain wishes to see us. Are you up to it?"

"Yes. I feel much better now."

"No," Ilka cut in. "Donovan can wait until after Elene's eaten. She may feel perkier, but she needs some sustenance. I'm guessing you and your men do, too. Katryne, don't dawdle, lass."

Elene smiled as Liam turned his head. She nodded, hoping he saw her. She hurried to help her sister finish her bath. Once Johan was in the tub and Katryne was presentable, the Highlanders entered. Ilka shooed them to spots around her table, bowls already placed before them. Smelling the pottage, Johan was quick to bathe. Soon the Highlanders and Elene, along with her siblings, were eating the hearty stew. Elene didn't realize how famished she was until Liam filled her bowl a third time. She grinned, then made her way through most of her extra serving.

"Ilka." A man's voice sounded on the other side of the door.

"Enter, Donovan." A blond man bearing a striking resemblance to Elene and her siblings entered. Liam aimed to appear relaxed, but his hand slid to the dirk in his right boot. He hadn't met the man yet, only heard that the chieftain wished to see them. It surprised him how young this chieftain was. Liam didn't recall ever meeting him during his many previous visits, but then he'd never been to Isbister before.

Elene rose from her seat and hurried to the chieftain, who opened his arms to her. She smiled as they embraced. The man dropped a kiss on Elene's head as he rubbed her arms. Liam watched. He waited for the jealousy, but it never came. Instead, hurt clamped his heart as he waited for Elene to remember him. He wondered if the man was married and if it would be safer for Elene to remain with someone who she clearly trusted. It was obvious the man was strong enough to protect her. The sword he wore strapped to his back wasn't for show.

"Don, I'd like you to meet my husband, Liam." Elene wrapped her arm around the chieftain's arm and pulled him to the table. Liam rose, his gaze locked with Elene's. When she beamed at him and released Donovan's arm to stand next to him, Liam extended his arm to the young chieftain. The Orcadian assessed Liam, but didn't hesitate to grasp forearms in a warrior's handshake.

"You didn't invite me to your wedding. You promised you would." There was a teasing lilt to Donovan's voice that eased some of the tightness in Liam's chest.

"We were children."

"And you swore you'd never marry. You promised to invite me if hell froze, and you wed."

"It was a quiet affair. I wasn't interested in a large feast." Elene wrapped her arms around Liam's middle, praying he would play along. As he pulled her against his side and stroked her shoulder, she knew she never should have worried Liam would give them away. He'd been the one to suggest they pretend to be married in the first place. The more she called him her husband, the more she wished it could be true.

"It's nice to meet you," Liam said as a greeting. His voice rumbled through his chest and against Elene's cheek. She closed her eyes, not realizing she sighed contentedly until Liam kissed her forehead. "Do you need to rest, *mo ghràidh?*"

"No. I'm still tired, but I'd like to visit with my family." Elene lifted her head and gestured for Donovan to join them. Liam gave up his seat for Elene, and Donovan sat where she'd been before he arrived. Liam stood behind her, one hand resting on her shoulder, when he felt her tense because she couldn't see him. "Donovan is a cousin of some sort through my father's mother. We used to play together when my family visited when I was little. Then we'd see each other when I came fishing with my father. It's been a few years."

"I've been away hunting the last two times you came. What brings you here now? The village is abuzz about your husband carrying you here. Another man carried Johan and Katryne. People said you were soaking wet."

"Johan and I didn't listen when Liam warned us not to lean too far over the curragh side," Katryne cut in. Her face showed an appropriate amount of remorse, making her lie sound remarkably truthful. "Elene jumped in to get us before Liam could pull us out. He had to rescue all three of us."

"It was my fault," Johan added. "I saw a fish so close to the surface, I bet Katryne I could grab it, and she couldn't."

Elene watched her brother and sister as they lied with ease. Her heart broke, knowing they were so adept from telling their mother fibs to keep the unpredictable woman from losing her temper. She prayed Liam and his men hadn't concocted some other story and already told someone.

"And will you listen to me next time?" Liam asked. "You gave your sister and me a horrible scare." Liam's thumb rubbed along Elene's nape, the sensation soothing.

"We're sorry," Johan and Katryne said together. Elene turned her attention back to Donovan, who watched Liam. She wished to see Liam's expression, but she had to trust that everything was all right.

"How long will you stay?" Donovan asked, changing the subject.

"We leave in the morning," Liam answered. "My

193

family expects us back in less than a sennight."

"We didn't plan this stop, but it's good to see you." Elene offered a warm smile, hoping it made their story even more plausible.

"I'm glad I stopped by." Donovan rose from the table. His gazed bored into Liam as he canted his head to toward the door. Elene rose, but Liam stopped her from moving away from the table. He pressed a soft kiss to her lips and tucked hair behind her ear.

"All will be well," he murmured against her mouth. She pressed her own kiss to him before turning to clear the table.

Liam followed Donovan outside, Dermot two steps behind. Donovan raised a questioning eyebrow when he noticed Dermot. Neither Liam nor Dermot appeared to notice. Donovan crossed his arms and waited. Liam offered him an obliging smile but remained silent. The men stared at one another until Donovan released his arms.

"We'll be here all night, and my wife will have my arse if I keep her waiting to serve the midday meal." Donovan glanced at Ilka's croft. "Gunter Haakonsson was here yesterday. Demanded to know where Elene was. He threatened to raze the village if we didn't turn her over. He never said why he searched for her, but almost everyone in the village heard him bellowing. Whether or not you're her husband, I don't care. It's not my business. I just need to know you will get her far from here. I can only imagine what her mother's got them embroiled in. But I know her father would be livid if he thought that Norseman had any claim on his daughter."

"Elene and the others are coming to Dunbeath with me."

Donovan's eyes narrowed, but he said nothing more. Liam knew Donovan was aware Varrich was his home, not Dunbeath. But the chieftain didn't question him about why he didn't say whether Elene would accompany him home. "Leave before dawn. I will send my fishermen with you. They can sail west until you get to the end of South Ronaldsay. Then you must make the crossing alone."

"Thank you." Liam thrust out his arm again. "He will never see her again."

Donovan accepted his forearm and nodded. "Take care of her. I've never seen her so at ease with anyone as she is with you." The chieftain didn't wait for Liam to respond, instead turning on his heel and walking toward his own croft. Liam turned to Dermot, who grinned at him.

"I've told ye that ye belong with the lass. Her great-aunt has told ye. He's told ye." Dermot gestured to Donovan's back, having understood much of the conversation. "I bet Ninian would if he didna already. Dinna be daft. Marry the lass for real."

Liam refused to tell Dermot anything before he spoke to Elene. He would share none of his feelings with someone else. He reached for the door and ushered Dermot inside. They passed the rest of the afternoon with the men cleaning and sharpening their weapons. Katryne and Johan convinced Elene to let them play with other children in the village, so Elene sat outside, topping and tailing green beans with Ilka.

After the evening meal, the men posted three at a time on watch outside the croft. The others found places to bed down in the barn behind Ilka's croft. None cared about the cow's low mooing or the chickens clucking. They were too exhausted to notice. Ilka retired to her bed while Katryne and Johan made their beds near where Liam spread his bedroll. Elene tucked her siblings in, and they were both asleep before Elene slid beneath the blankets beside Liam.

CHAPTER 14

$\mathcal{E}$lene and Liam lay among the sleeping family, covered with his spare plaid. He stroked back a blonde lock and tucked it behind her ear. His hand cupped her cheek as he feathered a kiss on her forehead. They remained quiet until they were certain Ilka, Katryne, and Johan were all deeply asleep.

"There is so much to tell you," Elene whispered. Regret, fear, shame, and guilt swirled within her. She wanted to spend the night in Liam's arms, sharing kisses and touches. But she knew they needed to talk. He'd said as much earlier. But while she feared he would run for his boats once she told him her story, she no longer wanted to keep it to herself. "We could have all died today. Yet again, you and your men risked your lives for me. Liam, you deserve to know the whole truth about why Gunter is so persistent. I need you to know before I can go to Scotland with you, before we..."

"Elene, tell me your story, but only if you want to. I don't expect aught from you. I want to know, but I won't hold your past against you." Liam settled his hand on her waist as she scooted closer. With a steadying breath, Elene began her story.

"Gunter arrived a year ago after being gone for probably five or six years. I was too young to notice him back then, and he took no interest in me. But when he came back, I was a woman. It wasn't long before we sat together at meals, and he invited me to walk in the evening. We talked about all sorts of things: our childhoods, our families, what we thought about life. He stayed a few sennights, traveling to the other isles during the day, but returning to Skaill most nights. After a fortnight of walking together, we shared our first kiss. At least, it was my first kiss. We said how much we missed each other. We talked about how we wished we never had to part. It was Gunter who brought up a future together. He described a life that sounded perfect. But I questioned often how a peasant farmer's daughter could ever share a life with a prince. It seemed too wild to believe. But he was persistent."

Elene gazed into Liam's eyes, completely at ease sharing her past. His hand stroked her hair again as the arm beneath her neck pressed against her back, drawing her closer. As she shifted her head, finding a more comfortable position against his shoulder, his hand returned to her waist. He spread his fingers wide, stretching to cover her hip, too. Elene could have interpreted it as a possessive gesture. Instead, it felt more reassuring than anything he could say.

"He sailed to Shetland for a fortnight and was so excited to see me when he returned. I'd pined for him. When we went for a walk the night he returned, we shared more than kisses, but I remained a maiden." Elene's gaze dropped.

"I know you are. But I wouldn't care if you weren't. We didn't know each other then, and our cultures are different enough that we don't share the same ideas about women being maidens when they marry. I know that isn't the Norse way."

197

"But it isn't our way," Elene corrected. "We Orcadians do value a woman being a maiden on her wedding night."

"I still wouldn't care."

Elene exhaled a puff of air. She doubted Liam would feel that way if she weren't. She doubted they'd be lying together if she wasn't.

"I wouldn't." Liam brushed a soft kiss against her lips. "I was wrong about my impression, and now I know. But the first time we kissed, I knew you'd had some practice. I thought you weren't an innocent, and I realized I didn't care. It was only later when you told me, then the first time I touched you, that I knew you were still a virgin. Whatever draws me to you is far stronger than any maidenhead."

Elene heard the conviction in Liam's voice and recognized the steadfastness in his gaze. She'd met no man who would say and believe such. Feeling more assured, she continued. "The way Gunter talked to me that night, I thought he meant he wanted me to marry him. He talked about coming back to Norway with him and the life we could build with a family. It still seemed outrageous that a member of the royal family would consider someone so far beneath him, but he was so convincing. I told him I had to think about it."

Elene hadn't noticed that she'd fisted Liam's leine where her hand rested at his waist. But her fingers cramped, and she realized she'd grabbed hold as her anger and regret grew.

"Two days later, a dragon boat arrived with a message for Gunter. I was returning from hunting and curious about the excitement. As I walked up, I realized it was a messenger. I understand enough Norse to follow most conversations. The man announced Gunter had another son, a bairn born a sennight earlier. I thought my heart stopped. *Another.* He already had a child. One that sounded like he acknowledged and a new one that he was excited for. I told myself that plenty of men had mistresses, and perhaps he would even give her up once we wed. I told myself I would accept any of his bastards since they were children, and no one chooses their parents."

Elene's grimace made it clear she thought of her own mother.

"I can't imagine that shock," Liam whispered.

"Oh, it gets far worse. I walked up to the group to congratulate Gunter on becoming a father again. One of his men asked if I would be next, and they all laughed. I said not until we married. It was with those words, my world shattered. A warrior woman cackled. It wasn't a laugh. It was definitely a cackle. She said Gunter doesn't believe in marrying more than one woman, and she was already his wife. All I could do was stare. I tried to sort through everything. Gunter was already married. His wife clearly didn't care if he had mistresses. He didn't mean to marry me but make me his mistress. And it sounded as though he had more than one."

Elene sighed a shuddering breath. Liam's soft kiss reassured her that he wasn't judging her as she feared. His slight nod encouraged her to continue.

"I looked at Gunter and dropped my catches—I remember there were three squirrels and a rabbit—and asked him what he'd planned for me. He laughed and said that as a free woman, I would be his concubine. I thought my head would explode. I asked how many he already had and what that meant for me. He shrugged and said that he had five. One had died three months earlier, and he allowed another to marry. He had seven children among those five remaining women, at least that's how many he knew for sure and acknowledged. He said I would live among these women and work within the village. He said he would visit me when he wanted me. Then he shrugged again. I knew before he explained that I would never go to Norway with him, but I needed to know. I needed to know just how stupid I'd been to believe a prince would marry me."

"You weren't stupid. You were naive and manipulated," Liam corrected.

"I felt stupid. And in front of his people, all who realized I thought he meant to marry me, he humiliated me. They laughed at me. Disappointment, shame, and embarrassment brought out my temper. I remember so clearly how I felt and what I said."

Elene's lips flattened, then pursed as her brow furrowed. Liam watched the anger return as her eyes narrowed.

"I told him, 'Since you have so many women already, it's not worth me traveling so far to share a man with a small prick. Had you made me a princess, I might have put up with the disappointment, but I couldn't be bothered now.' I stunned everyone, including myself. I spun around and marched away, but I made it a few feet before he grabbed my arm and dragged me across the village to my fields. I thought he would beat me. I thought he would kill me. I remember what he said, too."

Elene closed her eyes, taking a slow, even breath. When she opened them, she looked beyond Liam's shoulder and into the fireplace.

"He said, 'You will never embarrass me like that again and live. You are coming back to Norway, but I'm selling you. You'll come as my bed slave, and I'll fuck you until you scream in agony that you can't take my prick anymore. Then I will sell you to the oldest, cruelest man I can find who will beat you and force you every night until he dies. Then you will be passed to his sons. If I choose to, I will find you whenever I want, and I will remind you just how big my prick is.'"

Liam's hand that stroked Elene's hair froze. Shock immobilized him. He'd known something passed between Elene and Gunter that was severe enough to make her believe the Norseman intended to sell her. He hadn't imagined the threats Gunter made, but he believed every one.

"This happened a year ago, and you're still here?"

"Androw and Janet hid me when it was time for the Norse to leave. Gunter was too furious with me to stay near me, so he'd left me in the field that day. I avoided him when I could, and he believed I couldn't get away from him. When he couldn't find me, it forced him to abandon his plan at the time. He had to catch the tide because his brother expected him home by a certain day. When he came back three moons later, he pursued my mother. He cares naught for her. He did it to hurt me to, to scare me into submission. He knew that if he took my mother, that meant taking Katryne and Johan. He knew I wouldn't let them go. I knew he hadn't changed his mind about me. He just added to my punishment."

"And you didn't go then?"

Elene shook her head. "He couldn't take us. He was going to Shetland, then back to Norway, but not to his home. He couldn't feed us and house us. He knew that. He knew it would torment me, leave me terrified of when it would happen. He's done that thrice so far. But this time, I know he meant to take us. The only reason I considered leaving Katryne and Johan behind was because he'd said he would raise them as his own just to make me suffer. My mother either doesn't understand or doesn't care that he already has a wife and five women he swives. The Norse rarely trade slaves anymore, so I didn't fear my brother and sister being sold to retaliate if I escaped. I've heard enough over the years to know that people oppose buying children in particular. But now—now I know he can never get near any of us. Now I fear he would kill them before my eyes."

"With a noble wife to bear him legitimate heirs, and sons he already acknowledges, it wouldn't matter if he took a second wife. But I thought they ended that practice ages ago when they learned that Christ is our Savior."

"My mother will never marry him. She'll be another concubine." Elene shrugged a shoulder. "Who knows? Mayhap there'll be some type of ceremony, and she'll become his favored leman, but I doubt it. His true wife said it herself. Gunter would never have two wives."

"If Androw and Janet helped you the first time, why were they willing to let him take you now?"

"Because Gunter found out a few months ago that they hid me. He threatened to end all trade with our village and to ban other villages from trading with us. Androw can't afford that, and I would never accept that. We know Gunter believed someone hid me this time, but Katryne knew I left. I didn't tell her how or where I was going before I hid in the wagon. I haven't had a chance to ask her what she said to them."

"Do you think she told them you ran away?"

"If she had, she would say I went toward Shetland."

"That still wouldn't have given you much time before Gunter started searching."

"That's why I hid on your wagon and planned to stay hidden until we reached Mainland. You know I intended to find a way to sail to Scotland. I would get lost among the hills there. There are fishing ships that travel to Scotland all the time. Even if Gunter guessed I left Orkney first, he would still be a day or two behind me. I would have set sail already."

"And you believed the coin you carry would have kept you safe aboard a ship with only men? You don't speak Gaelic, but your Norn is enough to make Scots passable. You would have to get yourself to the Lowlands, then find somewhere to live, to work."

"As far as anyone needed to know, I was a widow who lost her husband and infant to a fever. I left Orkney because I couldn't manage the farm myself. I came to Scotland to find work because there was none at home. And I can speak Scots." Elene relayed the plan she'd devised months ago.

"There is so much that could have gone wrong. But I admire your courage, and I understand your choices."

"You don't think me a fool?"

"Never. I still think you're naive, but I don't think you're a fool. I think you're desperate and resourceful." Liam knew what he wanted as he leaned in for a tender kiss. When they drew apart, he offered her a gentle smile. "I've already told you I'll take you to Dunbeath if you want. My family will welcome you and protect you. But I want you to come to Varrich with me as my wife. I want to marry you, Elene. I want you beside me as my partner. I love you."

Elene's eyes grew misty as she nodded. She forced the words around the lump in her throat. "Yes. I love you, too. I never believed I would find a man I would love. Not after being played false by Gunter. I just wanted to survive, and I knew that meant I might have to marry. But I want to marry you because I love you."

"I told you that day in the stables when I found you that I didn't trust you. That wasn't right. I shouldn't have said it like that. I didn't trust you to stay and talk to me, but I've always trusted you. I know you've said yes, but I need you to think about it longer. One day I will be laird, and you would be our clan's lady. That comes with duties that I don't doubt you can manage.

Those strengths you'll need are the ones that make me love you and why I know you're the right woman to take to wife. But I want you to think about whether being the lady of a clan is what you want. If you marry me, then you accept not just me but that role."

"Would your clan accept me? Accept my brother and sister?"

"I wouldn't ask you to come to Varrich with me if I doubted my clan would accept all of you. I wouldn't ask you to take such a position if I thought my clan would reject you. I couldn't do that to you or to them, not as your husband and not as their leader."

"What would my life be like?"

"Busy." Liam grinned. "My mother will help you learn, and she will probably outlive us all. She's that stubborn. But when you would become the clan's lady, you would manage the servants and the keep. That means making sure the meals are planned, the servants attend to their duties, the larder is full, the ledgers are balanced, that everyone in the village has enough food and what they need within their homes. Their crofts will be my responsibility. You would be in charge when I ride out. If there's a raid, which there hasn't been in my lifetime but might be when the leadership passes to me and others wish to test me, you ensure all our people are safely hidden or locked in the keep." Liam knew he'd rattled off an overwhelming list. He drew her closer to whisper in her ear. "And at night, you'd let me make love to you in every way we can imagine."

"Let you?"

Liam chuckled. "That's all you got from what I just said. Of course let me. It's not my decision alone when we couple." Liam leaned back and cupped her face once more. "You will always have a say. If you don't wish to couple, then you tell me and that's the end. I won't question you, and I will never force you. Your body is your own to control, Elene. I wish to share pleasure with you and show you affection, but I do not own it or you."

"I don't know if I know any men like you."

Liam grinned again. "You will soon enough. There's my father, of course. Then my grandfather, Uncle Callum, Uncle Alex, Uncle Tavish, Uncle Magnus, and my brothers and my cousins. My father believes what my grandfather does and taught my uncles. It's why my grandfather agreed to let my parents marry. They believe in respecting their wives as their own person, to rely on them and trust them, to depend on them, and to cherish them. You are my equal in all things, Elene. It's the only way we can be strong leaders for our clan, and it's the only type of marriage I can have."

"You are the most remarkable man I've ever met. Though I think the other men in your family shall rather mesmerize me." Elene offered him a saucy grin, which earned her bottom a light pinch.

"Elene, I do not exaggerate when I say my family will accept you. They'll adore you because you're so much like the women in my family. You're independent, resilient, intelligent—" Liam rubbed his nose against hers "—and patient as the day is long if you're willing to put up with me. My mother and all my aunts are like that. That's how they and my uncles and my father are raising the lasses. Some of my cousins are shyer than others, but they will all be women a laird, or a farmer husband, can rely on to help build a home and a family that can survive any challenge. That's just the way of the Mackays and Sinclairs."

As Elene listened to Liam, his tone was so matter-of-fact that she knew what he shared was the truth. He sounded as though no other way was plausible, even imaginable, to him. She knew something deeply entrenched these values in who he was and the man he would be. She'd felt safe with him since the moment they met. She knew he would protect and respect her body, and she'd had faith that he could help her escape. But she realized she felt confident entrusting him with her future and her happiness. She knew he would never take for granted her love and her devotion. She'd never felt more precious than she did at that moment. He gave her something so perfect, something no one else ever had. He gave her hope. He'd done it before, and he did it once more.

"All of what you say is daunting. The duties you listed and the bond within your family. But I'm not scared. Not as long as you're there to help me learn and to stand by me as I adjust. I've done all those tasks before, but not with so many people depending on me. The only one that worries me are the ledgers. Liam, I can't read or write. I can do sums in my head, but I've never written a number." Embarrassment flooded Elene as she admitted her shortcoming.

"Elene, I had to learn those things. So did my mother and father. We may have learned them as children, but we weren't born knowing how to read and write. If you wish to learn, then we can teach you. I know you aren't of noble birth. I confess that worried me because I felt obligated to bring an alliance to my family. But it was stupid of me to harbor that doubt for even a moment. My family believes in love matches, not matching up clans. They believe a laird and lady who love one another are what strengthens a clan because it makes them indomitable allies. It's not the clans they come from, but the bond they form. I've met noblewomen, and none of them inspired confidence that I'd found the woman to lead beside me. And none made me happy. Only you do."

"If you believe I can learn these things, and you believe I can help you lead, then I wish to be your wife. I don't want you to regret your choice or ruin your life because I fail as your clan's lady. I believe you love me, and I know I love you. But I understand that duty can't be ignored either. As a nobleman, your life isn't entirely your own." Elene flicked her tongue against his lips before they exchanged a loving kiss. "I want to marry you and be at your side for the rest of our lives."

Liam rolled Elene onto her back, and both her hands came to cup his face as his right hand rested against her neck. Their kiss reflected their joy and the promise of a future together. As it drew on and their bodies pressed together, passion sparked. Elene's hand roamed over Liam's back and down to his buttocks while he cupped and kneaded her breast. His hand slid down to bunch the fabric of her skirts and draw it high enough for his hand to graze her thigh as she pressed her bent knee against his hip. It trailed along her leg until it reached her backside.

"Do we dare?" Elene whispered.

"The others are sleeping, and the guard changed ten minutes ago." As they gazed at one another, they were in silent mutual agreement that they wouldn't couple, but they would bring each other pleasure. Elene's hand dipped beneath Liam's plaid and wrapped around his turgid manhood. Liam's breath caught, the sensation nearly overwhelming. He slipped his fingers along her mons until he pressed them between her netherlips. Her dew coated his digits, making it easier to glide his finger over her pearl before he rubbed steady circles. Elene's free hand grasped his shoulder, her fingers digging into his muscle as her urgency grew. Liam couldn't keep his hips from thrusting into her hand.

"I love you, *leannan*." Liam's kiss swallowed Elene's moan as she came apart in Liam's arms, her body tensing, then shuddering.

"I love you, *me jarta.*" At Liam's confused expression, Elene's face softened. "My heart."

Liam felt like his heart and his bollocks might explode. He gave one more thrust as Elene stroked his length twice more, and his climax washed over him. He buried his face against her shoulder as he felt his seed pour forth. He inhaled deeply before raising his head and sharing another kiss. As they shifted apart, Liam pulled a corner of his spare plaid to wipe the evidence of his release from Elene's bare belly and thigh.

"One day soon..." Elene nodded, reading Liam's mind. They both thought about when they could join and find their release together, knowing Liam's seed might take root to start their own family. She pushed down her skirts as Liam adjusted the plaid they used as a blanket. It was only a few moments later that they were both asleep, nestled in one another's arms.

It was early afternoon, the day after they arrived at Isbister. The sun was high overhead, and the trip of South Ronaldsay was behind them. They'd boarded the birlinns before dawn, just as Donovan advised. The Isbister village fishermen had accompanied them until this point, but they'd just turned back as Liam's birlinns entered the open water of the North Sea. The distance they would traverse was among some of the choppiest and roughest water around the British Isles.

Liam deferred to Dermot and Alfred, trusting his captains far more than he trusted himself to get them safely back to Scotland. If the weather held, the sea cooperated, and the wind was in their favor, it would take them a day to sail through the perilous pass. If Mother Nature held a different plan, it could take them two or more days to battle the waves and current.

Liam watched the western horizon as they moved into the open channel. The wind favored them, so Dermot had no one rowing. Liam glanced at Alfred's boat, finding the captain at the tiller as men sat around the deck. He turned his attention to Elene, beaming at her as he approached. There'd been no time to talk since they woke, but she'd leaned against him when he slipped his hand into hers while they said their good-byes to Ilka. She'd stood beside him as he talked to Dermot about their plans before the sea captain relayed the directions to his partner on the other birlinn.

Now Liam squeezed beside Elene, teasing Johan as he pushed his hip against the boy's, making room for himself. Johan offered a half-gnawed apple to Liam, which he politely declined. He passed the waterskin to Katryne before he leaned to whisper in Elene's ear.

"If we cannot convince the priest to marry us sooner than three sennights, would you consider a handfast?"

"Would we still marry after the banns post?"

"Of course. I've grown too used to hearing you call me husband, and I'm too eager to call you my wife. I'm not giving that up after a year and a day."

"You're like a bairn on his saint's day," Elene laughed.

"And I have a special new toy I'd very much like to play with." Liam waggled his brow before he grew serious. "If you'd prefer to wait, then you need only to tell me."

Elene's sapphire eyes met Liam's. She saw the hint of nervousness in his gaze, even though his voice sounded confident. She tangled her hand in his hair and pressed his head forward. She swiped her tongue across his lips and flicked the tip until he opened to her. He fought to stifle his groan as she teased him, her tongue slipping into his mouth, then retreating. When he followed her, lured by the taste of the tart apple she'd eaten, she sucked on his tongue. He nearly carried her to the nearest bulkhead to thrust into her. She pulled away, grinning.

"Do you think I wish to wait?"

"By the saints, how I love you."

"I love you."

"Are you really going to be our brother?" Katryne interrupted.

Liam hadn't considered how Katryne or Johan would feel about joining his family, or rather, him joining theirs.

"Would you accept me as part of your family?" Liam asked solemnly.

"Yes!" Johan answered, as Katryne grinned and nodded. "I've always wanted a brother."

"Am I such a horrible sister?" Elene teased.

"You're not, but she—" Johan stuck his tongue out at Katryne, who cast him a snide look. The children giggled, unable to remain serious about their disinterest in one another.

"If you allow me to join your family, then you will also gain two other older brothers and another older sister."

"Another sister, and more brothers?" Katryne chirped.

"Aye. My brothers and sister are closer to my age and Elene's. My sister will be happy not to be the youngest anymore." Liam grinned.

"Would they let me train with you?" Johan asked earnestly.

"We would have to ask my father first. He's the laird." Liam wrapped his arm around Johan's shoulders as the boy's face fell. "But I'm certain he would be proud to have another warrior-in-training. And remember, my family will help you learn Gaelic and

Scots. It will take time for you to learn, but you will be welcome members of our clan."

Elene rested her head against Liam's shoulder as she listened to her siblings and Liam talk. She realized she felt content for the first time in years. She closed her eyes as their conversation carried on around her, filling her heart to near-busting. When there was finally a lull, she tilted her head back and looked up at Liam.

"I love you," Liam whispered.

"I love you just as much." Elene rested her forehead against his neck, but a wave jarred the ship's hull. She bit her tongue, unprepared for the sudden roughness beneath them. She scrambled to her feet as the others rose. She looked toward the west, shocked at the waves before them. She'd never seen the open expanse that led to Scotland; she'd only heard that the waters could be rough. What lay before them appeared like a squall, but there was no rain. Only bright sunlight and a churning sea.

"Come," Liam said as he took her hand. He led the three Isbisters to a somewhat-sheltered spot in the stern. "Stay here together. The wind is in our favor, so we should still make progress despite the waves."

Liam's prediction was correct. They crossed the North Sea and spotted land just before nightfall. Katryne and Johan stood before them as Liam's arm encircled Elene's waist as the Isbisters caught their first sight of Scotland, with Castle Dunbeath looming on the promontory. As they sailed into the natural harbor, bells tolled, announcing their arrival. Elene watched as a group of riders came to the edge of a cliff. It was a woman who dismounted first. Elene could barely see the woman in the nearing twilight, but she could tell the woman lifted her skirts and ran down the steep decline to the beach.

"Mama," Liam chuckled. As the boat nudged the

sandy shore, Elene could make out more of the woman's features. Her dark hair lifted in the wind behind her. It surprised Elene how fast the woman ran across the sand. She was so distracted that she nearly didn't notice the beast of a man following her. Liam called out, "Da."

Trepidation crashed down on Elene as she realized her introduction to Liam's family was imminent. She looked past the couple and saw a man following Liam's parents. Just behind him were four couples.

"They're all here," Elene whispered.

"I know, *leannan*. Don't worry. All will be right soon enough. You're safe now."

Dermot removed the rail and placed the ramp down. Liam urged Johan and Katryne to go ahead of them. He helped Elene until they were on solid ground, his fingers entwined with hers.

"Liam!" Mairghread Mackay opened her arms to her firstborn. Without releasing Elene's hand, he engulfed his petite mother in an embrace that lifted her off her feet. She peppered him with kisses before she leaned back and looked at Elene.

"Liam," a deep bass followed Mairghread's greeting. Tristan Mackay pulled his son into his arms, nearly squashing Mairghread in the middle. She thumped on her husband's and son's chests, giggling as she did so.

"Dinna be rude," Mairghread said in Gaelic as she squeezed out from between the men. She looked at Elene once more and switched to Norn. "Welcome to Dunbeath."

"Thank you, my lady." Elene attempted a wobbly curtsy, not yet feeling steady on ground that didn't rock beneath her feet.

"Mama, Da," Liam turned to his parents but waited as his extended family approached, his uncles and grandfather carrying torches. He opened his mouth, but snapped it shut as Liam Sinclair, his grandfather, stepped forward.

"Elene Isbister?" Liam the Older asked.

"Yes." Elene attempted another curtsy, this one steadier. She looked at the older man, something niggling at her memory. She glanced up at Liam the Younger, who wrapped his arm around her waist.

"Do you know my betrothed, Grandda?" Liam waited for the inevitable hum of questions, but none came. He looked at his grandfather, then his parents, and finally his four uncles and four aunts.

"I do, Wee Liam," Liam Sinclair answered, reverting to the moniker given to his grandson upon his birth to keep everyone from confusing the two. "I knew her father from when he was a lad. I haven't seen him in decades. How is he?"

"My father died several years ago, my laird." Elene prayed she addressed him properly.

"My grandson says you're his betrothed. If that's so, then it's Liam, lass. Mayhap one day even Grandda." With that, Elene realized he'd officially welcomed her into the family.

Mairghread stepped forward. "I remember your father, too. He was the same age as Alex." Mairghread turned and pointed to a man behind her. "You look so much like him. I knew who you were before Da said your name. He was a dear friend to all of us, and now his daughter is to be my daughter-by-marriage." Mairghread tentatively opened her arms to Elene, who hesitantly leaned forward. When the older woman closed her arms around Elene, the younger woman had a sudden sense that she'd finally found the mother she'd craved since childhood. She couldn't explain why she felt such comfort among the Sinclairs and Mackays, but it was instinctual to trust them.

"Thank you, my lady," Elene whispered.

"It's Mairghread, *nighean*." Mairghread leaned back and smiled. "It means daughter."

Elene's eyes welled with tears as she swallowed the lump in her throat. She could only nod. She looked toward Liam, and he could tell everything overwhelmed her. He eased her against his side as he nodded to his parents. They understood and made space for the couple to pass. The Sinclair men had already made their way to the village and their families. Dermot followed behind the men, leaving only the lairds' families on the beach.

Liam encouraged Katryne and Johan to go ahead of them, starting the trek up the cliff. He watched his aunts smile at Elene while his uncles grinned at him and elbowed one another. However, their mirth was short-lived when their wives swatted at them and pushed them toward the path. It surprised Elene to find a spare horse waiting for them. She was further shocked when a man lifted Johan onto a horse, handing the boy the reins. He set Katryne on another horse before helping a strawberry-blonde woman on behind Katryne. The man swung into the saddle behind Johan.

"That's my Uncle Callum and Aunt Siùsan. He's my grandda's heir and tánaiste." Liam pointed to each family member as he named them. Mairghread came to ride at his right, while Tristan rode on his left. He knew his parents had plenty of questions, but it made him breathe easier to know they wouldn't bombard him. When they entered the bailey, Liam helped Elene down from where she'd ridden in front of him. Mairghread ushered her toward the keep, but Elene hung back when she realized Liam wasn't beside her.

"Let him talk to his father," Mairghread whispered. "There will be much excitement when he enters the Great Hall, so there will be no chance for them to talk. Tristan and I can see Liam's well, but my husband will

214

want to hear it from him." Mairghread chuckled. "And I shall want to hear it from my husband. We'll wait for them at the top of the stairs."

"I—I don't speak Gaelic, my lady." Elene's cheeks flushed in the dim light.

"My brothers and I all speak Norn. My sisters-by-marriage understand and speak enough to get by." Mairghread shifted to stand in front of Elene and took her hands. "I know Liam wanted to go on this mission to prove he can lead his father's men. We all already knew he could. But I can already tell he's a more mature and more confident man than when he left. I don't think it had aught to do with delivering whisky and seeds. When you're both ready to tell your story, we will listen. But I trust my son's judgment. Elene, he looks at you the same way my husband has looked at me since the day we met. You look at him just the way I've been told I look at Tristan. You love each other. That's all I need to know for now. But I want you to know you're welcome here no matter what brought you two together."

"Thank you—Mairghread."

"That's better." Mairghread pulled her into another embrace. Elene rested against her, bending to place her head on the shorter woman's shoulder. "I told you I knew your father. I knew your mother, too. I know—what your family was—like. I'll never try to replace her, but I also know what it is to be a young woman without a mother. Mine died many years ago. I truly welcome you as my daughter, and I hope you know I am here if you need me."

Elene straightened and looked at Mairghread, confused by the woman's statements. She felt bombarded with longing to divulge her entire life's story to Mairghread while still feeling frightened by a stranger's kindness. She didn't know what to make of it, so she practically clutched at Liam's arm when he and Tristan joined them.

Liam watched his mother and Elene while he talked to Tristan. When he turned his gaze back to his father, realizing he didn't know what his father said, Tristan chuckled.

"She's a bonnie lass," Tristan mused.

"She is. She's a lot like Mama in many ways. She's intelligent, resourceful, too brave for her own good, and kind."

"That sounds like yer mama. Would ye marry a woman who makes ye think of yer mother?"

Liam's cheeks flushed, and his father clapped him on the shoulder. "Nae all of her reminds me of Mama."

"I didna think so. I willna rush ye to tell yer tale, but there is much I need to ken. It's clear ye love her as much as the lass clearly loves ye. But ye're bringing an outsider into our clan. She's skittish, and I dinna think it's just because she doesnae speak our language. I dinna expect ye to divulge her secrets, but I would ken what's amiss."

"I ken, Da. It's a long story, and this isnae the time or place to tell it. I ken Mama is taking care of her, but Elene's bound to be afraid. I didna prepare her for such a grand welcome, and I think it's shaken her."

"If we'd kenned, we wouldnae have all ridden out."

"Da, all I can say for now is that she and her siblings were in danger. They're still in danger, but I dinna wish to marry her just to save her. It willna take long for ye to see why I want her as ma wife. But I need everyone to be discreet and nae ask too much aboot her past until she feels safe here."

"I'll tell the others if that's what ye wish." Tristan watched as his wife embraced the young Orcadian woman. His expression softened as it did any time he gazed at Mairghread. It still felt like yesterday that she walked into his keep, set to marry his wastrel step-brother. He'd known the moment he saw her he would love her for the rest of his days. It hadn't been an easy beginning as the betrothal fell apart because of his step-brother's despicable behavior. But he'd counted it as a blessing when he could court Lady Mairghread Sinclair. He'd been in love with her for nearly two and a half decades, and his feelings hadn't faltered for a moment. He saw the same commitment in his son's eyes as he knew were in his own. They were mirror images of one another, but it hadn't been until that day that they'd stood together, and both seen the world as men in love.

With his father's approval reassuring him, Liam ascended the steps until he came to stand beside Elene. He noticed his mother's soft smile and how Elene stood close to the other woman, even though they no longer embraced. But when Elene realized he was by her side, she clung to him. He felt her trepidation and discomfort, his brow furrowing as he gazed down at Elene, then shifted to look at his mother.

"It's too much," Elene whispered. Liam saw his mother nod as she stepped away. She and Tristan held hands as they stepped inside the keep, leaving the younger couple alone. "I don't understand why they're all so nice. They speak as though I've always been part of their family. It's strange."

Liam laughed. "You're not the first person to say as much. We aren't like most families, I suppose. We're all very close, and we don't shy away from affection. We trust each other and value one another. We appreciate the lives our forebears built, so we may live as a loving family. We know that's not the way of it for most noble families, but it suits us. Whether or not I love you, they would welcome you just the same because we're to marry. But I'm certain knowing we love each other makes my parents feel better."

"Are there a lot of you in there?" Elene glanced at the keep's doors. She'd seen Johan and Katryne enter with the couple who'd given them rides to the castle. They'd happily chattered with the couple.

"There are a lot. I told you once before that there's a score or so of us. I'm the oldest of the cousins and the first to marry. But the Sinclairs are a large clan, even without the laird's family. There are two score Mackay warriors in there too, who accompanied us here. It will be noisy, and people will stare." Liam nudged Elene's chin up with the side of his forefinger. "I asked if you wished to handfast. I'm asking you again right now. They will give you the respect you deserve as my betrothed or as my wife. But I cannot share a chamber with you tonight as your betrothed. If you wish me to sleep on the floor because you're not ready, then I will. But I think you might feel better if I'm nearby."

"I'll always feel better when you're nearby." Elene winked and reached around Liam to pat his backside. "But you are not sleeping on the floor on our wedding night."

"Do you wish to handfast here, in private, or do you wish for my family to be part of it?"

"With your family. They're important to you, and I don't want to hurt your parents by excluding them. After how my mother was—it's a lot to get used to when it's so different. But I like your mother. She's kind and gentle."

"Mayhap with you." Liam snickered. "She wasn't so gentle when she used to skelp my arse."

"I assume you deserved it each time."

"Mayhap a few times." Liam leaned forward and kissed Elene softly. "Shall we get married?"

"I think we shall." Elene returned Liam's kiss before he pressed open the door for her.

Noise and heat met her as they stepped inside. She was unprepared for the enormity of Castle Dunbeath's Great Hall or the number of people within. Heads turned as they made their way toward the dais. Liam squeezed her hand as they stepped onto the raised platform. Liam came to stand in front of his grandfather and father. Tristan sat to Liam the Older's left, with Mairghread on the other side of her husband. Callum sat to the earl's right, and the family fanned out further along the table.

"After the meal, we'd like to handfast," Liam announced. "We wish for the family to be part of it, but I'd ask that we do it in Grandda's solar."

"Is that what you'd like, Elene?" Liam Sinclair asked as he gazed at the young woman.

"It is." Elene glanced at Liam the Younger. "Liam says we'll still have a church blessing, but I'd like to marry tonight." Her cheeks pinkened as she looked at her boots. The youngest cousins seated around the table giggled while the older ones offered their congratulations. Five married couples and a widower exchanged knowing glances as the young couple looked everywhere but at each other or the older relatives. It suddenly embarrassed both that Liam's adult family understood what they would do that night. If anyone had wondered if the couple anticipated their vows, it set their minds at rest.

"As soon as the meal is over. It shall be a tight fit, but we will make it work," Laird Liam announced. It seemed like only minutes later, not a five-course evening meal later, that the family filed into the laird's solar. The couple took their place before the fireplace, where Tristan wrapped the extra length of Liam's plaid around their joined hands. Elene whispered her middle name to Liam.

"I, Liam Brodie Mackay, pledge myself to you, Elene Catriona Isbister. I will be faithfully at your side from this eve until my last breath. I shall find you in the next life and any after, so I can love you, honor you, protect you, and make you happy. I will do this all the days of my life. I plight thee my troth."

"I, Elene Catriona Isbister, pledge myself to you, Liam Brodie Mackay. I will honor and cherish you, abide by your side in this life and the hereafter. I will be your partner in all things, the person you can trust, a helpmate through struggles, and a friend during happy times. I will do this all the days of my life. I plight thee my troth."

Liam's free hand skimmed up her arm until he cupped her jaw, his broad palm brushing her throat as his fingers tunneled in her hair. She rested her free hand over his heart. For a moment, their foreheads pressed together as they smiled at one another. Then their mouths fused, and passion erupted. Elene bent her arm bound to Liam's behind herself as he encircled her with his. She stepped forward at the same moment he pulled her closer. Their tongues tangled, as need surged through them both. They ignored the laughs and coughs until they were breathless.

"He's certainly a Sinclair," Alex announced in Norn before his wife, Brighde, elbowed him and he oomphed.

"He's a Mackay, thank you very much," Tristan responded, also in Norn.

"We've made a Sinclair of you, brother," Magnus said as he clapped his hand on his brother's-by-marriage shoulder. "He takes after all of us. None of us could help ourselves with our bonnie brides."

"We still can't," Tavish chuckled before he whispered something in his wife's ear. Ceit winked at him.

"What my brothers mean," Callum spoke up, "is welcome to our family, Elene."

Liam the Older unbound the couple's hands and embraced them both. The newlyweds accepted embraces and well wishes from the adults, smirks from the older cousins, and quick hugs from the youngest members of the family. Liam swept Elene into his arms and marched to the door, where his brother Hamish stood waiting to open it. Before they crossed the threshold, Liam paused. He twisted to look back at his family.

"Mama, Da, please look after Katryne and Johan. As family tradition dictates, don't disturb us for a sennight. Food and baths are all I'll open the door to." Liam pressed a smacking kiss to Elene's cheek before she buried her face against his chest, but he felt her laughter. She didn't disagree, and he knew she was as eager to be alone as he was. He took the stairs two at a time as he headed to the chamber he'd used since he was a child and during his fosterage. They fell into each other's arms once Liam locked the door, and Elene stood before him. They were finally married and finally alone.

CHAPTER 15

$\mathcal{L}$iam skimmed his hands up Elene's arms, then grazed one hand over her chest as the other tugged at her laces. The swells of her breasts rose and fell with each shallow breath, tempting then withdrawing. He pressed scorching kisses from her collarbone up the right side of her throat until he nipped at her jaw. With a moan, she turned her head to meet his kisses. She'd never appreciated being tall until she met Liam. Wrapping her arms around his neck with ease, she held onto him as he pulled the laces from her gown's first few eyelets. When he released her with a frustrated growl, she watched him draw a dirk from his belt. She froze as she felt the blade saw through the ribbons. She felt warm air across her back as Liam exposed her skin. She lowered her arms to let him pull the sleeves down her shoulders. Her husband's impatience made her feel more alluring than she ever had before.

Liam's kisses followed the gown, feathering over her breasts, stopping to suckle each nipple through her linen chemise until Elene moaned, then down her belly before he let the gown fall to the floor. He pushed her chemise up to her waist, and she didn't hesitate to whip it over her head. Kneeling before his bride, he nudged her legs apart as he rolled down her stockings, kissing her inner thighs as each inch of bare skin tempted him. Once he'd steadied her, and her shoes and stockings were in the heap beside her gown and chemise, he turned his singular focus to the thatch of blonde curls at the apex of her thighs.

He kept his hold on her waist light as his tongue flicked out and caught the tip of her bud. Pleasure rippled through her, making her sway. Liam tightened his grip as she rested her hands on his shoulders. He looked up from the feast he intended to enjoy and found Elene watching him. Curiosity and desire filled her gaze. He drew the flat of his tongue along her seam, dipping the tip into her entrance just before he reached her bud once more. A gasp sent heat straight to Liam's throbbing manhood.

Take yer time. Ye have all night. Dinna end this before ye've begun. If ye dinna slow down, ye'll be spilling yer seed on the rushes rather than in yer wife. Wife? By God, that sounds good. All I want is to taste her. Drive maself into her. Feel her wanting me as much as I want her. I've never felt aught like this. Now I ken what Da meant when he said it's different with a woman ye love, and that it's worth waiting for. I'm glad I ken enough to make her moan. God, those sounds. Mayhap I can fist maself and ease this bluidy ache.

"Liam," Elene whispered.

"Mmm," Liam responded as his teeth grazed the sensitive bundle of nerves.

"I want to do that." At the tentative tone, Liam looked up once more and found Elene watching him as he stroked himself. She jutted her chin toward him, heat suffusing her cheeks. He realized she'd been as brave as she could be for now. She hadn't hesitated to tell him what she wanted in the past, but he understood much had passed between them that night and with his family. He rose to his feet, then kissed the skin behind her ear.

"Do you wish to touch me, my bonnie bride?" Liam murmured beside her ear.

"Very much," Elene responded, her voice just as soft. He removed the brooch from his shoulder as Elene unbuckled his belt. He caught the heavy leather band, placing it on the floor as he pulled his plaid loose. Elene watched every movement, eagerness and shyness warring within. She took the yards of wool from him and turned to set it on the end of the bed. When she turned back, Liam was bare.

She reached forward, her fingers brushing the velvet heat that protruded from between Liam's muscular thighs. She wrapped her hand around it, sighing as she stroked him. The feel of his wife's hand around him drove Liam to a frenzy. So much for trying to calm his need. His fingers bit into her backside with each glide of her hand. Their kisses devoured one another, rough and without finesse. Liam spun them and backed Elene to the wall beside the door.

When her back met the bricks, Elene widened her stance before Liam drew her right leg over his hip. She brought the tip of his cock to the moisture dripping along her inner thighs. She coated it as she brushed it along her entrance. Their hips rocked together, and Elene felt her arousal become a burning ache as her nub rubbed against Liam's pubic bone. She raised up on her tiptoes of her left foot, tilting her hips forward, the invitation clear.

"I'm not making love to you for the first time with you pressed against a door, *mo chridhe*. Maybe the second, third, and fourth time. But I wish for us to be in bed."

"What does that mean?" Elene panted, still rocking her hips.

"My heart. You're everything to me, Elene. I don't want to make love trying to balance. I want to touch every part I can reach. I want to feel you holding me because you desire me, not because you need help to stay on your foot."

"Take me to our bed, husband. But I insist you ravish me as much as you make love to me." Elene's seductive grin reassured Liam that she was moving past her earlier bout of nerves. He swept her into his arms and carried her to the bed in which he'd slept since he'd left the cradle in his parents' room. He'd never brought a woman to his chamber at Dunbeath or at home at Varrich. He knew his father regretted doing so before Tristan met Mairghread. He also knew the Sinclair men always saved their bed for only their wives. He was glad he'd done the same.

"It is our bed," Liam whispered. "Before today, it has only ever been mine. Now it is ours. It will only ever be ours. The very same as it is at Varrich."

Elene's eyes widened as she realized what Liam implied. She looked at the pillow beside her head and stretched her hand out to run it over the sheets. She turned her gaze back to Liam's, and she thought her heart might burst from the love she felt and the devotion she found in his steadfast expression. She knew there would be trials and struggles in their future. But she also knew she would never—not for a minute—have to worry about Liam's faithfulness.

"I love you, *me jarta*," Elene whispered as she pulled him toward her, calling him "my heart" in Norn just like the night they agreed to wed. Their kiss began as a tender melding of their lips, but in a flash, it was back to the tempest it had been as they stood against the wall.

Liam brushed his fingers along her slick entrance, groaning as he felt the proof of her desire. Once more,

CELESTE BARCLAY

Elene wrapped her hand around Liam's manhood. They toyed with one another until they both became restless with need.

"I know there will be pain, and I wish I were the one to bear it," Liam said as he stroked hair from Elene's cheek.

"I don't want to rush us, but let's be done with that part. I know it'll get better. I've wanted to know what it feels like to couple with you since the first night at the loch. I was so tempted…"

"You and me both. I thought to swim just a wee closer, just try for a little peek. Then when I saw you leave the water…I feared you'd discover I fisted myself while you dressed."

Elene grinned, making Liam's eyebrows rise. "I eased my desire, too."

"You did?" Liam's grin matched Elene's.

"Far too often since I met you. Mmm, not often enough." Elene shifted beneath Liam. He'd been kneading her breast while they talked, and now he once more suckled. She'd never imagined an invisible cord connected behind her breast down to the throbbing center of her core, but each draw on her swollen flesh registered a wave of desire between her thighs. She begged, "Please."

Liam nudged the tip of his rod into her channel, waiting for Elene to grow accustomed to the feel. When she gripped his buttocks and pressed him toward her, he thrust into her, tearing her maidenhead, and consummating their marriage. He watched her, praying he wasn't hurting her as he entered her tight sheath. He was proportionate everywhere, his thick manroot matching his broad and thick frame. While he thought being inside his bride was divine, that no woman had ever fit so well, he feared she thought he was tearing her asunder.

226

He observed her take a deep inhale and flinch, but she soon opened her eyes and looked up at him. There was a softness he hadn't expected. She rolled and flexed her hips, adjusting to the new sensation, then nodded. Liam eased back and nudged forward as gently as he could.

"It burns a bit, but it's not unpleasant," Elene admitted. She bent and raised her knees, bracketing his hips. "You can move more."

Liam heard the need in her voice, even if she phrased her request as a statement. Without drawing back, he rocked forward, pressing his cock deeper into her. Elene's head tilted against the pillow, her neck bowing. Liam kissed hungrily at her throat as he eased a few inches of his length out of her before surging forward. Her fingernails dug into his back, but her throaty moan and squeezing thighs told him she wanted more. Their pace increased, a silent agreement that they both wanted to oblige their urgent need.

Their kisses once more conveyed their lust as Liam rested on his forearms, and Elene's hand roved over his chest. Her other arm wrapped over his shoulder, her nails grazing his back. It sent a shiver along Liam's spine, urging him on. He pressed his left hand under her shoulder, then slid it along her back until he reached her hip. He grasped her buttocks and lifted, angling her so he could dive deeper still.

Love and lust swirled in a savage storm as they moved together, colliding together, then retreating over and over. The sounds of their lovemaking filled the chamber. Neither remembered a world existed beyond their chamber door. Neither thought to care if people heard them. They centered all their attention on each other. Liam watched a flush rise from Elene's breasts and course up her neck before her core spasmed around him. Her body tensed, her inner muscles milking him with more strength than he imagined any part of a woman could possess. He slammed into her twice more before he felt his seed fill her. He pulsed inside her, leaving her body still needy. When she continued to move beneath him, Liam obliged. He pistoned his hips until she shattered again, once more tilting her head back with a carnal moan.

As they fought to catch their breath, their hands roamed in now tender touches. Liam leaned back, his arms hooked under her shoulders, and drew her up with him. He shifted, so he sat with her straddling his hips. She settled her head against his chest, her eyes closed. Liam rested his cheek on her crown, his eyes drooping closed too. They held one another, the calm after the storm. The intimacy of sitting together, still joined, was as powerful as their cataclysmic coupling. When their hearts no longer raced, their mouths sought one another. The kiss was languid, love flowing between them.

"Are you all right?" Liam asked as he ran a gentle hand over her shoulder and back.

"When can we do that again?" Elene giggled.

"Give me five minutes. I'm still catching my breath."

"I shall count and not give you a second more." Elene nipped at his jaw before she once more leaned against his broad chest. With heavy arms draped over her, and his broad shoulders rounded, she'd never felt more petite and feminine than she did in that moment. She'd spent years protecting her younger siblings and providing for her family. She'd thought herself fully independent and self-reliant. But the moment she met Liam, she realized two things. She was as she believed, and she didn't need someone else to help her survive. She also knew she no longer wanted to shoulder her burdens alone, and Liam was the only man—only person—she knew with whom she felt comfortable being vulnerable.

"Do you know how much I admire you?" Liam said as he leaned back. When Elene's brow furrowed, he continued. "When we met, I was impressed how you kept your voice calm even as you surely lost your temper with your mother. You were never rude, but you made sure I knew you didn't appreciate me listening and not making it known that I understood your argument. I saw you in the fields working alone. I watched you with Katryne and Johan. I learned what you'd endured after your father died. I worried you thought I wouldn't see all that, that I just wanted to swoop in and fix what I assumed you couldn't. Part of me wishes I could have, but more of me was so bluidy impressed with your strength, inside and out. When I realized all of that, I knew I could marry you. I knew that I would have a partner when it's my turn to lead. I feared having to walk away from you because of duty to my clan. I wish I'd understood sooner what I do now."

"What's that?"

"The reason I fell in love with you was because you're everything I have ever wished for in a wife. I never wished for a particular clan to ally with mine. I always imagined a wife I could confide in and trust, a wife I could share my life with. I regret I didn't put it all together sooner. I would have found a way to get you and your brother and sister away from Rousay without you running away first."

Elene studied Liam's emerald eyes, touched by the honesty she saw and heard. "Do you think you let me down?"

"I did."

Elene shook her head. "I knew how I felt about you, but I never imagined who I am is who you would look for in a wife. I believed you would look for an alliance, and the wife would come with it. You couldn't let me down because I didn't expect you to save me. I wished there was a way you could, but I never felt like it was your responsibility. But when I climbed into that wagon, I just knew I could trust you."

"I didn't do well by you when I found you. I told you I didn't trust you."

"And you've explained and apologized for that. Does it still bother you?"

Liam nodded. "I spoke without thinking. I think I scared you, and that wasn't my intent. I hate thinking I ever scared you, ever made you doubt for a moment that you could rely on me."

"I think your mother and aunts would argue with me, but I shall go to the grave knowing I have the best husband. I never doubted I could rely on you, Liam. I wish this still didn't bother you. You're holding yourself to an expectation of perfection that only you see. I didn't blame you for being angry. I tricked you. I did what I wanted and assumed you'd deal with it. I deserved your anger. I even expected it. But it was knowing deep within me that I would still be safe with you—that you wouldn't abandon me—convinced me to take the chance. If aught, I feel guilty that I used you. I manipulated you and forced your hand."

Liam pressed a quick kiss to Elene's lips. "It wasn't our finest moment, but I can tell you I've never been so tempted to maul a beautiful woman as I was with you in those stables. Sweet heaven and fiery hell, I wanted to do with you what we just did."

"I don't think I would have stopped you. I was hoping you would because I was too scared to be the first to start something."

"I hope you know now that you never have to wait for me to be the one to initiate our coupling."

Elene beamed. "You shall regret that when I chase you around this keep, flipping your plaid up and riding you like a stallion."

"Stallion," Liam chuckled. His body had withdrawn from Elene's while they talked, but the thought of them finding secret places to make love throughout Varrich, and even at Dunbeath, made his cock thicken. Elene rose on her knees, guiding Liam back to her sheath. She sank onto his sword, mesmerized at how different it felt in a new position. Liam scooted them, so his back rested against the bed poster. He encouraged Elene to set the rhythm and motion, watching her breasts bob as she rode him. She rested her hands on his shoulders as she tested different movements, finally settling on circling her hips and rocking back and forth. It wasn't long before Liam's hold on her hips pressed her down on to his shaft as he thrust up.

"More," Elene demanded. Liam flipped them, so they lay with Elene beneath him. He drew her hands above her head, holding her wrists in one of his as the other scooped her breast and brought it to his mouth. He suckled like a man starving, and his wife was an oasis. Their movements grew wild and uncoordinated as Liam and Elene threw caution to the wind. She encouraged him to be rougher, and Liam gratefully obliged. Neither cared that the bed scraped along the floor, shifting from its regular position as it rattled against the wall.

"Fuck," Liam hissed. "I'm going to hurt you, Ellie."

Their eyes locked, both surprised by the diminutive, but a moment later, it spurred them on further. A damn broke between them, both needing to feel like their partner desired them more than their next breath. Both straining to show their partner that they could never get enough of the other. They reached a precipice and teetered there as their hearts pounded and air burned their lungs. Then they plunged over the side together, soaring as their bodies tautened together, release engulfing them. But they coasted back to Earth, clinging to one another, hands cupping one another's cheeks as they exchanged tender kisses.

When he was certain his legs wouldn't give out beneath him, Liam crawled from the bed and wet a linen square in the basin with cool water. He wrung it out and came back to the bed, where Elene watched his every movement. He placed the cool compress between her thighs, easing some of the tenderness already aching. Elene would never complain, but she knew he'd been right that their roughness would hurt. But she cared not. She couldn't imagine a more perfect wedding night than the one they were sharing. They'd made love and talked, both bringing them closer together.

Once she felt more comfortable and took over her own ablutions, Liam wetted his own cloth and cleansed the evidence of her maidenhood from his cock. They drew the covers around them and snuggled close. With their arms around one another's waists, and Elene's leg once more over Liam's hip, they sighed contentedly in unison. It was only moments later they were both asleep. Exhaustion kept them in the land of Nod until midmorning. True to his word, Liam only opened the door to food trays and baths. And in keeping with tradition, the newlyweds tucked themselves away for a sennight, just as Liam forecasted. They talked, played chess and other games, slept, bathed together, and made love. But eventually, they both admitted they could no longer ignore the outside world, and Elene feared the impression she was making on her new extended family.

When they were ready to emerge from their honeymoon, Brighde lent Elene a gown. They were closest in build and size, but Elene could tell her new aunt-by-marriage had to let out the hem as long as she could to make the gown a passable length. It made Elene fear she would be a giant among the Highland women, but she felt less self-conscious when Liam tucked her against his expansive chest and wrapped a brawny arm around her shoulders. She felt ready to face the world once more.

Liam watched Elene as she joined his mother and aunts in front of the hearth in the Great Hall. He'd waited apprehensively as the women disappeared abovestairs to the chamber he now shared with Elene. They'd barely finished their first breakfast among their family when the women urged Elene back upstairs to be measured for gowns and undergarments. Now the women sat together, each with lengths of fabric pinned to form gowns.

"She'll have a full wardrobe by sunset," Tristan mused as he watched the six women working. He sat beside his oldest son, each with a mug of ale before them. He glanced at Liam and clapped his hand on his shoulder. "Ye've heard the story of how yer mama and I fell in love. I should like to hear the story of how ye found the good fortune to convince such a stunning woman to marry yer scrawny arse."

"She doesnae think it's so scrawny," Liam crowed. Their deep and booming laughter made the women turn toward them. Five inquisitive faces stared at them, and one glowered. Mairghread could imagine what her husband and son discussed. They were far too much alike. She mouthed, "behave," to which she received two innocent shrugs.

"Ye were to represent yer grandda and reassure the

233

Orcadians that their lives wouldnae change just because they're Scots now. We didna send ye to find a bride."

"I didna go looking for one." Liam still watched Elene, nervous that she would feel intimidated. But it relieved him to see her smile and join in the animated conversation. He thanked the heavens that all the women in Laird Liam Sinclair's family spoke Norn. He didn't want to think about when Elene had to navigate life without his extended family to make her feel welcome.

"Ye worry for her." Tristan's tone lost the teasing note, and he offered his son a sympathetic smile.

"I met her by eavesdropping on an argument between her mother and her. In fairness, they were having it by the village well, and I ken she suspected I understood. But I should have walked away or let her ken I could follow what they were saying. Da, mayhap I should wait to tell ye this until we meet with Grandda, too. There's more to this than me finding a bonnie woman and falling in love. It's much more complicated than that."

Tristan nodded and sighed. He'd assumed as much. "Tell the ladies we're going to yer grandda's solar. I'll find the others in the lists."

"Da, Mama and ma aunts should be there too. This involves everyone, but I'm scared having everyone there will overwhelm Elene."

"Ask her what she wants." Tristan shrugged as though the solution was obvious. Liam nodded. His father's simple response that Liam should consult his wife was a notion foreign to most men. But it was something that seemed as natural to Tristan as the sun rising in the east and setting in the west. Liam knew his father trusted his mother's counsel more than anyone else's. As he looked at Elene, he realized he felt the same way about his wife. He left the dais and went to the fireplace as his father went in search of the Sinclair men.

"Ellie," Liam whispered as he leaned over his wife's shoulder. He'd taken to calling her that since their wedding night. "I need to tell my father how we met. My grandda needs to know too, which also means my Uncle Callum. I can't tell the three of them and not tell my other uncles. If I tell them, then their wives must know, too. None of them keep secrets from one another. My mother deserves to hear it from us, just like my father and grandfather."

Elene swallowed, her stomach tightening into a knot. She'd known they'd have to tell everyone, but she suddenly felt ashamed and terrified. She looked back at Liam, her eyes welling with tears, but she nodded. She rose and set her sewing on her seat. She was unprepared for Liam to pull her into his embrace, but she needed it.

"I'm scared to tell any of them. Do they all have to be there?"

"No. I can ask that it just be my parents and Grandda, but they will all know soon. I'd rather they hear it from us than someone retelling the tale." Liam stroked Elene's hair, trying to ignore the other women. Siùsan canted her head toward the dais, and the ladies slipped away, leaving the couple alone.

"Why'd they leave?" Elene felt nauseous.

"Wheest, *mo chridhe.*" Elene recognized the two phrases, and they soothed her. "They're giving us space. I wish I'd thought to tell you how my aunts and uncles came to be together. None of them had an easy start. Something or someone tried to keep them each apart, not so unlike what's happened to us. All my aunts had to learn how to belong to such a large family and clan. None of them grew up with loving families. Mama became Lady Mackay the day she married Da. She went from being the youngest sister to helping run a clan. She'd done the same duties for years since my grandmama died young, but it was different once she had to do it with only Da to support her. Ellie, marriage isn't easy, and neither is being a newcomer. My family understands that better than most."

"Do we have to tell them everything about when I thought Gunter was courting me, that I let him kiss me?"

"No, *mo ghràidh*. That can remain private between us. That's no one's business but our own."

"What if they ask why he's so persistent? They'll all guess." Elene turned her head against Liam's chest. "I'm already mortified, and we're not even talking to them yet."

"Ellie, Aunt Siùsan discovered the man she thought would save her from an arranged marriage only wanted to marry her to become laird of their clan and even plotted to kill her father and brothers. Aunt Brighde nearly died when her father tried to betroth her to a violent man, so they could both gain more coin. Aunt Deirdre and Uncle Magnus handfasted when they were young, but her parents dragged her away when they found out. They hid her at court for seven years and tried to marry her to a man Uncle Magnus kept from raping her. Aunt Ceit used to trek through the night to pass messages to and from the Bruce. I can only imagine the men she faced before she met Uncle Tavish. Naught that we tell them will make them judge you, lest they be judged too."

Elene stared at Liam, her mouth agape. "Mayhap you should have been telling me these tales instead of chasing me around our chamber."

"Instead of playing chess and knucklebones.

Chasing you around our chamber will always be more important." Liam winked.

"I feel a little better, but I'm still scared."

"I know. I'll be by your side the entire time. If you don't want to talk, then I will. If we get too close to something you don't want discussed, squeeze my hand, and I will change the subject."

Elene nodded and turned toward the sounds of men entering the Great Hall. She hadn't fully appreciated the intimidating sight the Sinclair men and Laird Mackay made when she first arrived since it was night-fall. She'd been too engrossed in handfasting with Liam to pay attention to the men. Each of Liam's aunts and his mother had taken turns bringing up trays and ar-ranging baths, so she felt comfortable with them. But Laird Liam Sinclair, his four sons, and Laird Tristan Mackay were terrifying as they moved through the gathering hall together. It was like watching a walking, talking, siege engine move toward her. She was certain they were as tall and as wide as the most impressive mountains in the Highlands.

"According to Grandda, I piddled on all of them as a bairn," Liam whispered. Elene choked on a laugh as she turned back to Liam, grateful that he tried to distract her. "You haven't seen them with their weans yet. They're all giant softies around them. Don't underesti-mate any of them in battle or when they protect their family, but they aren't so ferocious when they're rolling around on the floor, pretending and playing with the weans."

Elene had a hard time believing that, but she ac-cepted what Liam said. She tucked her hand into his and offered him a weak smile. He pressed a kiss to her lips and led her to his family. They filed into Liam the Older's solar, where they'd gathered the night Elene and Liam the Younger arrived.

"Wee Liam, Elene," Laird Liam greeted them. Elene covered her mouth to stifle her giggle as she looked at her husband. She'd heard him called that the night they arrived. Now that she'd spent days with her naked husband, she knew there was nothing wee about him.

"Laugh all you want, *mo chridhe*. They shall likely call me that until my last tooth falls out and my head is as bald as it was the day I was born and christened with that nickname." Liam guided Elene to a chair and pulled one so close that he was nearly sitting atop her when they took their places. He wrapped his right arm around her and used his left hand to hold hers.

"Tristan says you'd like to tell us how you met," Laird Liam stated. He offered Elene an encouraging smile. "I knew your father since well before you were born. He and Alex were close in age. I've met your mother a few times, as well."

Elene tried not to wriggle, already uncomfortable with the conversation. She caught the hesitancy in the older man's voice, and she assumed he knew about her mother's reputation. When the laird said nothing more, Elene glanced at her husband.

"I already told Da this," Liam began. "I met Elene when I arrived in Skaill and overhead her arguing with her mother. I should have been clear that I understood, and I should have given them privacy. But I admit I couldn't stop watching Elene."

Liam's cheeks heated, and he couldn't bring himself to look at his mother, father, grandfather, or any of his uncles. He settled for looking at his Aunt Deirdre. She offered him an encouraging smile.

"They were arguing about a Norse trader who they expected back soon. Elene warned her mother than the man had foul intentions for her, but her mother refused to listen. She didn't seem to understand Elene's point."

Elene covered their joined hands with her free one. "My mother has always drunken too much. It wasn't so bad while my father was alive, and I was very young. But he died several years ago, and she started drinking far too much, far too often. She's—" Elene looked at her lap as she mustered her courage. She focused her attention on Laird Liam. "She's not of sound mind these days."

"What do you mean by 'foul intentions'?" Mairghread asked.

"He means to sell me as a bed slave," Elene blurted. She figured it would be best to just say it and be done with it. She couldn't meet anyone's eyes, so she jumped when a warm, manly hand rested on her shoulder that she knew wasn't Liam's. She looked into emerald eyes, an exact match to her husband's. Tristan offered her a smile so paternal that her heart ached. His touch was gentle but reassuring. She realized her husband inherited many traits, both physical and character, from his father.

"You don't have to say any more," Tristan offered softly.

"Androw and Janet confirmed this," Liam picked up the story. "Even if they hadn't, I met Gunter. I—"

"Gunter Haakonsson?" Laird Liam interrupted.

"Yes, Grandda."

Laird Liam steepled his fingers and leaned back in his chair. His right eye narrowed as he surveyed the young couple. He remembered meeting his wife, Kyla, when they were betrothed. It had been an arranged marriage to end a feud between the Sinclairs and Sutherlands. He remembered how his bride's beauty veritably knocked the wind out of him. He remembered how skittish and uncomfortable she'd been when he complimented her. And he remembered the day he'd seen the fresh bruises his cousin gave her and the nearly healed ones her father caused before she arrived at Dunbeath. He'd been ready to set the Highlands ablaze to avenge and protect her.

The older man's gaze shifted to Mairghread, and his heart ached. He hadn't seen Mairghread tied to a bed as two men made ready to assault her. Tristan and his sons told him the tale, what they encountered just in time to rescue her. She was a wonderful and constant reminder of his beloved wife. He couldn't imagine living without both Kyla and Mairghread. He'd never been so grateful for four strapping sons and a mountainous son-by-marriage as he was when he saw Mairghread riding safely in front of Tristan as they returned to Varrich.

With a deep inhale, he looked at his first daughter-by-marriage. He'd never imagined he could love four women as much as he did the daughter born from his own seed. He couldn't have asked for better helpmates for each of his sons. Siùsan was the daughter of Kyla's best childhood friend. She'd been emotionally abused and abandoned her entire life by a negligent father and wretched stepmother. He'd arranged the marriage between Siùsan and Callum in part to save her, and in part because he'd heard about her character and believed she would be a strong influence on his oldest son. But it hadn't been without its challenges. History had repeated itself, and it was Callum and his youngest son, Magnus, who saved Siùsan as two men attacked her. He'd nearly lost three precious women in his life to violence at a man's hand. He had no tolerance for mistreatment of women. He hadn't before he met his wife, and he still didn't as a grandfather to a passel of young girls.

"I know the man's reputation, Elene. I've met him many times, and I trust him not at all. What you say doesn't surprise me, unfortunately. He's a petty and violent man. Those two qualities mixed make him unpredictable and dangerous. I'm glad you are away from him."

Laird Liam turned to the young man named for him. It felt like yesterday that he was crooning nonsense to his oldest grandchild, then carrying him around on his shoulders, pretending to gallop like a horse while the toddler used his hair as reins. A man now sat before him. One he was immensely proud of and loved with a devotion he'd never imagined possible as a young man.

"I also know he's a man with a fragile ego and a temper to boot. He must know by now that you escaped."

"He does, Grandda. He found us on Mainland. We tried to keep Elene hidden, but he spotted Elene as she entered Dingieshowe. She hid in Ninian's croft. Gunter sent warriors into the croft in the earliest morning hours. We pushed them back out, but rather than fight us alongside his warriors, he tossed a burning log onto the thatch. He trapped Ninian, Sonneta, and Elene inside. Elene was in the cellar. I got all three of them out, but we couldn't save the croft. Two more logs wound up on the roof."

"Ninian and Sonneta, are they all right?" Callum asked.

"The last we saw, they were. Bernard, Hugh, Mans, and Meg were there. They saw everything and swore to help Ninian and Sonneta. They won't forgive Gunter any time soon. He's likely ruined his trade relations on that island. We went back to Rousay to gather Johan and Katryne." Liam looked to his aunts. "Thank you for caring for them while we…"

"Katryne and Johan are adjusting so well," Elene turned the attention away from Liam and the hint that they'd spent a week coupling. "They told me while we broke our fast this morning how much fun they're having with the other children. Language doesn't seem to keep children from making friends."

"They're brave, too." Liam smiled as he considered what they'd endured. "Gunter found us as we tried to squeeze between Egilsay and Shapinsay. He spotted us from near Tingwall. Elene suggested they hide in barrels and go into the water. It was the only choice since there was nowhere to hide them on either birlinn, and we couldn't get to shore before the Norse reached us. They nearly froze, but we reached them in time."

"If you had them hiding in barrels out at sea, Gunter must have boarded your boats," Ceit observed.

"He came aboard mine. He cut open some sacks and knocked over empty barrels." Liam looked at his father, then his grandfather. "I didn't complete all the trade."

"I'm the earl whether or not we trade seeds and whisky. That's not what's important. However, I govern those lands, and attempting to capture and sell someone violates our laws. I'm within my rights to apprehend Gunter and imprison him. Prince or not."

"We're here now," Elene whispered. "Can we not just let it go?"

Liam kissed her temple and drew her closer. He looked at his grandfather, imploring him to let the matter rest for now. He flicked his gaze to his mother, hoping she would know what to say, since he was at a loss to how to soothe his frightened wife.

"I'll think about what you've told us. We don't have to do aught right this moment," Laird Liam assured Elene.

"There's a market in the village today," Mairghread said, changing the subject. "My sisters and I are going. Would you come with us?"

Elene's brow furrowed until she realized Mairghread referred to her sisters-by-marriage with no qualifier. She nodded, appreciating the invitation and marveling at the family who surrounded her. She'd felt like she was drowning in a sea of people when she first arrived, but she was gradually growing accustomed to how the Sinclairs and Mackays treated one another. It was the stuff of fairytales in her mind. She'd never met a family like the one she'd married into. She prayed she never woke up if it was a dream.

"I'd like that," Elene beamed.

"When we return, we can work on your gowns some more," Siùsan suggested.

"I have a shawl you can borrow. It can be a wee blustery," Deirdre explained.

Elene rose, accepting a chaste kiss from Liam, before she followed the other women. Liam hung back, nodding his encouragement, when she paused at the door. He looked around the room at the men he'd admired all his life. He still felt like an imposter, but he felt closer to fitting in than he ever had before this mission and before marrying.

"Ye've found a strong woman to love." Tavish switched the conversation to Gaelic and smiled before tousling Liam's hair. Perhaps he didn't quite fit in as an equal quite yet. "She'll take none of yer guff, but she'll be the best partner ye could ask for. She reminds me of ma Ceity."

"I hope nae." Magnus rolled his eyes. "We dinna need to listen to them bickering as much as we do ye two. She seems intelligent and quiet like ma Deirdre."

"She prefers her books to ye because ye're boring," Alex teased.

"But ma wife never ran away from me," Magnus tossed back.

"That was nearly a score and a half years ago, mon!" Alex scowled. The most brooding of all the brothers, his face was a thundercloud. "At least I wasna the first one to lose track of his wife."

"Dinna bring me into this," Callum warned. "But if Elene is like anyone, it would be ma Siùsan. Brave, intelligent, sharp-witted. The lot of ye were just jealous of ma luck and found women as fine as ma wife."

"I was married years before ye," Magnus reminded them. It had been long enough that the gut-wrenching pain Deirdre and he experienced during their forced separation had dulled enough for the family to talk about that time.

"Ye all found women as fine as yer mother." Laird Liam ended the playful debate when his sons nodded.

"I dinna think I should tell her too often, but Elene reminds me of Mama in many ways. It's how I kenned I'd found ma match." Liam shifted his weight before he looked at his father. "I ken ye and Mama have always told us we can choose our own mates, but I didna get yer permission to marry. She doesnae have a dowry, and she brings nay alliance."

"Those arenae things we need, lad." Tristan came to stand in front of his son. "The strongest alliance in Scotland was forged before ye were born. It started with yer grandparents marrying, bringing the Sutherlands and Sinclairs together. We strengthened it when I married yer mama. It's only gotten stronger as yer uncles married and so did their cousins. We're already connected to every clan we want to ally with. As for the dowry, I dinna care aboot that. We Mackays are prosperous in our own right. We dinna need to buy ye or yer brothers a wife, nor do we need dowries to keep us afloat. Yer aunts didna come with dowries, and nae a one of us ever looked down on them or their grooms for it. Much to yer mother's annoyance, ye've been the spitting image of me since the day ye were born. I hope ye're like me and ken a woman's worth will never be measured in coin. Ye left here already a mon, but ye needed to prove it to yerself. None of us doubted it. I think ye've come back the mon ye set out to find. I'm proud of ye, just as I always have been and just as I always will be."

Tristan pulled Liam in for a tight embrace, the two men pounding one another on the back. Liam looked over his father's shoulder at his four uncles, who looked everywhere but at them, their eyes suspiciously glassy. It was only his grandfather, his namesake, who unabashedly allowed a tear to fall.

"I think it's time we put some hair on that wee chest of yers," Tavish chortled. The Sinclair and Mackay men passed around a jug of whisky, imbibing several drams as they teased one another about their various prowesses. Liam was mindful not to have too much, not wanting to make Elene uncomfortable or make her nervous that he would be a drinker now that he was practically home. When offered a fourth dram, he explained his reasoning. Without a word, the others put aside their mugs. Then the men headed to the lists while the women visited the market.

CHAPTER 16

$\mathcal{E}$lene followed Mairghread and the other women through the postern gate. She looked around as an army of guards encircled them. Her eyes widened as she recognized the Mackay and Sinclair plaids. She grew apprehensive as she wondered where the women were taking her if they needed so much guarding.

"Our husbands are protective." Deirdre wrapped her arm around Elene's waist. "Naught means more to any of us than family. We each have two guards. It's the same for the weans until the lads enter the lists. Then they have one each. It was annoying for each of us when we first wed. None of us were accustomed to having so many people around and someone worrying so much about us. But the Sinclairs and the Mackays are powerful clans, and with that comes envy and spite. Few are foolish enough to attack, but never assume it can't happen."

"Deirdre is right. Our husbands are protective, but they're also warriors who've seen enough battles to know what could happen if we're not vigilant. Liam will be the same." Ceit smiled. "Do you know how to wield a dirk? Throw one?"

Elene shook her head. "I can defend myself well enough. But I'm not skilled, and I've never tried throwing one."

Siùsan laughed, drawing attention from the surrounding people. "Mairghread, you must teach her! Callum will be beside himself if he discovers his niece-by-marriage can out-throw him too."

At Elene's confusion, Mairghread explained. "I had no sisters growing up, so I followed my brothers everywhere. They gave up trying to get rid of me when I popped up wherever they headed. I eventually got to an age where they didn't really know what to give me on my saint's day, so they started giving me dirks." Mairghread chuckled. "You've met them. Not so surprising, is it? I used to practice with them, but it was Magnus who encouraged me to compete against the other women at the Highland Gatherings. It was soon clear my competitors didn't have the same—experience —as me. Magnus and Tavish taunted Callum one year, and other people heard them. The other men thought it was hilarious that Magnus and Tavish said their wee baby sister could best Callum. Wanting to win the wagers, the two daft men came and got me. They told me the men insulted me and said I couldn't do more than cut a loaf of bread with a dirk. I had no idea about the wagers or about Callum. I marched over to the knife throwing contest, picked up Callum's five blades and chucked them at the targets. They all landed dead center. I'd bested Callum's last try. I didn't understand why everyone laughed so hard. I thought they were laughing at me. But Callum's face was scarlet. I thought he was having an apoplexy until Magnus explained. Callum is the best knife thrower of all the men in the Highlands. He has been for decades. I just happen to be better."

"That's only because Siùsan refuses to compete," Ceit chirped as she elbowed Mairghread.

"I keep my knife throwing for defending my husband and weans," Siùsan said casually as they arrived at a booth with ribbons and laces. Ceit leaned back to look past Siùsan and shook her head, grinning. Her irrepressible smile made Elene giggle. The younger woman looked back at the material on display. She thought about the laces Liam cut the night they handfasted, both of them impatient to make love for the first time. Her cheeks heated.

"Let me guess," Deirdre grinned. "My nephew shredded at least one set of laces."

Elene choked. It mortified her as she looked at Mairghread, who pretended not to hear. Elene gave a quick nod, then went back to browsing. She picked up a lavender ribbon and was about to ask its price when she realized that she'd spoken Norn with her new family since she arrived. Now that she was among the villagers, she had no way of communicating. Her brow furrowed. She didn't want to ask one of her aunts-by-marriage or her mother-by-marriage. It embarrassed her to talk about money, especially since she had none with her. She was merely curious.

Mairghread shifted to stand beside Elene. "*Dè a tha seo a 'cosg?* That's how you ask, 'how much is it.' Repeat each word after me while you ask."

Elene shook her head. The words sounded too foreign for her to mimic. She was already embarrassed and didn't want to descend into humiliation. She'd hoped to learn Gaelic with Liam, or even with his family, but in private. She watched the merchant grow impatient as he looked between Elene and Mairghread. He grunted in annoyance and turned his back.

"*Dè a..*" Elene stumbled over the first two words, forgetting the rest. Mairghread whispered each one, giving Elene a chance to say it in her head before saying it aloud.

"Trì sgillinn," the merchant responded. Elene turned to Mairghread, who interpreted and said three pennies. Elene nodded with a smile. The man waited, but when Elene made no move to pull out the required payment, he muttered something in Gaelic. Mairghread's response was immediate and harsh. Elene watched as her mother-by-marriage glowered at the man. She watched as Mairghread pulled out a handful of coins, turned around, stepped across the aisle to another merchant with ribbons, dropped the coins on the makeshift counter, and scooped up a handful of laces and ribbons. She came back and handed them to Elene, her eyes narrowed at the offensive man.

Elene looked at Siùsan, whose authoritative voice made the man blanch. He shook his head but said nothing. Siùsan continued to issue an order Elene couldn't possibly understand. The man fumbled as he reached for a crate and pushed his wares into it. Elene realized he was packing his goods. She looked at Siùsan, who continued to stare at the man.

"Are you sending him away? Please don't. Whatever he said couldn't be that bad. He probably has a family who needs what he earns." Elene didn't know what else to say or where to look. She couldn't meet the man's eye, and it embarrassed her in front of her new family.

Mairghread led Elene and the others away, while Siùsan remained behind to ensure the vendor left without further trouble. Elene trembled as she looked back and caught the man staring at her. Siùsan said something more, making the man jump. Elene noticed that Siùsan had her hand on the hilt of a dirk.

"What did he say?" Elene whispered.

"He used an unkind word for foreigners." Mairghread spoke with finality, so Elene didn't press. She repeated in her head what she'd heard him grumble. She would ask Liam later. But as she looked at the four women around her, then glanced at the guards who'd reached for blades during the verbal altercation, she realized it would be wise not to involve Liam.

When they reached a stand with meat pies, Mairghread and Deirdre ordered enough for the women and their guards. While they paid the merchant, Elene whispered to Ceit. "I need to know what he said. I don't dare ask Liam. But I can't go around not knowing what people are saying about me. It's not safe for me or my brother and sister."

Ceit nodded. "He called you a foreign whore."

Elene sucked in a breath. She didn't appreciate the insult, but she didn't understand why it was enough for even the guards to become defensive or why Siùsan ordered him to leave.

"Elene, you're with Lady Mackay and, for all intents and purposes, Lady Sinclair," Brighde spoke up. She'd been silent throughout the exchange, but Elene didn't miss her aunt-by-marriage shifting to stand between Elene and the merchant. "You're with the laird's three other daughters-by-marriage and the laird's daughter. It's obvious you are of importance to our family. You're shopping with us, and the quality of the gown you wear speaks to your nobility—which you are now. Not everyone may know you're Wee Liam's wife, but they will soon enough. The man's lucky Mairghread didn't skewer his bollocks and Siùsan didn't sever his tongue."

"Elene, as angry as they are, they likely saved his life," Ceit said. "The guards won't say aught to Wee Liam unless we tell them they may. But other people heard, and they will repeat it. Wee Liam will see red when he finds out. The merchant would be wise to put as much distance between him and Dunbeath as he can."

"But he didn't threaten me." Elene worried her

upper lip as she looked back at the man as he pushed a handcart in front of him.

"Not in so many words." Mairghread handed Elene a meat pie as Siùsan handed one to Deirdre, Ceit, and Brighde. "But to allow him or anyone to think they can speak such foul things about Clan Mackay's tánaiste's wife will endanger you. Elene, you may not understand this yet, but you married into an exceedingly powerful clan, and you married a man who will one day be as powerful as his father. I'm not saying this to frighten you, but I want you to understand."

Elene nodded but remained quiet for the rest of the time the women visited the village. Mairghread offered her a warm embrace that Elene leaned into, appreciative to finally have the maternal figure she'd always missed. As the women entered the keep, Elene spotted Liam, who changed course and came to greet her. He took her hands and press a soft kiss to her lips. As he watched her, his brow furrowed.

"What happened?" Liam whispered.

"Naught."

"Elene?"

Elene glanced at the women moving around the Great Hall, returning to their duties. She sighed, knowing Liam would eventually learn what happened. She supposed it would be better if he heard it from her.

"A merchant said something unkind that I didn't understand. Your mother and Siùsan handled it. The man left." Elene shrugged and made to step around Liam, but he didn't release her hands. Instead, he led her to an alcove.

"What did he say?"

Elene repeated the words she'd heard. She watched fury unlike anything she'd imagined wash over Liam. His entire body tensed, his hands fisted, and the anger practically vibrated from him. She took a step back and shook her head.

"I really wasn't that offended. It was annoying, but naught to get this angry about." Elene's gaze swept over Liam. "You're scaring me."

Liam immediately relaxed, repentant that he'd intimidated Elene. "I never want you to fear me. I would never hurt you, Ellie."

"I know that. I'm not scared that you'd hurt me or blame me. I'm scared you're going to murder this man."

"Beat him to a pulp." Liam sighed and looked at the floor before he met Elene's gaze once more. "What did my mother tell you he said?"

"It was Ceit actually. She said he called me a foreign whore."

Liam squeezed his eyes closed and shook his head. "Ellie, it was a lot worse than that. I need to talk to Grandda about this. He won't allow a clan member to say such to any woman."

"He wasn't a clan member. He didn't wear your plaid, or the plaid of the Sinclairs. What did he say?"

"He called you foreign. But he didn't just call you a whore like a tavern wench. He called you a woman who services many men at the same time. He implied I would share you or that you've already been shared. I can't let that stand."

"Please let it go, Liam. I don't want more people to know. It's embarrassing enough."

Liam opened his arms to Elene, and she didn't hesitate to step into his embrace. She found comfort from his gentle touch, especially after glimpsing what Liam was like as a battle-hardened warrior. They had hidden her in the cellar when Liam fought the Norse.

"Only this one time. If it happens again, then I have to say something. These are issues that are bigger than you and me. They're leadership issues for Grandda."

"I understand."

"Ellie, did it scare you? Did you feel threatened?"

"No. Insulted, but not scared. But your mother explained how it could be threatening to me. I would just like to think that this is a single incident and not something that's going to be bigger. He was just a rude man who now can't carry out his business on Sinclair land."

Elene shrugged and pecked Liam's cheek, hoping that was the end of the discussion. When her stomach rumbled, Liam laughed and gestured for her to lead the way out of the alcove. They took their seats among their family as the meal began. Everyone spoke Gaelic as they joined the others, but they immediately switched to Norn. Elene understood they wanted her to feel included, but it embarrassed her when they accommodated just her. She didn't want to inconvenience the others.

Mairghread, Tristan, Laird Liam, and the Sinclair brothers all spoke like native Orcadians, and the wives spoke near perfect Norn. It would have felt perfectly normal if it weren't for the people at the lower tables staring at the Sinclairs and Mackays. Elene wanted to slide under the table. She was hardly fitting in when her lack of Gaelic drew so much attention.

"I don't want your family to feel like they have to change to suit me. They should continue as they were. If they wish me to join the conversation, then they can use Norn."

"We wish you to join in. That's why they're speaking Norn."

"I just don't feel comfortable with this much attention. Everyone is staring." Liam watched as Elene's gaze darted to the clan members assembled for the evening meal. He nodded and looked to his mother, who sat to Elene's right. Three seats down was Laird Liam. Tristan sat between his wife and father-by-marriage, a position

CELESTE BARCLAY

of honor at the laird's left hand. Callum sat to the laird's right.

"Bhiodh mo bhean nas comhfhurtail nan leanadh a h-uile duine sa Ghàidhlig." Liam told his family, "My wife would be more comfortable if everyone continued in Gaelic."

With a few smiles flashed to Elene, the lairds' families reverted to the Highlanders' language. When a servant brought a platter with roast duck, Elene smiled at the offer.

"Liam, how do you say thank you?"

"Tapadh leat."

Elene stumbled over the words, but the serving woman offered her a warm smile, acknowledging Elene's effort. In return, the servant offered her, *"S e do bheatha."*

Elene looked at Liam with confusion as the woman moved on. He explained, "That means 'it's your life.' It's our way of saying you're welcome." When Elene looked no less confused, Liam continued. "It's like we're saying that your life needed whatever the person did, so of course they helped."

"That's a rather beautiful sentiment. It shall take me a while to master it, but I will try."

Liam rested his hand on her thigh and leaned to whisper so only she could hear. "It warms me to know you wish to learn even a little Gaelic. I shall teach you a few other phrases, but no one else needs to know you learned them." He winked as he straightened. "Would you go for a walk after we finish? The sun shouldn't set for a little while."

"I'd like that."

The meal continued with ease, and Elene relaxed. People switched to Norn when they wished to talk to her directly, but otherwise, she happily chatted with Liam and Mairghread quietly. After the meal, Liam guided her toward the keep's massive, iron-studded wood doors. He placed his palm on the wood before he opened the door, then pointed to it.

"*Doras.*" When they stepped outside, Liam pointed to the steps. "*Ceumannan.*"

Elene attempted the new words, doing better than she expected. When they reached the top of the battlements, they held hands as they strolled to the eastern corner. From there, they had views of the loch and the cliffs beyond. Liam pointed to the setting sun.

"*Grian.* When the moon appears, that's *gealach.* I think that's enough for now, but if you'd like, I'll teach you a little more each day."

"Liam, why haven't I met your brothers or your sister?" Elene had wondered about that the night they arrived, but then they'd barely seen any family for a sennight. She'd supposed Liam's siblings might be busy during the day, but they weren't at the evening meal.

"You haven't met too many people because I've kept you locked away in our chamber where I've feasted on you every meal of the day." Liam waggled his eyebrows. "Alec, Hamish, and our cousin Thormud are away hunting. They left the morning after we arrived. Do you remember the couple I pointed out? The lady with hair as white-blonde as Aunt Brighde, and the man who sounds English? Isabella and Dedric Hartley's son, Kirk, is also with them. My sister, Ainsley, and Thormud's twin, Rose, were already visiting our Sutherland cousins. Thormud's and Rose's younger sister, Shona, is with them. They should all return within a day or two. I think we will leave for Varrich within the sennight."

"There are so many names to remember." Elene grinned. "Is anyone in the Highlands not related to you?"

"One or two." Liam chuckled. They turned to look down to the bailey when they heard children's voices.

Elene spoke to Katryne and Johan that morning, and she was happy to discover that between their Norn and the noble children's Scots, they were all able to play together. The Sinclair children interpreted for the Isbisters, so they could play with the clan's children who only spoke Gaelic.

Elene wished adults made friends so easily and cared so little for language barriers. While she and Liam were sequestered during their honeymoon, Mairghread and Liam's aunts gladly welcomed the two younger Isbisters as though the children had always been part of their clan. Now Elene's lips twitched as she watched Katryne saying something to a child she believed belonged to Magnus and Deirdre. The girl turned around and scolded a village child in Gaelic.

"They seem to have worked out a system. They didn't ignore whatever displeased Katryne." Elene leaned forward to hear her sister, but she couldn't make out anything specific. Katryne and the other girl linked arms and dashed away. "What will happen at Varrich when they don't have your cousins to play with?"

"If you agree to it, they can join you for lessons and learn how to read and write Scots. Since they're young and are now my brother- and sister-by-marriage, they can grow up as nobles if you wish. If you'd rather they didn't, they can still learn just Gaelic with you."

"Won't people talk about them? They're not nobly born. Neither am I."

"Birth and marriage are the ways into the nobility. Ellie, you're Lady Elene now. That's how people will address you. One day it will be Lady Mackay. We have basically adopted them. If you wish Katryne to carry the title 'lady,' then she can. If you and she don't want that, then she doesn't have to. It's your choice, *mo chridhe*."

"Can I think about it? Talk to her and Johan?"

"Of course." Liam wrapped his arm around Elene's shoulders as they walked back into the keep. They made their way abovestairs where they shared a bath. Liam respected Elene's need to reflect on the day. He didn't press her to talk more. It wasn't long before they were both distracted by the feel of their bodies pressed together in the wood and copper tub. Once they'd scrubbed one another, Elene turned to straddle Liam's hips. He guided her onto his length as they kissed.

The passion existed as it always did, but their coupling was slow and gentle. The water rippling around their bodies added an erotic aura. They were both lost in sensation and love. The rest of the world seemed far away. They existed in a bubble where they were all each other needed. As they lay together in bed afterward, Elene couldn't remember being more content after an emotional day. Before Liam, her mind would have jumped from one worry to another, until she was too exhausted to remain awake. With Liam, she felt calm and fortified to handle whatever the days ahead presented. While neither spoke it aloud, they knew there was much still unresolved about their new lives.

The next sennight passed in a blur for Elene. Liam would accompany her to the Great Hall where they would break their fast together. He would leave to join the men in the lists, while Elene shadowed Siùsan, who taught her about managing a keep. She knew Mairghread would take over her lessons at Varrich, but it was Siùsan's household to lead. The other aunts continued to help Elene with her wardrobe. By the end of the week, she had six new gowns, four chemises, and three pairs of stockings.

Throughout the day, Elene added to her Gaelic vocabulary. She repeated words over and over until she encountered a new one. She strung them together as best she could in her head before she practiced speaking them aloud. A few attempts garnered snickers from the servants, but a piercing gaze from Ceit soon subdued the women. Elene discovered most of the Sinclair clan members were patient and kind to her. She'd feared being an outsider after her initial encounter with the merchant at the village market. But she had no such experience again. If people talked about her, they did so well behind her back and those of her family-by-marriage.

Some days Liam returned for the midday meal, but he remained in the lists for most. In the afternoons, Mairghread gathered the three Isbister siblings in her father's solar and began teaching them to read and write Scots and to speak Gaelic. It embarrassed Elene how much more easily her brother and sister caught on. There was a strong Scots influence in Norn, so she already understood and spoke proficiently. But it frustrated her she couldn't learn to read and write with her siblings' ease. Mairghread patiently reminded her that it wasn't a competition. Mairghread's reassurance mollified her.

But it was the early evenings that Elene enjoyed most. Liam took her for walks near the loch or out to the beach. They shared what filled their days between kisses. It surprised Elene when Liam asked her opinion about an argument between two men he'd watched. She weighed in, and Liam said he would share her suggestion with Tristan. She came to a compromise Liam hadn't considered.

During the evening meal, Elene slowly joined in more. She found she comprehended more Gaelic by the day. When she couldn't respond in the language, she used Norn or Scots. Among the three languages, she could take part more. Much of her anxiety lessened. At night, Liam and Elene escaped to their chamber, where Elene far more enjoyed her linguistic lessons with her husband than with anyone else. She soon became well versed in all their body parts and how they liked to use them.

It was with a heavy heart that she left Dunbeath. She'd found an extended family she'd never imagined. She'd always felt out-of-place in her village; her mother's behavior isolated her from others. Her need to work in the fields from sunup to sundown kept her from mingling with other people her age, and caring for her siblings often made her feel older than her years. But among the Sinclairs, and the Mackays who'd traveled with the laird's family, she finally felt like she belonged. It scared her to imagine starting over at Varrich when she'd just found a place that made her happy.

Elene impressed her parents-by-marriage and the guardsmen who traveled with the Mackays when she easily fished with her bare hands in rivers and lochs. Johan and Katryne worked alongside her, none of them thinking their strategies particularly special. She quickly learned how to make bannocks from oats rather than beremeal, so she helped Mairghread each morning. Her first attempt when she traveled with Liam and his men had been passable, but now she mastered them. She liked Alec and Hamish, but they were young men more interested in spending their time with their guards. She discovered she and Ainsley had much in common with their interests and their temperaments. She prayed her introduction to Clan Mackay went as smoothly as their journey.

When they skirted Clan Gunn's land, Mairghread explained the ongoing animosity between the Mackays and Gunns, as well as the Sinclairs and the Gunns. Elene had never imagined such rivalry or fierce hatred between neighbors. It was unlike anything with which she was familiar. She took to heart Liam's and her parents'-by-marriage warnings that she should never walk or ride out alone.

When the Mackays reined in their horses on their fourth day of travel, Elene, Katryne, and Johan caught their first glimpse of their new home. Elene's chest swelled as she gazed at the castle with a sturdy tower and a barmekin that appeared impenetrable. She could smell the salty air blowing toward them from the Kyle of Tongue.

"There was once a Norse fort where the keep is now," Liam explained. "There are caves below where the Mackays made their homes while they built the castle. It was also a place where Norse pillagers hid their plunder. Nowadays, we keep naught down there." Liam drew closer to Elene as the party nudged their horses closer. "There is a tunnel from the keep down to the caves. If ever you must flee, there are three birlinns always kept within the caves. The birlinns aren't a secret among my clan, but no one outside the laird's family and the clan council knows where the tunnel begins or ends. It's imperative that it always remain a secret, or it will no longer be a safe escape."

"I understand." Elene nodded as she peered at the castle that grew larger with each step their mounts took.

"Do you see the third window from the right? That's our chamber, Ellie." Liam reached out to take Elene's hand. He guided Urram with his other hand while Elene held the reins to the mare she rode in her free one. It was an awkward position to ride in, but it felt intimate despite the five members of the laird's family and the two-score warriors who accompanied them.

"Where will we sleep?" Johan chirped, interrupting the couple's moment.

"There are chambers for you and Katryne on the other side of the second floor," Mairghread explained.

"Chambers?" Katryne asked. "We each get one?" They'd shared a chamber at Dunbeath since it was bursting at the seams with the added Mackays in residence. The children had shared a pallet their entire lives that was off to the side in their family's croft on Rousay. Elene's pallet was next to theirs, and more recently, Katryne began sharing Elene's.

"Yes, you each get one," Tristan confirmed.

"You need your own," Ainsley chimed in. "Boys are disgusting."

Hamish, the youngest of the Mackay brothers, leaned over and not so subtly belched in his sister's ear. He barely dodged her elbow as it came perilously close to his windpipe. Ainsley cocked an eyebrow and was the mirror image of her mother. When Elene turned to look at Mairghread, she nearly laughed aloud. Mother and daughter bore the same unimpressed expression. As they drew close enough to hear the bells announcing their approach, the family and their guards spurred their horses. They entered the bailey with a clatter of hooves and clouds of dust.

Elene swept her gaze around the bailey as people poured forth to greet their returning laird and lady. Liam dismounted and hurried around to help Elene. His strong hands branded her waist, and he skimmed her body along his as he lowered her to her feet.

"I have never wanted to see my bed more than I do now. Our bed." Liam wrapped his arm around Elene's waist, steadying her as her exhausted legs threatened to give out. She was unaccustomed to so many hours on horseback. Her plow horse at home in Skaill hadn't trotted in at least a decade. He barely plodded through the fields. She'd ridden hard when they traveled from Dingieshowe to Kirkwall, but it hadn't been a long ride.

"Can I have a bath first?"

"Are you in pain, *mo chridhe*?"

"A little," Elene confessed.

"You should have ridden with me. I should have insisted. Then you could have sat with your legs over one side."

"Wheest," Elene teased. "I enjoyed riding my horse. I'm just stiff. That's all. A bath will bring everything to rights. Then I can share that bed with you."

"I shall ask for one immediately." Elene's brow furrowed as she watched Liam scowl. He shook his head and grinned. "I forgot we will have to wait until my parents finish. It will be awhile." Liam rolled his eyes. It hadn't taken Elene long to realize that all five of the Sinclair siblings and their mates were still as in love and in lust as the days they wed. While they were moderately discreet, there were plenty of times when Elene overheard or caught glimpses of the couples when they intended a private moment. It wasn't hard to understand where Liam learned to give affection freely. While it reddened her cheeks often, she appreciated the family tradition.

Tristan and Mairghread came to stand with the younger couple. Tristan surveyed Liam before grinning. "I can have a second tub made within a few days."

Elene thought she might go up in flames. Liam merely nodded. Mairghread took pity on her and took her by the hand. Standing to Mairghread's left, the older woman guided Elene to the keep's steps. Liam walked to Elene's left, with Tristan on his other side. The family paused when they reached the top step. Hamish, Alec, and Ainsley took spots one step below.

"Today, Clan Mackay welcomes a new member. I am proud to introduce our clan to ma daughter-by-marriage," Tristan announced in Gaelic. Elene understood much, but as Tristan continued she found herself lost. She only recognized her name. "Ma tánaiste and auldest son has taken a bride. Lady Elene is fair of face, but more importantly, she is hardworking, intelligent, and a match for Liam. She will one day be yer Lady Mackay. I am proud to call her daughter."

Liam quietly interpreted into Norn as his father spoke. Elene watched Tristan, honored by his introduction but somewhat intimidated, too. When Tristan finished, Liam spoke. Mairghread whispered to Elene what Liam said.

"I met ma bride, Lady Elene, while in Rousay. I met a woman with a sharp mind, and an unwavering loyalty to her family." Liam gestured to Johan and Katryne. "She has many talents. She—"

Elene watched as Liam snapped his mouth shut when a man spoke in the crowd. Liam's glower was enough to send anyone up in smoke. Tristan gestured to someone, and a guard appeared. They removed the offender from the crowd as the surrounding people stared, aghast, at whatever the man said. Elene turned to Mairghread, but the older woman shook her head. Elene turned her attention back to Liam as he wrapped his arm around her shoulders.

"Ye all ken the story of ma parents falling in love. Ye all ken that ma mother's brothers married for love. Do nae think for a moment that I am any different. Lest anyone be confused, I love ma wife unconditionally and without reserve. Anyone who speaks ill of her speaks ill of me as yer tánaiste, and speaks ill of ma parents, yer laird and lady. Ye'd all do well to remember that I am ma father's son, inside and out. How ma father would react if anyone said such filth aboot ma mother is how I will respond to anyone who insults ma wife."

Liam scanned the crowd, certain his clan members understood his meaning before he continued.

"Lady Elene is still learning Gaelic as are her younger brother and sister, Johan and Katryne. While they are sometimes slow to answer, all three understand most of what we say. They are sweet children, and Lady Elene is a hard worker. I'm proud to bring them into ma family and into our clan."

Elene was unprepared for the cheers that went up among the crowd. She noticed some people were less enthusiastic than others, but she figured the man who insulted her was an outlier, much like the merchant had been. She glanced at Liam as the crowd dispersed.

"What will happen to him? What did he say?" Elene looked at Liam, but her gaze flicked to Mairghread and Tristan. Ainsley chatted with her mother, and Tristan spoke to an older man Elene assumed was on the clan council and giving the laird a report. Alec and Hamish had slipped into the crowd, but when she turned away from Liam, she saw them headed in the same direction the man was taken.

"My brothers will take care of it."

"Liam, stop." Elene refused to budge when Liam tried to guide her toward the keep's doors. "You aren't protecting me by not telling me. It's scary not to know. And I don't like feeling like you'll keep secrets from me. I'm not your child. I'm your wife. I deserve to know."

"Ellie, I never intended to hide this from you. I wanted to speak to you in private. Even if people don't understand, I don't want anyone listening in. Will you please come inside?"

Elene nodded, feeling horrible that she'd jumped to conclusions. Once inside, Liam watched Tristan lead the clan council into his solar. Mairghread and Ainsley went straight to the kitchens. Liam entwined his fingers with Elene and led her abovestairs to a ladies' solar. She smothered her grin as she watched her mountainous husband nearly crush a low stool. She took a seat in front of him, their knees brushing together.

"The man said I must have traded the whisky with a Norseman to get you in exchange." Liam watched Elene, ashamed that she'd received a poor reception within minutes of arriving. The man, Stuart, had never been of sound mind and was prone to blurting out profanities and threats he never meant. There was no way Elene could have known that, but he tried to explain. Elene listened to him and could do little more than nod.

"Everyone else seemed happy enough," Elene noted.

"They are. My parents have never pushed the issue about me marrying, but other people have asked when I was going to settle down. I think people are eager for my parents to become grandparents. Bairns are exciting, but new generations in a laird's family promise stability and future prosperity. It gives people hope."

"What if I don't get with child right away?" Elene felt immense pressure that she hadn't considered before.

"You are not my broodmare. We will have bairns when the Lord decides we should. Whether it's in nine moons, nine years, or never, I care not. I have two brothers who will probably have weans one day. My family line will not end with me. What I want is to make a happy life with my bride. If that includes weans, all the better. But I love you for you, Ellie. Not your womb."

"You're quite the bard," Elene teased.

"You make me say the floweriest things." Liam playfully batted his eyelashes. A knock on the door interrupted their conversation. A maid announced a bath was being prepared in their chamber. Liam pointed out the other chambers on the floor before leading her to theirs. Elene thanked the servants as they left. The chest Laird Liam gave her was already at the foot of the bed. It was only moments later that they were both stripped bare and soaking in the tub. After a jarring introduction, Elene felt much more prepared to meet the clan once more at the evening meal.

CHAPTER 17

$\mathcal{L}$ ate summer passed into early autumn as Elene and her siblings adjusted to life among the Highlanders. The three Isbisters grew more comfortable speaking Gaelic and were all apt pupils once they started to read and write Scots in earnest. Elene appreciated the warm welcome the clan offered not only her, but her siblings. She realized the two men who'd insulted her, one at Dunbeath and one at Varrich, were the exception and not the norm.

Elene wasn't sure what her position within the laird's household would be. Siùsan taught her what she could in a sennight, and Mairghread taught her far more. But she wasn't chatelaine, and at first, she felt out of place. It wasn't long before Mairghread consulted her about many household decisions making Elene feel valued and accepted. As her Gaelic improved, she found the servants receptive to her instructions and requests. There were times when the Highlanders' customs seemed strange, and she was certain people questioned some of her own ideas, but they all adjusted.

Despite finding a place among the clan and growing closer to Liam every day, she could not quell her fears that Gunter would find her. Castle Varrich and Castle Dunbeath were roughly equidistant from Orkney, even though Dunbeath lay on the eastern coast of Scotland, jutting into the North Sea. Varrich was along the north coast, only eight miles from the Atlantic. The Norse could easily sail their dragon boats into the Kyle of Tongue and attack.

Elene often looked toward the kyle and north toward the ocean. When Liam took her for walks along the battlements, she tried to be inconspicuous as she strained to see the waterway. The first time a ship arrived from the Hebrides, goods coming from the Mac-Leods of Lewis, Elene had been prepared to seek the hidden passage and escape through the tunnels and caves. Liam calmed her terror, explaining the Mac-Leods were yet another branch of extended family as well as trade partners. When they awoke to bells clanging, warning of a fire in the village, Elene dashed to the window embrasure to see if tall blond warriors descended on them.

Finally, as autumn moved toward winter, Elene felt at ease. She doubted the Norse would sail through the violent waters where the North Sea and Atlantic Ocean met during the coldest days of the year just to hunt her. She reasoned with herself that Gunter had given up and was no longer interested in what became of her. At times, she thought of her mother and worried about how she fared. But then she recalled what she'd seen, and what Liam told her, when they returned to Skaill for Katryne and Johan.

Snow blanketed the ground as the Mackays gathered to celebrate Yule. Elene and her siblings told of Orcadian traditions for Yule and Hogmanay, many of which harkened back to their Norse heritage and were foreign to the Highlanders. They explained about the *Jul Bok*, or Yule goat, that was sacrificed each year.

Elene admitted it was a leftover tradition from when the Norse were pagans, but it meant a feast within her village and a time for families to gather and tell the Christ Child's story.

Elene swirled the mug of warm mead Liam handed her as she gazed at the yule log burning in the Great Hall's giant hearth. They'd gone ice fishing that morning on the loch, and their catches were served at the evening meal. Katryne and Johan, supervised by Elene, Liam, and his siblings, taught the village children how to fish through a narrow hole with only a string to lure the fish. As she sat before the fire, Elene glanced at Liam, who took her hand while he spoke to Tristan. Mairghread exchanged a knowing look with Elene and lifted her chin in encouragement.

"Liam," Elene whispered when Tristan shifted his attention to Alec and Hamish. "It's not too cold. Mayhap we could go out and look at the stars."

Stargazing became a habit for them once they settled at Varrich. They would walk to the loch and lay near the water, just as they had during the first days they'd known each other. They never ventured beyond the castle walls without guards, but the warriors kept a respectful distance.

As they left the keep, Liam adjusted the Mackay plaid arisaid Elene now wore daily. He pulled the extra wool over her head and drew it together beneath her chin. Their breath created icy clouds between them, but the night air wasn't unbearable. Holding her skirts high so she wouldn't trip in the dark, Liam and Elene made their way onto the battlements. They looked out toward the Kyle of Tongue and began pointing out constellations and their own star shapes.

"Liam, I've been waiting to tell you something until I was sure. I saw the—" Bells clanging interrupted Elene mid-sentence. They didn't announce the arrival of a welcome visitor. Liam gathered Elene against his side, grabbing her skirts to help her hold them up as he rushed her toward the steps. "Liam?"

"They're warning of attack."

"Where?" Elene craned her neck. It was in a single shaft of moonlight that she saw her nightmare approach. Below the cliffs, she made out the masts of ten Norse longboats. They were just below the keep, having made their stealthy approach unnoticed.

"Hurry, Ellie. I have to get you inside. Mama will know what to do."

"She has to help the villagers."

"I know. She'll tell you what she needs, then she'll make sure you're all safely hidden."

"It's Gunter, isn't it?"

"I can't think of anyone else."

"This is all my fault."

"It's his fault. His stubbornness and ego. He thinks me little more than a boy, so he believes he can attack my clan because he assumes everyone must be as weak as he sees me. He's seriously underestimated me, my father, and our people."

"Be careful." Elene stopped and spun around. She clasped Liam's jaw. "We're going to have a bairn, Liam. I need you to come back to me, to us. Don't be rash."

Liam pulled Elene in for a passionate kiss, her news ringing in his ears. He understood that she told him in an effort to make him more cautious, but it only made him more determined to protect her and end this threat for good.

"I love you, Ellie. And I already love our bairn. I'll be damned if some arrogant Norseman arse keeps me from my wife and child." Liam kissed her again, hard and quick. "Go inside."

Elene returned his kiss before she turned on her heel and rushed toward the keep doors. Mairghread and Tristan burst through just before she reached them. Tristan bellowed orders, Hamish and Alec following in his footsteps. The four Mackay men made for the battlement stairs, each taking torches from men near the barracks.

"Come with me," Mairghread ordered. "Ainsley is gathering the women and hiding them beneath the floors in the storerooms. The villagers are already coming in. We need to get them into the storage buildings and the undercroft. You take this first group to the undercroft. Once they're safe, you go to your chamber and bolt the door. You do not open that door unless it's Liam. Do you understand?"

"Yes. But I should help more."

"You should keep my grandbairn safe and yourself alive. He must not see you. The best thing you can do to keep your husband alive is to hide. Go." Mairghread gave Elene a soft push toward the group of villagers streaming in through the gates. Elene herded the people toward the undercroft, looking over her shoulder as Mairghread fired rapid orders for more villagers to hide in the smaller building around the bailey.

Once Elene was certain she hid all the villagers with her beneath the stone floor in the undercroft, she hurried toward the kitchens. She could hear a voice bellowing and knew it was Liam. Temptation got the better of her, so she changed course and tucked herself against the wall just outside the kitchens.

"Being made a fool of in Orkney wasn't enough. You've sailed a long way to be embarrassed in a foreign land," Liam called out.

"Give me my woman, and I shall sail home in peace."

"I can't give you something that I don't have. I've never had your woman. Inburgh was in Skaill last I saw."

271

"That bleating bitch isn't who I want," Gunter jeered. "You can try to stall, but we are already on land."

Elene could only hear Gunter. She had no way of seeing where he was. She wasn't certain if that was more terrifying than being able to watch him approach. A blood-curdling scream rent the air, followed by several more.

"The only bleating I hear are your people as they die. Mighty hard to see where those arrows come from in the dark," Liam snarked.

Elene tried to picture the landscape near the kyle. There were trees that grew along the clifftops, so she assumed the archers hid amongst them. She wondered if there were even some in the caves. She knew guards had rotations watching the caves. She guessed that was how they knew to sound the alarm, but the Norse were far closer than Elene imagined the Mackays would intentionally allow them to arrive.

"I'll say it again since you're either hard of hearing or just fucking daft. Give me my woman," the Norseman demanded.

"I hear just fine. The only daft bugger is you. You sailed in winter for the sake of your pride. Let me ask you this. How big a funeral pyre will satisfy your ego? You don't deserve so much as a campfire."

"Bastard," Gunter snapped.

"Shut your fucking mouth, you stupid piece of shite." It was Tristan's turn to enter the parlay. "Speak of my wife like that again, and I shall shove my own son out of the way and run you through myself."

Another scream tore through the night air, this one much closer. Elene looked up at the battlement when light flashed in her periphery. Flaming arrows shot through the air toward the encroaching enemy. The Mackays used their elevated position and knowledge of the land to their advantage. Their archers picked off one man after another.

A noise behind her drew Elene's attention. With everyone's attention directed at the front gate and the screams of pain coming from the other side, they overshadowed the thuds she heard. She shifted her gaze up to the battlements in time to see a man fall backwards, landing with lethal force into the bailey. Another man staggered on the wall walk before pitching forward toward the enemy. Elene looked around in desperation.

"Mairghread!" Elene hissed as her mother-by-marriage hurried past her hiding place. The older woman shifted course. Before Mairghread could chastise Elene, the younger woman blurted, "They're at the postern gate. Gunter is distracting them while they take a battering ram to the gate. I heard the thud. Look." Elene pointed to the dead man.

"Hie yourself up to that chamber now. I will deal with that. If they get through either gate, you cannot be standing here. Go."

Elene didn't hesitate to follow Mairghread's command this time. Something in Lady Mackay's tone told Elene life would bode poorly for her if she disobeyed. Elene ducked into the kitchens; the last thing she saw outside was Mairghread pulling dirks from her gown. She didn't wait to discover what the woman did with them.

Mairghread kept close to the wall, expecting arrows to land soon within the bailey. She slipped into the keep through the gardens and ran toward a flight of stairs. She went up past the family and guest chambers to the battlements. A memory flashed before her: the first time she and Tristan stood together looking at the early morning sun. They'd agreed to court while they

CELESTE BARCLAY

watched the sunrise, Tristan's extra length of plaid wrapped around them. She was certain she was half-in-love with him, and they'd only known one another for a day.

Pushing open the door, Mairghread eased onto the wall walk. She crouched and walked, hidden, to the portion of the battlements above the postern gate. She was grateful for her dark hair rather than the blonde locks of her daughter-by-marriage, as her own brunette hue disguised her against the night sky. She counted the ten men who stood with a battering ram. It was smaller than what the Norse would use for the front gate, but it would still break through the postern hatch. When the remaining Mackay guards spied her, she waved them away.

Still crouched, Mairghread pulled a dirk from each boot and two from the sheaths around her thighs and beneath her gown. She tugged at the seam at her waist, ripping the skirts but freeing the three *sgian dubh* sewn into the clothing. She had already withdrawn two from her belt before entering the keep, and she pulled a final one from a wrist bracer. Pressed against the stones, the knives in her lap, Mairghread aimed her first one. It embedded in the man's neck at the end of the battering ram. In quick succession, she picked off one man after another. She'd moved so quickly, the men were dead before they found their assailant.

With her skirts gathered close around her, Mairghread crept along with her head below the crenelation. The Mackay guards knew better than to question their lady, but she knew there would be plenty of talk after the raid. As she approached her husband and sons, she listened to the ongoing exchange.

"You claim I have something of yours, but I haven't seen you in months. Did you get lost?"

"Hardly. But I've found several people along the way

274

who've been happy to tell me all about your whore."
Gunter sneered. "Your arrogant family assumes they
command everyone in sight."

Liam snorted. "Just as on the outside you appear to
people as righteous, but on the inside you are full of
hypocrisy and wickedness."

"You would quote the Bible, yet you conveniently
forget 'thou shalt not steal'."

"You grow boring. You can keep repeating yourself,
but you cannot claim theft of something that never belonged to you. Elene is her own woman. One you intended to enslave."

"She pledged herself to me."

"She did not. But you played her false. You led a
young woman to believe you would marry her. Fortunately, she realized you're a whoreson before making
mistakes she couldn't fix. When you couldn't have the
daughter, you made a whore of the mother. Does Inburgh know she isn't your only wife?"

"Idiot wench drank herself to death two moons
after her brats left."

Liam hadn't expected that piece of news. He was
about to respond when he realized his mother stood
behind himself and his father and brothers. Without
acknowledging her, he turned his head slightly to hear
her whisper.

"He had warriors at the postern gate. Be sure ye get
ma dirks back before they leave."

"Mair," Tristan huffed, but he couldn't fault his wife.
She'd stood beside him for over two decades defending
their people. Her reputation was as fierce as his and
was in no small part a reason no one had raided them
since before Wee Liam was born.

"I'm going inside. But there will be more."
Mairghread didn't wait for any of the men to respond
before she followed her own advice to Elene and hied

herself off to the keep. There, she checked on people hiding throughout, then locked herself in the chamber she shared with Tristan.

"I tire of this, Gunter," Liam called down.

"Then come out and meet me like a man."

"Single combat," Liam announced.

"Bah. Is your father getting too old to fight? Are those boys standing with you too small to wield a sword?"

"We don't want to waste the wood on the funeral pyres," Liam retorted. "This is about naught but you and me. Are you too craven to fight on your own?" Liam knew challenging Gunter's manhood was an insult the Norseman wouldn't overlook. While they were now Christians who paid lip service to turning the other cheek, it was clear Gunter's beliefs harkened back to the days of yore, when vengeance was justice to the Norse.

"And a man doesn't fight little boys," Gunter mocked.

"Coward." With that one word, Liam threw down the gauntlet. There could be no backing down for Gunter, not without losing face before all his warriors.

"Your father shall watch his heir die tonight. I'm not the one hiding behind a wall. Come down here if you dare to be within my reach."

Liam drew his sword. "You and one other warrior may enter. This warrior may fight in your place if you are wounded and cannot continue. But this battle is to the death, not first blood. Once you are dead, the fight ends. Neither your second nor mine may fight if one of us is killed."

"Who are you to set the rules?"

"I would accept my rules, since we've already set one of your boats on fire. Leave your people the chance to leave, or it won't just be you who meets our Maker."

Gunter swung around, spying the growing flames from below the cliffs. They cast eerie shadows on the rocks across the kyle. He'd ignored the death cries from his warriors, disinterested in who he lost as long as he won the battle. He remained confident that he would win any challenge against Liam, but he dreaded explaining to his brother why he returned with one less ship and several fewer warriors. Gunter fooled King Haakon into believing he was sailing farther south toward Europe to justify an expedition in winter.

"Fine," Gunter called up.

Liam made his way down the steps to the bailey, his father and brothers following close behind. The portcullis rose just enough for Gunter and the largest man Liam had ever seen to squeeze beneath. He knew the men in his family were large, all standing nearly six and a half feet and weighing fifteen stones or more. But the mountain before him had to be weigh more than twenty stone, and little of it was fat. He had no choice but to defeat Gunter because he doubted anyone could defeat Goliath.

The Mackays encircled Liam, Alec, Gunter, and the behemoth. Liam understood that his father wished to be his second, and was in fact the best choice to fight in his stead, but his duty to the clan made it impossible for the laird and the tánaiste to enter a single combat. But if Liam had to rely on anyone within his clan other than his father, he knew both of his brothers were the best choices. All three had trained for years, emulating their legendary father, grandfather, and uncles. They all strove to be the men they'd hero-worshipped since they were old enough to toddle. The result was three young men with the strength and knowledge of seasoned warriors and the energy of youth.

"I'm giving you one last chance to leave, and for this disagreement to be forgotten."

"I won't forget," Gunter threatened.

"Then don't." Liam shrugged. "But be gone." He flapped his hand as though he waved away a gnat. Gunter lunged forward, his sword raised. But Liam swung his sword upward, blocking the attack as his hand wrapped around Gunter's throat. He dug his fingers into the Norseman's corded muscles, feeling the frenzied pulse beneath his fingertips. He didn't release his nemesis, even as Gunter's fist plowed into his temple. He only squeezed harder. When Gunter raised his sword, prepared to decapitate Liam, the younger warrior shoved him away.

They danced around each other, circling one way and then the other, taking each other's measure. The night sky made it difficult for the men to decipher each other's facial expressions, but the torches in the bailey shed enough light for Liam to observe Gunter, while Liam searched for any telegraphed moves. He noted how Gunter carried his weight, tipped toward the right and forward on the balls of his feet. He swept his gaze over the sword, estimating Gunter's reach with the weapon. As he moved in each direction, he watched for any openings that Gunter might offer where a vulnerable part of his body would be exposed.

Gunter lobbed insults at Liam, but the time for banter was over. Liam ignored them. He kept his focus on his opponent's movements, not his taunts. No matter where he moved, he always kept Gunter's second in sight, trusting the man not at all. Liam increased the pace subtly as they danced around each other, forcing Gunter to adapt to maintain his defensive posture. Between the movement and his talking, Liam watched his opponent breathe harder with each passing minute. He might look like he stalled to an outsider, but everyone save Gunter realized that Liam was tiring him.

"Now that you've broken her in, she'll be a fine concubine. I will enjoy her more than my others." Gunter grin was equal parts lecherous and defiant.

"Why her? You have other women. You even have a wife. You fucked her mother countless times."

"She is a prize that I already won."

"Not from what I heard. Something about a small prick not being worth it without being a princess," Liam taunted. "She turned you down."

"She believed what she wanted to hear. I never said I would marry her."

"Has your country run out of beautiful women? Why her?" Liam kept his breathing regulated, forcing himself to keep from getting winded.

"A virgin like her was worth taking back to court to be made my woman."

"You just said yourself that she was never yours. 'To be made.' It never happened. She rejected you, and now you're in a snit like a little girl."

"I loved her," Gunter bellowed as he lunged at Liam once more. Liam nearly missed his chance to block Gunter's attack, so stunned was he by Gunter's admission. It suddenly made sense to Liam why Gunter held such a grudge. Just as Liam had, Gunter had fallen in love with Elene, but unlike Liam—who never denied the depth of his feelings—Gunter's pride kept him from admitting the truth. He assumed his title and position would be enough to lure Elene, but when she refused him, he turned vindictive and tried, unsuccessfully, to bully her into submission.

Their swords clanged together, creating the shriek of metal sliding against metal, sending shivers down everyone's spine. Their hilts locked as they pushed against one another, neither giving an inch. Liam kicked out, his foot contacting Gunter's shin, but the Norseman didn't move. As they stared at one another, both snarling, Liam eased a dirk from his belt. Leaning to his right, as though he might lose control, Liam distracted Gunter long enough to stab him between the ribs. Gunter howled and jumped back.

Liam was already prepared. He withdrew the knife and stabbed again, this time into Gunter's belly. He raised his sword parallel to the ground, ready to drive it through Gunter's throat. Before he had the chance, Gunter headbutted him, breaking Liam's nose. Blood geysered and sprayed across both combatants. It wasn't the first time someone had broken Liam's nose, and he supposed it wouldn't be the last. It hurt like hell, but he was accustomed to the pain.

Reflexively, Liam darted back and spun sideways as Gunter followed the headbutt with a swing of his sword that was intended to cleave the Highlander in half. Liam spun sideways and brought his sword across his body, landing a disabling blow to Gunter's left shoulder. Gunter roared in pain as his back arched, and his shoulder hung nearly severed from his body.

"This is to the death. You will soon run out of blood. Do you wish to call it now? No healer can save you," Liam offered.

"Fucking cunt," Gunter panted. "You're fucking her cunt."

Liam puffed a disdainful breath and stepped back, waiting for Gunter to raise his sword again. But the Norseman stumbled for several steps. His second stepped forward to take his place, but Liam had no intention of fighting the human mountain. Neither would he slay Gunter from behind, which is where he stood as the Norseman staggered. Liam eased his way around the two Norse warriors until he stood before Gunter.

"You shall die, Gunter," Liam stated simply. "Do you wish for me to put you out of your misery like a sickly beast? Or do you wish to finish fighting like the man you claim to be?"

"Fu—" Gunter stumbled as he struggled to lift his sword, blood pouring from his wound. With a deep inhale, tapping into a strength no one believed he possessed, Gunter raised his sword. Liam observed Gunter's bleary eyes watching him. It wouldn't be long before the Norseman bled to death. He could wait out Gunter's attempt at a defense or he could end things quickly. While he didn't feel particularly merciful, a sudden, all-consuming need to find Elene and be assured of her safety took hold.

"*Bratach Bhan Chlann Aoidh!*" With the Mackay's battle cry of "The White Banner of Mackay" on his lips, Liam surged forward. He brought his claymore high over his right shoulder and head, gripped in both hands, and swung it downward. His blade cut through bone and sinew, cleaving Gunter's head and right shoulder from his body. The two pieces of Gunter crumpled to the ground, a river of blood surging toward Liam. He stepped away as it stained the dirt and grass. Gunter was hardly the first man Liam killed in battle, but never had he done so much damage in one strike.

"It's done," Tristan declared.

The bells tolled once more, this time in victorious jubilation. Liam wiped blood and sweat from his face. It stunned him to watch the Norse giant merely turn around and walk away from his leader, willingly leaving the dead man's body behind. He watched the man pass beneath the portcullis, signaling to his comrades to retreat to their boats. None argued. None demanded Gunter's body. None looked in the slain man's direction. It was clear this had been Gunter's personal vendetta, one that no one else shared. The Norse warriors went where they were ordered, but none supported Gunter. It seemed like a just ending to the tyrant's life.

"I need to find Elene," Liam stated as he turned toward the keep.

"Nay. Find a bar of soap and a fresh leine. Ye will terrify the lass if she sees ye like that. She'll think ye're more dead than alive from the looks of ye." Tristan nodded toward the barracks.

"Da—"

"Two more minutes willna kill ye, but it will ease yer wife's fears. Listen to a mon who's been married longer than ye've been alive." Tristan grinned and pointed his sword toward the barracks. Dismissing Liam, the laird turned to his other two sons. "Get a grave dug and dump him. Father Daniel can care for his soul. I want the bastard out of our sight."

Liam saw no point in arguing with his father, and he realized the more experienced warrior and husband was likely right. He sprinted to the barracks, yanking his leine over his head as he went. One man met him with a fresh shirt and plaid. Using the trough outside the building, placed conveniently for the men to use after training, Liam hurried to scrub as much blood and grime from himself as he could. Once he had donned the borrowed leine, he swapped the filthy plaid for the clean one. With his sword sheathed on his back, he sprinted back across the bailey and took the keep's steps three at a time.

"Mama, I'm fine," Liam called once he raced toward the stairs, taking those two and three at a time until he reached the landing. With only his door in sight, Liam charged forward, pounding on the portal when he arrived. "Elene! It's me!"

CHAPTER 18

*E*lene paced the width of her chamber as she waited for someone to tell her Liam was dead. She desperately wanted to believe that he would live, that the Mackays would be victorious, that she would make a long and happy life with her husband. But far too much disappointment in her life told her that fate would likely be cruel once more.

She'd peered through the window embrasure several times, hoping she might spy activity below and gain a sense of what transpired. But it was far too dark to see much beyond the flickering glow of the torches. She could make out no details. She heard voices from time to time, but the words were too hard to decipher, even though she was certain it was Norn.

Elene found Johan and Katryne searching for her when she finally heeded Mairghread's directions. They'd slipped away from the group of children with whom they were supposed to hide. They needed their sister. She'd gathered them close to her as they ran up the stairs and along the passageway to Elene and Liam's chamber. Once inside, Elene bolted and barred the door, and they all stacked chests before it. She had one chest that unfortunately held little, but Liam had three

283

chests, one of which she discovered had weapons and light armor.

Elene withdrew several dirks from that chest and two cotuns. They were far too large for Johan and Katryne, but she insisted they don them anyway. She used girdles Mairghread gave her before they left Dunbeath to cinch the garments around the children's narrow waists. With the chest tower in place, she'd sent her siblings to hide beneath the bed. She thought about joining them, but she was too anxious to remain still. She feared she would cry or scream, and she wouldn't be able to stop in either case. So she paced instead.

It felt like hours, if not days, passed as the Isbisters waited. Elene nearly jumped out of her skin when the bells tolled again. She leaned through the window embrasure, attempting to see what caused the second set of bells to ring. She heard Norse voices calling out orders in the distance, but she didn't understand them. She made out shapes moving throughout the bailey, but she couldn't identify anyone.

More minutes ticked by as she expected either Liam to arrive and prove he was safe or someone to announce that he was dead. The longer she waited, the more she panicked Liam didn't survive. Her heart raced until nausea overpowered her. She retched over and over into the chamber pot. The sound was so loud she nearly missed the knocking at the door.

Then she heard it, the most glorious sound she'd ever heard. Liam called to her.

Wiping her mouth with her sleeve, she snagged a twig of mint as she passed the ewer and basin where they conducted their morning ablutions. She glanced at the bed as Johan and Katryne scrambled to climb out from beneath it. The three siblings hurried to unstack the chests.

"Liam?" Elene called as they moved the last container out of the way, but before she unlocked the door.

"It's me. It's over, *mo ghaol*." My love. He'd called her that many times over the months they'd been married. He'd named her his darling, his heart, his treasure. But never had the endearment moved her more than to hear him call her that as he arrived safe from battle.

Elene lifted the bar and turned the key in the lock. The moment Liam heard the latch release, he pushed open the door. Elene yanked it open; the force of their movements made them collide. The couple clung to one another for a long moment before each one's mouth sought its mate. The kiss was desperation and relief. It was love and hope. It was perfect and what each craved. When they could no longer go without air, they pressed their foreheads together, embracing.

"Liam!" Johan yelled as he and Katryne wrapped their arms around the couple. Elene and Liam clasped the children against their sides as they continued to gaze at one another.

"I'm hale," Liam assured them.

"It's really over?" Katryne wondered.

"He's gone. He can never threaten or harm any of you ever again."

"It didn't sound like a battle," Johan asserted, as though he were an expert.

Liam glanced down at his siblings-by-marriage. "It was a battle of single combat. Just Gunter and me. They lost a longboat and several warriors before he and I fought. But we resolved the matter by the two of us fighting."

"You killed him?" Johan marveled, excited by the prospect of Liam's manly dominance.

Liam squatted to bring himself to eye-level with Johan. "I did. I didn't do it for pleasure or sport. There is never aught wonderful about taking another person's life, Johan. It's naught to celebrate. He was someone's son, someone's brother, and someone's father. But he was also a threat to my family and my people. I killed him to protect the people I love most. That's not something to relish. I did it because I value naught more than my family, not because I enjoyed it."

Johan nodded, his excitement dimmed. Liam pulled the boy into a tight embrace, drawing Katryne in, too. He kissed the girl's forehead and ruffled Johan's hair.

"Johan, one day soon you will join me in the lists. You will learn to swing a sword and to fight. But you will also learn about duty and responsibility. I asked you once before to be brave, and you asked if it would make you a man like me. Bravery is only part of what makes a man. You wield power when you wield a sword. A man knows how to use that wisely."

"I understand, Liam. Thank you for saving us." Johan leaned forward, squeezing Liam before releasing him. Liam rose, pulling Elene in for another kiss.

"Can we go belowstairs?" Katryne asked, old enough to recognize the couple wished for privacy.

"Yes. My mother and others are gathering in the Great Hall." Liam didn't wait to hear the door close behind them before he lifted Elene off her feet, his arms resting beneath her bottom. She cupped his jaw as they once more shared a passionate kiss that threatened to set everything around them ablaze.

"I love you," Elene chanted between kisses.

When their second wave of reassurance passed, Liam carried Elene to the edge of their bed. He sat with her perched on his knee, her legs between his thighs.

"I remember you telling me something before we parted. What was that again?" Liam grinned.

"We'll be calling you da in a few months." Elene beamed.

"A bairn, Ellie?"

"Yes."

They laughed, exchanging more kisses. Liam tucked a loose lock behind Elene's ear. He prayed their children looked like his wife because he'd never seen a face more lovely than hers.

"How far along are you?"

"I saw the midwife this morning. Your mother told me to. She guessed before I did. The woman said I'm at least four moons."

"That far?" Liam's brow furrowed.

"I know. What I thought were my courses a few months ago was very light. I've never gotten them every month like some women. I didn't realize because I've felt fine. My breasts have been sore, but I just figured we'd been a little too—vigorous." Elene's cheeks blushed, even though she giggled.

"How did my mother guess?"

Elene shrugged. "She's had four bairns and seen other women carrying. She just knew."

"How do you feel now?"

"Excited. You?"

"The same. But that wasn't what I meant. I guess I wondered if your body feels different now that you know. I've never talked to a woman about carrying a bairn. I don't know—aught."

"I thought eating better meals and just being happy was why I've put on weight. I guess not. It's a happier explanation for why some of my gowns don't fit the same. I feared I was becoming a pudding."

"Feared? Because you would need new clothes? Never worry about asking for aught you need, Ellie."

"That's not what I meant. I—" Elene shrugged.

"Would you love me less if I were no longer so lean? Would you love me less if I gained ugly scars?"

"Of course not," Elene countered.

"Then you can let go of that idea before it takes

hold. I love you. All of you, not just your body. I crave you, not just because I enjoy your body. I crave you because I feel whole when we are together." Liam tickled her ribs. "Besides, you're a wee bony. Your hips dig in me." He winked.

"I can think of something of yours that I'd like digging in me." Elene unfastened the brooch at Liam's shoulder as he tugged at her laces. Their clothes soon lay in a heap as they laid stretched on their bed. Their hands roamed over one another, enjoying each peak and valley. It wasn't long before desire drew their bodies together. Liam surged into Elene's sheath as she tilted her hips to receive him. Months of practice synchronized their movements, drawing out their pleasure as they melded their bodies just as they'd melded their lives.

Their bodies grew slick as Liam suckled Elene's breast, flicking her nipple before grazing it with his teeth. All those months ago when they found each other at the loch, they'd both wondered what it would feel like to couple. Then they spent weeks longing to find out. Now they both knew their imaginations hadn't done reality justice. It was far better than either had ever dreamed. In bed together, they found bliss. But their partnership outside their chamber, working together to serve Clan Mackay, was a powerful one that no one could put asunder.

As they reached the peak together, Liam roared like the Highland lion Katryne once dubbed him. Elene's moans blended with his groans in a perfect harmony of love and lust. When the euphoria calmed and it left them wrapped in one another's arms, Elene looked up at Liam.

"I'd convinced myself that I could walk away from you. That I could say goodbye once I reached Scotland. I'd have fond memories of a brief time together, but I would move on. Now I can't imagine a day without you in my life." Elene offered him a half smile, her gaze soft.

"I nearly passed up the chance for happiness with a woman I admire and love. I thought I had a duty that never existed but in my mind. It was Dermot who made me see sense. Thank the angels and saints that he did because I don't know that I could have survived walking away from you."

"I love you," they said together. Just as they had since the beginning, they lay beside one another and looked at the stars that were visible through their window. They pointed out constellations and devised stories of their own until exhaustion claimed them both. They drifted into oblivion, holding one another, and knowing they were each exactly where they belonged.

EPILOGUE

*L*iam and Elene stood together with their children outside the Castle Varrich kirk. Together, they watched an anxious Johan brush his hand over his plaid for at least the twentieth time as the nervous twenty-five-year-old waited for his bride to appear. Katryne bounced her baby daughter in her arms while her husband held their sleeping toddler son.

Fifteen years had passed, and four children entered their lives, enriching every moment of Liam's and Elene's marriage. There had been times of struggle and times of happiness. Barely six months had passed since the last time Tristan and Liam led their men into battle against Clan Gunn. Marriage had settled the feud between the Gunns and Sinclairs, but it hadn't entirely ceased the tension between the Mackay and Gunn clans.

Liam glanced back at his parents. Gray hair replaced the dark locks they'd both had, and fine lines formed around their eyes and mouths. But they were still as striking a couple as they'd ever been. Liam was grateful that his father was still alive. Even nearing his fourth decade, Liam learned something from Tristan nearly every day. Mairghread and Elene had grown as close as any mother or daughter could, especially after Ainsley married. He knew that one day Elene would fill his mother's place as Lady Mackay, but just as he'd told his wife when he asked her to marry him, he still believed Mairghread's stubbornness would make her outlive them all.

Elene's hand slid into Liam's larger one as the crowd shifted to allow the bride and her father to pass. Their wedding had been a small affair once they'd arrived at Varrich, with only their immediate family present. Elene had felt uncomfortable at the time with the attention when she still struggled to converse with clan members. Now she and her siblings spoke Gaelic and Scots as though they'd done so since the day they were born.

"Ye look vera braw. Stop twitching," Elene whispered to her brother.

"I canna believe she agreed to marry me," Johan whispered as his bride approached.

"Neither can I," Liam teased. Johan cast him a brotherly scowl, but soon his attention was fixated on the young Mackay woman he was about to wed.

As the ceremony progressed, Liam released Elene's hand in favor of wrapping his arm around her waist. She leaned her head against his chest, once more surveying their family. Her siblings would both be married before the sun finished setting. Their children were healthy and lively. Alec and Hamish stood with their wives and children. And Tristan and Mairghread still impressed Elene with their stoic strength, the love they shared clear to everyone as they stood watching the wedding with their arms wrapped around each other.

The day after Gunter's defeat, Liam told Elene what the Norseman said about her mother. They shared the news together with Johan and Katryne. The three Isbister siblings made the perfunctory comments of sadness and grief, but none found that these expressions were heartfelt. That caused its own time of sadness and grief for Elene. But she'd joined a family and clan that valued her. It hadn't taken long for her to realize she'd made a home among people who respected and appreciated her. She'd married a man who devoted his life to her, their children, and their clan.

"Are ye happy, *mo chridhe?*" Liam whispered in Gaelic as the vow exchange ended, and the laird's family moved inside the kirk for the Mass.

"More than I deserve."

"Ye deserve the sun, the moon, and the stars, along with everything beneath them."

"And ye've given me that. So, aye, I'm happy. Are ye?"

"Blissfully. Especially after this morn." Liam grinned with a wink. His hand slid along her back and tapped her bottom. Neither knew which of their children released the beleaguered sigh, but neither cared. They'd woken together, making love as the sun peeked around their window covering. Their desire never waned, their abiding love ensuring it never would.

"It's a good thing I love ye, ye cheeky mon. I shall make ye roar like a lion again tonight." Elene pinched his backside before they took their seats on the laird's pew.

"I love ye, ma bonnie lass of the Northern Isles."

THANK YOU FOR READING
HIGHLAND LION

Celeste Barclay, a nom de plume, lives near the Southern California coast with her husband and sons. Growing up in the Midwest, Celeste enjoyed spending as much time in and on the water as she could. Now she lives near the beach. She's an avid swimmer, a hopeful future surfer, and a former rower. When she's not writing, she's working or being a mom.

Subscribe to Celeste's bimonthly newsletter to receive exclusive insider perks.
Subscribe Now

www.celestebarclay.com

Join the fun and get exclusive insider giveaways, sneak peeks, and new release announcements in
Celeste Barclay's Facebook Ladies of Yore Group

THE HIGHLAND LADIES

A Spinster at the Highland Court

BOOK 1 SNEAK PEEK

Elizabeth Fraser looked around the royal chapel within Stirling Castle. The ornate candlestick holders on the altar glistened and reflected the light from the ones in the wall sconces as the priest intoned the holy prayers of the Advent season. Elizabeth kept her head bowed as though in prayer, but her green eyes swept the congregation. She watched the other ladies-in-waiting, many of whom were doing the same thing. She caught the eye of Allyson Elliott. Elizabeth raised one eyebrow as Allyson's lips twitched. Both women had been there enough times to accept they'd be kneeling for at least the next hour as the Latin service carried on. Elizabeth understood the Mass thanks to her cousin Deirdre Fraser, or rather now Deirdre Sinclair. Elizabeth's mind flashed to the recent struggle her cousin faced as she reunited with her husband Magnus after a seven-year separation. Her aunt and uncle's choice to keep Deirdre hidden from her husband simply because they didn't think the Sinclairs were an advantageous enough match, and the resulting scandal, still humiliated the other Fraser clan members at court. She admired Deirdre's husband Magnus's pledge to remain faithful despite not knowing if he'd ever see Deirdre again.

Elizabeth suddenly snapped her attention; while everyone else intoned the twelfth—or was it thirteenth—amen of the Mass, the hairs on the back of her neck stood up. She had the strongest feeling that someone was watching her. Her eyes scanned to her right, where her parents sat further down the pew. Her mother and father had their heads bowed and eyes closed. While she was convinced her mother was in devout prayer, she wondered if her father had fallen asleep during the Mass. Again. With nothing seeming out of the ordinary and no one visibly paying attention to her, her eyes swung to the left. She took in the king and queen as they kneeled together at their prie-dieu. The queen's lips moved as she recited the liturgy in silence. The king was as still as a statue. Years of leading warriors showed, both in his stature and his ability to control his body into absolute stillness. Elizabeth peered past the royal couple and found herself looking into the astute hazel eyes of Edward Bruce, Lord of Badenoch and Lochaber. His gaze gave her the sense that he peered into her thoughts, as though he were assessing her. She tried to keep her face neutral as heat surged up her neck. She prayed her face didn't redden as much as her neck must have, but at a twenty-one, she still hadn't mastered how to control her blushing. Her nape burned like it was on fire. She canted her head slightly before looking up at the crucifix hanging over the altar. She closed her eyes and tried to invoke the image of the Lord that usually centered her when her mind wandered during Mass.

Elizabeth sensed Edward's gaze remained on her. She didn't understand how she was so sure that he was looking at her. She didn't have any special gifts of perception or sight, but her intuition screamed that he was still looking.

THE CLAN SINCLAIR

His Highland Lass **BOOK 1 SNEAK PEEK**

She entered the great hall like a strong spring storm in the northern most Highlands. Tristan Mackay felt like he had been blown hither and yon. As the storm settled, she left him with the sweet scents of heather and lavender wafting towards him as she approached. She was not a classic beauty, tall and willowy like the women at court. Her face and form were not what legends were made of. But she held a unique appeal unlike any he had seen before. He could not take his eyes off of her long chestnut hair that had strands of fire and burnt copper running through them. Unlike the waves or curls he was used to, her hair was unusually straight and fine. It looked like a waterfall cascading down her back. While she was not tall, neither was she short. She had a figure that was meant for a man to grasp and hold onto, whether from the front or from behind. She had an aura of confidence and charm, but not arrogance or conceit like many good looking women he had met. She did not seem to know her own appeal. He could tell that she was many things, but one thing she was not was his.

His Bonnie Highland Temptation **BOOK 2**

His Highland Prize **BOOK 3**

His Highland Pledge **BOOK 4**

His Highland Surprise **BOOK 5**

Their Highland Beginning **BOOK 6**

PIRATES OF THE ISLES

The Blond Devil of the Sea **BOOK 1 SNEAK PEEK**

Caragh lifted her torch into the air as she made her way down the precarious Cornish cliffside. She made out the hulking shape of a ship, but the dead of night made it impossible to see who was there. She and the fishermen of Bedruthan Steps weren't expecting any shipments that night. But her younger brother Eddie, who stood watch at the entrance to their hiding place, had spotted the ship and signaled up to the village watchman, who alerted Caragh.

As her boot slid along the dirt and sand, she cursed having to carry the torch and wished she could have sunlight to guide her. She knew these cliffs well, and it was for that reason it was better that she moved slowly than stop moving once and for all. Caragh feared the light from her torch would carry out to the boat. Despite her efforts to keep the flame small, the solitary light would be a beacon.

When Caragh came to the final twist in the path before the sand, she snuffed out her torch and started to run to the cave where the main source of the village's income lay in hiding. She heard movement along the trail above her head and knew the local fishermen would soon join her on the beach. These men, both young and old, were strong from days spent pulling in the full trawling nets and hoisting the larger catches onto their boats. However, these men weren't well-trained swordsmen, and the fear of pirate raids was ever-present. Caragh feared that was who the villagers would face that night.

The Dark Heart of the Sea **BOOK 2**
The Red Drifter of the Sea **BOOK3**
The Scarlet Blade of the Sea **BOOK 4**

VIKING GLORY

Leif BOOK 1 SNEAK PEEK

Leif looked around his chambers within his father's longhouse and breathed a sigh of relief. He noticed the large fur rugs spread throughout the chamber. His two favorites placed strategically before the fire and the bedside he preferred. He looked at his shield that hung on the wall near the door in a symbolic position but waiting at the ready. The chests that held his clothes and some of his finer acquisitions from voyages near and far sat beside his bed and along the far wall. And in the center was his most favorite possession. His oversized bed was one of the few that could accommodate his long and broad frame. He shook his head at his longing to climb under the pile of furs and on the stuffed mattress that beckoned him. He took in the chair placed before the fire where he longed to sit now with a cup of warm mead. It had been two months since he slept in his own bed, and he looked forward to nothing more than pulling the furs over his head and sleeping until he could no longer ignore his hunger. Alas, he would not be crawling into his bed again for several more hours. A feast awaited him to celebrate his and his crew's return from their latest expedition to explore the isle of Britannia. He bathed and wore fresh clothes, so he had no excuse for lingering other than a bone weariness that set in during the last storm at sea. He was eager to spend time at home no matter how much he loved sailing. Their last expedition had been profitable with several raids of monasteries that yielded jewels and both silver and gold, but he was ready for respite.

Leif left his chambers and knocked on the door next to his. He heard movement on the other side, but it was only moments before his sister, Freya, opened her door. She, too, looked tired but clean. A few pieces of jewelry she confiscated from the holy houses that allegedly swore to a life of poverty and deprivation adorned her trim frame.

"That armband suits you well. It compliments your muscles," Leif smirked and dodged a strike from one of those muscular arms.

Only a year younger than he, his sister was a well-known and feared shield maiden. Her lithe form was strong and agile making her a ferocious and competent opponent to any man. Freya's beauty was stunning, but Leif had taken every opportunity since they were children to tease her about her unusual strength even among the female warriors.

"At least one of us inherited our father's prowess. Such a shame it wasn't you."